Advance Praise for *The Debt* by Angela Hunt

"*The Debt* is a wonderful story that reminds us not to follow in the footsteps of men, but in the footsteps of Jesus."

—FRANCINE RIVERS,
author of *When the Shofar Blew* and *Redeeming Love*

"*The Debt* is a powerful story, captivating and superbly written. I couldn't put it down. Angela Hunt touched my heart. When I finished, I thanked Jesus for speaking to me. That's the highest compliment I can pay any book."

—RANDY ALCORN,
author of *Safely Home*

"Angela Hunt's *The Debt* is a must read! It will challenge you in many ways, and it just might shake you loose from your comfortable church pew and send you out to follow in the footsteps of Jesus."

—ROBIN LEE HATCHER,
author of *Beyond the Shadows* and *Firstborn*

"If any novel deserves to be called 'a life-changing book,' it is *The Debt*. This story not only engages your emotions—anger, sorrow, tension, laughter, and joy—but it truly resonates in your soul. *The Debt* has changed the way I look at my relationship to the world, to God, and to the people around me. When was the last time a novel changed *your* life?"

—JIM DENNEY,
author of *Answers to Satisfy the Soul* and the *Timebenders* series

"*The Debt* is a clever parable and an engaging novel about the dangers of playing church in a real world with real sinners. *The Debt* will push you out of your comfort zone and make you rethink that deceptively simple question—what would Jesus do? The answer may just change your life."

—RANDALL INGERMANSON,
Christy-award winning author of *Oxygen* and *Premonition*

"*The Debt* is a deeply moving tale of one woman's journey toward a more vital, vibrant faith. Emma's story, in Angela Hunt's skillful hands, inspires and challenges us in a way fiction rarely does."

—JAMES SCOTT BELL,
author of *Deadlock* and *A Higher Justice*

"Written from the heart, with a passion for truth that sears the pages, *The Debt* is Angela Hunt's most powerful novel to date—and that says quite a lot. This is a triumph of a novel from an author willing to challenge our preconceptions and confront the reality of where the contemporary church is today...and where it ought to be. What makes Hunt's achievement more remarkable still is that she accomplishes it with such uncommon skill and compassion."

—BJ HOFF,
author of *American Anthem* and *An Emerald Ballad*

"*The Debt* is a great book. With a timely message for today, Hunt throws open the doors of the church and encourages all believers to leave comfort and safety behind to fulfill Christ's highest command: love God, love one another. *The Debt* is a skillfully written, beautiful read that will challenge those who claim to follow Christ. If you've forgotten the thrill of his still, small voice, this parable will make you fall in love all over again."

—JANE ORCUTT,
author of *Lullaby*

"If you're ready to stop 'playing church', read Angela Hunt's *The Debt*. This amazing book shook me out of my comfort zone, and I haven't been the same since. Every Christian should read it."

—COLLEEN COBLE,
author of *Without a Trace*

"Angela's book touches upon so many relevant questions for today's Christian, but what I came away with was a new understanding about the way God sees life, and perhaps the way I have chosen not to see it. This timely parable searched my heart and I'm better for it."

—RENE GUTTERIDGE,
author of *Boo*

OTHER NOVELS BY ANGELA HUNT

The Canopy

The Pearl

The Justice

The Note

The Immortal

The Shadow Women

The Truth Teller

The Silver Sword

The Golden Cross

The Velvet Shadow

The Emerald Isle

Dreamers

Brothers

Journey

With Lori Copeland:

The Island of Heavenly Daze

Grace in Autumn

A Warmth in Winter

A Perfect Love

Hearts at Home

www.angelahuntbooks.com

THE DEBT

A STORY *of a* PAST REDEEMED

ANGELA HUNT

WestBow
PRESS

A Division of Thomas Nelson Publishers
Since 1798

visit us at www.westbowpress.com

Published by WestBow Press, Nashville, Tennessee, in association with the literary agency of Alive Communications, Inc., 7680 Goddard Street, Suite 200, Colorado Springs, Colorado 80920. All rights reserved. No part of this book may be reproduced, stored in a retrieval system, or transmitted in any form or by any means—electronic, mechanical, photocopy, recording, or any other—except for brief quotations in printed reviews, without prior permission from the publisher.

Scripture quotations are taken from the *Holy Bible*, New Living Translation, copyright © 1996. Used by permission of Tyndale House Publishers, Inc., Wheaton, Illinois. All rights reserved.

This is a work of fiction. Names, characters, places, and incidents either are the product of the author's imagination or are used fictitiously.

Library of Congress Cataloging-in-Publication Data

Hunt, Angela Elwell, 1957–
    The debt / by Angela Hunt.
        p. cm.
    ISBN 0-8499-4319-1 (softcover)
    1. Spouses of clergy—Fiction. 2. Married women—Fiction.
3. Kentucky—Fiction. I. Title.
PS3558.U46747D43 2003
813'.54—dc22   2003020545

Printed in the United States of America
04 05 06 07 PHX 9 8 7

Dedicated to the memory of Robert Briner,
who is still encouraging lambs to roar

Then Jesus told . . . this story: "A man loaned money to
two people—five hundred pieces of silver to one
and fifty pieces to the other.
But neither of them could repay him,
so he kindly forgave them both,
canceling their debts.
Who do you suppose loved him more after that?"

LUKE 7:41–42

CHAPTER ONE

*A*s the President of the United States slips his arm around my husband's shoulder, I think I might just bubble up and burst with pride. I'm standing and applauding with everyone else, of course, trying to keep my smile lowered to an appropriately humble wattage, while Abel, bless him, bows his head, obviously embarrassed by the deafening applause.

We're among the few who have been seated at the head table of the National Prayer Breakfast, and my head is still reeling from the honor. Dizzy as I am, I try to look around and gather as many impressions as I can. The support team back home in Wiltshire, Kentucky, will want me to recite every detail.

The woman next to me, a senator's wife, bends to reach for her purse and jostles the table, spilling my cranberry juice. She glances at the spreading stain, apparently deciding it's more politic to continue applauding than to help me mop up the mess.

Faced with the same choice, my heart congeals into a small lump of dread. If I ignore the stain, the president might glance over here and decide that Abel Howard's wife is a clumsy country bumpkin. If I stop to clean it up, I'll look like a woman who can't cut herself loose from the kitchen.

Fortunately, life as a minister's wife has taught me a thing or two about diplomacy and compromise. Steadfastly smiling at the president, I stop clapping long enough to pick up my napkin and drop it onto the wet linen. The senator's wife gives me an apologetic look as the applause dies down and we settle back into our seats.

"Abel Howard and his affiliated ministries," the president says, moving back to the lectern, "have provided us with an excellent example of how religious television broadcasts can promote quality in programming and restore morality to our nation. Not only does Abel Howard deliver a worship service to millions of American homes each week, he and his organization have spearheaded drives to lead our country back to its spiritual, ethical, and moral roots. In this special presentation for religious leaders, the Points of Light Foundation is pleased to honor Reverend Howard for his courage and many years of dedicated hard work."

Behind the president, Abel laces his fingers and keeps his head lowered. Beside him, the Catholic bishop who has also been honored looks at Abel with open curiosity . . . or is that skepticism in his eye? From where I sit, I can't tell.

"Abel Howard," the president continues, "and the other worthy people who stand before you today represent all we can achieve through determined effort, concentrated vision, and dependence upon God. Our nation has no official religion, no state-endorsed faith. All are free to worship or not worship, to exercise faith or sustain doubt. Yet faith, and those who practice it, brings out the best in us. Scripture describes people of faith as salt, and salt not only adds spice to a substance, it acts to retard spoilage. The men and women standing before you have decided to be salt in a society that can, at times, seem terribly decayed. I hope and pray that these men and women will be joined by thousands of others who realize that salt kept in a saltshaker is useless."

The crowd responds with another boom of applause. The president grips the sides of the lectern as he waits for the sound to fade, and I catch my husband's eye. Abel smiles, but his folded hands and stiff posture tell me he is eager to leave the platform. Abel has never minded attention, but this is a lot for a Kentucky preacher to handle.

The president clears his throat. "In a letter to a friend, George Washington once wrote, 'I am sure that there was never a people who had more reason to acknowledge a Divine interposition in their affairs than those of the United States; and I should be pained to believe that they have forgotten that agency, which was so often manifested during our Revolution, or that they failed to consider the omnipotence of that God who is alone able to protect them.'"

The president throws back his shoulders as his gaze sweeps across the crowded ballroom. "May we all remember that God can and will intervene in our affairs to keep America strong. May God bless you all, and may God continue to bless America."

As the audience rises to deliver a final thundering ovation, the president turns to shake the hands of a few people on the podium. He reaches for Abel's hand first—a fact I can't help but notice—then moves on to congratulate the nun who oversees a soup kitchen, the Muslim cleric who founded a literacy program, and the rabbi honored for his efforts to combat racism.

A host of noteworthy people stands on the platform, but the President of the United States turned to shake Abel's hand first.

That thought pleases me to no end.

Like children who've just been excused from the grown-up table, our group is relaxed and giddy as we spill out of the limo and cross the tarmac. The February day is cold, but the sun has gilded the asphalt and the gleaming white jet with "Abel Howard Ministries" painted on its side. The ministry pilots, Dan Moon and Jim Spence, are waiting by the pull-down steps, shivering in their navy peacoats. They grin and wave as we approach, then they climb the stairs.

At least a half-dozen steps ahead of me, Abel walks with Josh Bartol, his administrative assistant. While my husband rattles off a list of names and titles, Josh murmurs into the tiny tape player he always carries in the pocket of his suit coat.

Without being told, I understand what my husband is doing. The names belong to dignitaries he saw at the break-fast, and whether he shook their hand or merely glimpsed them from across the room, he'll send those VIPs a personal note within the next forty-eight hours. Abel recognized the value of networking before *networking* became a buzzword, and he has never hesitated to embrace business ideas for use in the ministry. "We're salesmen, after all," he tells young preachers who flock to his annual ministers' conference, "offering the best possible product to people who desperately need it. So why should we be any less motivated—or any less savvy—than companies peddling fancy tennis shoes and overpriced automobiles?"

Beside me, Crystal Donaldson is huffing to keep up, her boots clomping heavily on the pavement. I smile inwardly at her efforts—after nearly twenty-four years of marriage to Abel, I've mastered the long stride necessary to keep pace with him. But Crystal is new to traveling with the Reverend and probably a bit starry-eyed from riding in limos and the ministry jet. She couldn't attend the breakfast, but on our way out of the Hilton lobby I glimpsed her chatting up other staffers who couldn't get a ticket to the exclusive event.

She quickens her step. "Will we be here long?" She reaches up to grab the purse strap slipping from her shoulder. "On the ground, I mean?"

I look toward the tiny cockpit windows where I can see our pilots. "Dan and Jim are usually pretty good about moving us out. I'm sure they're as anxious to get home as we are."

"I'm not anxious to get home." Excitement sparks her eyes. "This has been absolutely incredible. Honestly. I mean, we were in the same building as Franklin Graham! And you won't believe—well, maybe you would—all the famous people I saw walking through the lobby!"

Somehow I resist the urge to pat her on the head. Crystal is probably twenty-three now, a recent college graduate, but to me she'll always be a "sunbeam" from my children's choir. I remember visiting her mother in the hospital just after Crystal's birth . . . and wishing that little pink bundle of sweetness were mine.

A few years later, after the establishment of our tentative television ministry, she became the first child baptized in a televised Sunday morning service. When she came up out of the water, wet and shivering, eight-year-old Crystal shone her blue eyes into the camera and shouted, "Thank you, Jesus!"

That single exclamation, Abel says, probably boosted donations by two hundred percent. After the sudden spurt in contributions, my husband decided God meant for us to remain in television, so we signed a contract to purchase a full year of weekly programming on our local station.

Now Crystal has come home to take her place among the scores of homegrown kids we've hired to work in the ministry. I don't know much about what goes on in the payroll department, but I suspect the average twenty-something working for us earns only slightly more than minimum wage. But they're learning as they work, gaining invaluable experience and maturity, not to mention the opportunity to list "Abel Howard Ministries" on their employment résumé.

Abel says we're teaching these young people to be servants while they follow the highest calling any believer could receive. When I see the enthusiasm in their eyes, I have to agree with him. Sometimes I'm stunned by their single-minded dedication. God has been good to bring so many committed people to our ever-expanding organization.

Crystal is working for *Purity*, our ministry's monthly magazine. She graduated from a Bible college with a degree in journalism, and as editor of the magazine, it's my job to approve her articles. She's a gifted writer, but sometimes her writing seems stilted, as though she is hesitant to write anything that might rock anyone's boat.

Her hesitation is probably my fault; when she took the job I sat her down for a frank discussion and told her that our readers could be a persnickety group. The previous month's guest column had featured the story of Gomer and Hosea, and the author happened to mention that Hosea's wife had lived as a prostitute. We're still getting mail about that issue— apparently the word *prostitute* has no business in a Christian family magazine.

I should have caught it before we went to press.

"Emma Rose," Crystal hustles to keep up with me, "mind if I ask you some questions on the plane? Impressions of the breakfast and all? I figure I can work your comments into an updated feature article about you and the Reverend."

"That's fine, Crystal."

We have reached the stairs, where Josh has fallen back to allow Abel to climb first. Wes Turner, a freelance photographer along for the ride, snaps photos of my husband striding up the steps. I can imagine the caption: *Despite a hectic schedule, the Reverend takes time to receive presidential honors at the National Prayer Breakfast in Washington.*

As Abel disappears into the cabin, Josh puts one foot on the stairs, then removes it. A deep flush creeps up from the top of his collar as he steps aside.

I grab the handrail and pretend not to notice his belated gallantry. "Thank you, Josh."

I climb into the jet and move past the cockpit. Winnie Barnes, the air hostess, gives me a warm greeting. "Mornin', Emma Rose. Did you enjoy the breakfast?"

Winnie, Dan, and Jim are the ministry's flight crew, kept on the payroll to fly wherever the Reverend Howard needs to go. Originally brought on as part-time employees, lately they've been traveling three or four times a week. The pilots don't seem to mind much, but I suspect Winnie finds it hard to leave her eight-month-old son.

I give her the grateful smile she deserves. "The breakfast was wonderful, thank you for asking. How was your rest last night?"

"Fine." Her radiant expression diminishes a degree. "Except when I called home and Charlie told me the baby has another earache."

"I'll be praying for him, then."

"Thank you, ma'am. I appreciate that very much."

I move forward, noticing that Abel has taken the seat nearest the left window. Because he didn't head to the conference table at the back, I know he's not in the mood for conversation. I slip into the seat across from him, grateful for the solidity of a window at my shoulder. If the flight makes me drowsy, as most flights usually do, I might nap on the way home.

Josh enters next, and it's obvious that his manners fell

short of extending gallantry to poor Crystal. Answering the hostess's greeting with an absent grunt, he spies the empty seat next to Abel and drops his briefcase into it, then blocks the aisle while he removes his overcoat and insists that Winnie hang it in the small closet across from her jump seat.

But he doesn't take the seat next to Abel. Understanding my husband nearly as well as I, Josh respects Abel's signal for silence. He takes the seat directly behind his boss, then hauls his briefcase from the space next to Abel.

I look away lest Josh read the irritation on my face. Abel loves the young man, says he has great potential, but I'm not so sure. Yes, he's efficient; yes, he's bright and sophisticated. But he's also brash and a little too blunt for my taste. He grew up in a well-connected political family; the father practically begged Abel to give Josh a position. Abel has not regretted a day of Josh's tenure, but I've had more experience with people, and I know Josh's type. The moment a bigger and better offer comes along, he'll be gone, leaving us to deal with whatever mess he leaves behind.

Josh just seems . . . I don't know. Sometimes I think he's giving the ministry every ounce of his intellect and energy, but nothing of his heart.

Abel thinks my fears are groundless. He says we might owe this National Prayer Breakfast honor to Josh's family. I don't know about that, but I'm content to watch and wait.

As the others troop aboard, I turn my face to the window,

hoping Crystal will follow Josh's lead and grant me a few moments of peace. I haven't forgotten my promise to give her an interview, but at the moment I want to relax and collect my thoughts.

I adore my husband, I love working by his side in the ministry. But when we are locked away in a private space with only our most trusted aides, I cherish the freedom to let my face relax, my shoulders droop.

Even the most vigilant Christian soldier needs a cease-fire now and then.

We have been airborne only a few minutes when I hear the high-pitched warble of the jet's telephone. Josh springs to answer it; both Abel and I look at him, waiting.

A faint look of disappointment flits across Josh's face as he hands the phone to me. I smile and accept it, knowing that Josh was probably expecting a call from one of the movers and shakers at the prayer breakfast this morning.

I bring the phone to my ear. "Hello?"

"Emma Rose! Good morning!"

Celene Hughes, who serves as my administrative assistant and our director of women's ministries, wouldn't have called unless something important had come up. "Everything okay, Celene?"

"Pretty much." Despite her assurance, I hear a note of worry in her voice, and my tension level rises a few points. I sink into my seat. "What's up?"

She exhales a breath that seems to whoosh straight into my ear. "It's probably nothing, just one of our usual fruit-cakes. But the young man insisted that I contact you right away. I tried to stall him, but on the off chance he really did need to talk to you, I thought I'd better call."

I shift my gaze to the window, where a quilted blanket of low clouds blocks my view of the landscape below. "What'd he want?"

"He says he wants to meet you privately. I told him you would be speaking at Sinai Church four times in the next month and you'd be happy to meet him after any of those services, but he said a public meeting wouldn't do. That's when my alarm bells started ringing. He said he had impor-tant news for your ears alone."

A soft groan escapes my lips. Last year I attracted a stalker, a lonely middle-aged man who watched the TV program every week and somehow convinced himself that I was his soul mate. His early letters went into the massive bins sorted by our mail department; when he began to mark them "personal," they came to my office. I ignored them at first, not wanting to encourage him, but when three or four letters began to arrive every afternoon, I showed them to Abel, who handed them off to Jon Stuckey, chief of security for the ministry.

After Jon wrote the fellow a terse warning, the personal letters stopped coming.

I put all thoughts of the man out of my mind until one July Sunday when a disheveled stranger began to walk up the center aisle. Though Abel saw him he kept preaching, assuming that the man wanted to pray at the altar. But when the fellow called my name and pulled a gun from his overcoat, Abel and half the choir hit the floor like wheat before the reaper.

I have a dim memory of Abel gesturing frantically, motioning for me to get down, but for a full five seconds, I couldn't think. Half-formed thoughts stuttered through my brain as my eyes registered our minister of music inchworming on the carpeted platform and my husband cowering behind the reinforced pulpit (bulletproofed in the year we launched our campaign against homosexuality depicted on television). I sat frozen beside the piano, not knowing whether to crawl beneath the Steinway or slip behind my chair, as the wild-eyed man kept coming, his eyes locked on me.

Fortunately, I didn't have to waver long. Jon and his security team—who'd probably been half-hoping for an opportunity to test themselves—rushed from pews and behind pillars and charged the platform like NFL linebackers intent on victory. While several team members covered Abel and other staff members, Jon tackled my deranged Don Juan. As they hit the floor, I glimpsed the black gleam of steel and heard the crack of the gun and an answering *chink* from one of the crystal chandeliers.

In the days to come, people often remarked on my composure. But what they took for grace under pressure was nothing more than paralyzing fear.

Within sixty seconds, it was all over. The security men hustled the man away; the choir members brushed dust from their robes and climbed back into their seats. The music director smoothed the long strands of hair atop his bald head and sat back down, though his hands trembled on the armrest.

But without so much as a tremor in his voice, Abel pulled himself erect in the pulpit and told our people that God had just protected us against a flagrant satanic attack. The congregation broke into spontaneous applause, a veritable offering of praise.

Later, after the police had interrogated the man and learned his identity, Abel drew me into his arms and asked why I hadn't crawled into the bulletproof pulpit with him.

"It all happened so fast," I answered, surprised by the question. "I never dreamed anyone would come after me."

He promised we'd be more careful about investigating suspicious letters. "It's sad to think people can't relax when they come to church," he whispered in my ear, "but this is a different world, Em, and we're charging straight into it with our weapons drawn. We might as well be prepared for trouble."

Now discreet metal detectors stand outside the entrance doors of our worship center and office complex. I'd been afraid our church members would despise the new security measures, but their reaction surprised me. "Why, look at that," one woman told me, pausing to admire the technological marvels. "Not every church draws Satan's attention. Just goes to prove you and the Reverend are making a real difference for the kingdom of God."

That supportive attitude is just one of the things I love about our church people. Outsiders, though, often worry me.

Now Celene is calling about another strange man—if he came to church, would he set off the metal detectors?

My hand tightens around the telephone. "This guy who called"—not wanting to alarm Abel, I lower my voice—"do you think you need to alert security?"

"I don't know." I can almost see Celene chewing her lip. "He seemed harmless, really. He kept saying he didn't want to bother you, he just wanted to leave his number and a brief message."

I close my eyes, imagining what the message might be. Abel gets lots of letters from well-meaning viewers who wake in the grips of a bad dream convinced God has chosen them to tell the Reverend that the world will end in forty-six days, or sixty-two, or on January 15 in the year 2005 . . .

"What's the message?"

I hear the sound of shuffling paper. "He said his name is Christopher Lewis—"

The name doesn't ring a bell.

"—and he's calling about someone whose birthday is January 6, 1976."

A sudden spasm grips my heart.

Ignorant of her words' effect, Celene continues: "This is the odd part—he told me to tell you that someone wrote an address on his birth certificate: 4839 Hillside Drive. He said it was important I tell you that."

A dark cloud sweeps out of the past and blocks my vision; the empty hand resting in my lap trembles as the life I once locked away bursts through the dam of memory and floods my heart. I have not spoken of January 6, 1976, in decades; even my husband has no idea why that date is significant.

But I know. And the young man who called has to know why I have silently marked that anniversary for the past twenty-eight years.

My voice, oddly enough, is calm when I can speak again. "That's the only message?"

"That's all. He thought the address might mean something to you."

Might. Oceans of mercy flood that word; in it I hear the possibility of saying he's mistaken, the address and date mean nothing to me, somehow he has tracked down the wrong Emma Rose Harbison Howard who once lived at 4839 Hillside Drive in Hudson Falls, New York.

But he has found me. Despite the sealing of the court records, despite legal promises and emotional assurances, he has gone through the challenging work of searching me out.

For an agonizing moment I can't decide if the thought terrifies or thrills me.

"Does it?" Celene's voice snaps at my nerve endings.

"What?"

"Does the address mean something?"

The corner of my mouth twitches. Though I experienced a dark and troubled adolescence, I have fond memories of the rectangular ranch house on Hillside Drive. Mercy House, the place was called in those days, and though its function did not appear on a single sign, no one in Hudson Falls mentioned Mercy House without adding a subtitle: The Home for Wayward Girls.

"I'm not sure why he would mention that address," I answer, taking care to wrap the truth in ambiguity. "But save the message, okay? I'll look at it when I come in."

"Fine."

Celene's voice rings with relief and I'm touched by her concern. I know when I return to my office the pink message slip will be sitting on a stack of others, arranged on my desk with a pile of carefully screened mail.

"Is that all you have for me?" I ask, looking across the plane at Abel. He gives me a tired smile, silently acknowledging the waning of the morning's adrenaline rush.

"That's it," Celene answers. "See you later today, then."

I click off the phone and drop it into the empty seat. Across the aisle, Abel leans against the curved wall to face me.

"Everything okay at the office?"

"Fine. Celene just wanted to run something by me."

"Nothing urgent, I hope. Our schedule's pretty tight for the next few weeks."

I take pains to keep my voice light. "Nothing urgent."

The message on my desk could be earth-shattering, life-changing, and completely destructive. But it can wait. After all, the stranger who called has been waiting twenty-eight years.

From the corner of my eye I see Crystal approaching, steno pad in hand. She has questions—probably a long list of them.

Despite my promise to her, I can't be interviewed now. My head is swirling with too many questions of my own.

I turn to the window and prop my brow on the molded plastic. Crystal—astute girl that she is—correctly guesses that I'd like to be left alone, for after a moment I hear soft footsteps heading toward the back of the plane where Josh has joined Wes to drink coffee and crow about the VIPs they spotted at the prayer breakfast.

I close my eyes against a sudden spurt of tears.

How completely the world can change in the space of a moment! This morning my head had been filled with sights and sounds from the powerful world of government. I'd been a little star-struck by the senator's wife sitting at my right, a little dizzied by the fact that the President of the United States wished to honor my husband.

But those memories pale in significance as other visions fill my mind. I see a reddened, squalling baby boy, pulled from my swollen belly and held aloft just long enough for a nurse to wrap in a blanket before she whisks him away.

They took him from me—at my request—but in the winding length of twenty-eight years, nothing has been able to remove him from my heart.

CHAPTER TWO

*T*en minutes out of Wiltshire, Dan Moon's voice crackles over the intercom. I haven't slept a single minute, but I open my eyes, feign a yawn, and slip my feet back into my leather pumps.

Behind the bulkhead, Winnie perches on the jump seat and snaps her belt. "A good flight," she says, meeting my eye. "Were you able to rest at all?"

I nod like a simpleton. In more than twenty years of marriage to a very public preacher, I've had to develop a gift for small talk; in the face of Celene's message that gift has vanished as utterly as morning dew. I find it impossible to babble about banalities when a particular pink message slip waits on my desk.

Leaning forward, I slip my right arm into my wool coat, then work the bulk of the material over my shoulders. The wind sliding over the mountains will be frigid, and our tiny airport offers little shelter for corporate passengers. We'll disembark on the tarmac and scurry to our cars, which will be cold and wet from melting frost.

After struggling into his overcoat, Abel glances at his watch. "We're going to have to run to make that twelve o'clock lunch meeting," he calls to Josh, who has returned to the seat behind Abel. "Is your car at the hangar?"

"Yes, sir, it is."

Abel shifts his gaze to me. "I'm sorry, Em, but I've got a Christian businessmen's luncheon down at the Ramada. Josh will take me, if you don't mind driving my truck."

Though the last thing on earth I want to do is drive my husband's bulky black Navigator, I manage a smile.

"Or," Abel gives me an exaggerated wink, "you could always join me. I'll bet the businessmen would love it if you came along."

His words reverberate along the walls of my unsteady heart, sending me back to the winter day in early 1980 when he proposed. We were both seniors at Calvary Bible College, eager and slightly apprehensive about the future. We'd been best friends for nearly two years, and though I had begun to suspect God might want me to remain by Abel's side through life, I didn't dare dream of anything specific. We were close, but I hadn't shared my secrets.

He knew I hadn't become a Christian until the age of seventeen. He knew I loved Jesus with all my heart, for I had openly declared my devotion to the Savior on the first day we met. Something in my simple speech must have either touched or amused Abel, because he frequently sought out my company. Together we talked and studied and prayed, earnestly seeking God's will for our lives.

I didn't know what God had in mind for me, and it felt dangerous to voice any assumptions. I had privately thought about becoming a social worker for a place like Mercy House. In college I learned that because God is sovereign, the darkness he has allowed to enter our lives could serve his purposes. Given my past, I figured God would put me in some out-of-the-way place, allowing me to quietly feel sorry for my sins and do what I could to prevent others from making my mistakes.

I never, ever thought that God would use me in what my fellow students called "full-time ministry." Those who had received a calling were revered on campus; even the professors looked at them as front-line warriors in training. I respected those who chose to major in ministerial studies; I studied English and psychology and prayed that someday I could make a difference in some other girl's life.

One cold afternoon in 1980, Abel walked me from the chapel to the entrance of the girls' dorm. We talked of the sermon we'd just heard, and somehow the conversation veered toward what we would do when we left school. Abel spoke of his dream of ministering in his hometown of Wiltshire, Kentucky. His father pastored a small church in that college town, but the church had suffered a split and dwindled to a handful of members. Abel wanted to resuscitate his father's ministry and encourage the local people to reach far beyond the mountainous borders of Wiltshire. Kentuckians were proud, hardworking people, he told me, and most of them were devoted to God. A man would have to be persuasive, though, to convince them to use new methods of spreading an old message.

"God can use a man who is willing to sell out," he told me, his eyes shining. "And I'm sold out to be whatever the Lord wants me to be. I expect to be serving the Lord for the rest of my life and . . . well, I'd love to have you come along on the journey."

"Really?" I joked. "As what, your secretary? I should remind you that my typing isn't all it could be and I'm an absolute dunce when it comes to computers—"

"Emma Rose Harbison." He turned, blocking my path. His gloved hand took my mittened one, pushing the boundaries of what was considered proper male/female behavior on campus. His eyes bored into mine. "I'm asking you to be my wife and ministry partner. Will you serve the Lord by my side for as many years as God chooses to give us?"

For a moment I thought he was joking. Other students walked by, their conversations blowing past us along with scattered autumn leaves. I felt a blush burn my cheek—how could he propose in the open, in the middle of the day, without any sort of warning?—but when I looked into his eyes I saw sincerity . . . and love.

With all my heart, I wanted to say yes. But though I admired Abel tremendously, appreciated his dedication to God, and loved the way he protected me, the thought of being his wife scared me silly.

"Abel," I lowered my eyes lest he see too much, "I don't think I'd be a good partner for you. We have such different backgrounds."

"Everybody's equal at the foot of the cross, Em. And I've watched you over these last two years. I know you could be a great pastor's wife. I know you could help me be the man God wants me to be. Besides"—his hand rose to lift my chin, and again I was surprised he would risk this display of physical contact in full view of professors and resident assistants—"I've learned to love you. I can't imagine going into ministry without you by my side."

I pulled my hand from his. "You have no idea what my life was like before I came here. I haven't told you about—"

"I don't need to know anything about your past, Em. Life

THE DEBT

for a Christian begins the day we accept Christ; on that day all things are forgiven, the past is wiped clean by God's forgiveness. I don't need to know, I don't want to know what you've done. What matters now—the only thing that counts—is that you are as forgiven as I am, and just as alive in Christ."

He looked at me, his smile crinkling the corners of his blue eyes. "Honey, if Jesus can forgive the sins of this red-haired spoiled brat, he can forgive anyone. So please, Em, promise you'll marry me after we graduate."

I have never been able to resist that little-boy grin. And so, believing in Abel's affirmation and the Lord's leading, I married Abel Howard the night after graduation. Our first year held lots of adjustments and hurt feelings—mostly mine—but after a few months we learned how to live and work together. I learned that the wife of a pastor must lower her expectations; Abel learned to elevate his. I learned that I couldn't have my husband to myself every night; Abel learned that I could be trusted to handle some matters without his direct involvement.

Over the years we established a home, a church, and a television ministry. Together we toiled with God's people to touch thousands, perhaps millions, of souls.

Prayer and Praise, our weekly telecast, reaches into over forty million households every Sunday morning; each month the Prayer and Praise mailroom processes over five hundred thousand dollars in contributions. Abel's college dream has come true, and nearly every penny of the television ministry's income goes to fund some aspect of outreach extending far beyond the city limits of Wiltshire, Kentucky. The influence of television has allowed us to support missionaries in Uganda, smuggle Arabic Bibles into Iran, and feed children in the hidden hollers of Kentucky.

The thought of my husband's success softens my smile as I watch him from across the cabin. Abel likes to reminisce about his devilish childhood, but you don't have to have a Ph.D. in psychology to realize that what he and his late mother called utter depravity was nothing but typical childish mischief. My dear husband thinks he understands life on all its levels, but his understanding is intellectual, at best. He reads about horrible atrocities in *Time* and *Newsweek*, but the world's evil has never seared his soul.

And while he may be content to believe that my spiritual birth at seventeen enabled me to shed my mistakes like a butterfly casting off its cocoon, I know traces of the past remain.

One of them has just cast its shadow across my heart.

Abel pauses by the passenger seat of Josh's aging BMW and hands me the keys to the Navigator. "So you're going home, hon?"

I wrap my fingers around the keys, feeling their chilly bite.

"Eventually. I think I'll go to the church first. Celene seemed to think I should look at a few of my messages."

"I'll catch up with you later, then."

Abel slides into the car and I grab the door, not quite ready to let him go. Abel is my husband, partner, and best friend. He deserves to know that a door to my past has just sprung open.

I bend to catch his eye. "Will you be home later today? I think I might need to talk to you about something . . . and I could use your advice."

He glances at his watch. "I'm booked all afternoon, and don't forget we have that deacon dinner tonight. But I should be home at five to change clothes." A slight furrow appears between his brows when his eyes meet mine. "You okay?"

I straighten and look toward the horizon, where a cloudbank is edging over the mountains. "Just tell me you love me."

"More than anything but Jesus." Abel gives me a wink before closing the door.

I step away as Josh starts the engine. I am burning with the desire to share my news, but it wouldn't be fair to spring this kind of surprise on my husband in anyone else's hearing. Especially Josh's.

The Navigator is cold and smells vaguely of coffee when I unlock the door and climb inside. The passenger seat is cluttered with yesterday's copies of the *New York Times* and the *Wall Street Journal*, as well as the *Wiltshire Record*. The discarded papers are a good sign—if any of the three had printed negative articles about our ministry, Abel would have stuffed the offending paper into his briefcase and spent hours working on a rebuttal. We'd have been lucky to get him out for dinner last night, but Abel had been relaxed and happy, buoyed by the thought of the National Prayer Breakfast. The sharks had been lazy and content this morning; not a single reporter had yelled out a comment about Abel's stand against homosexuality or pornography.

A tremor cascades down my spine as I slide the key into the ignition. What sort of frenzy would erupt if the press sniffed out the story behind the young man who called me? My private life is no one's business, but when an individual becomes a public figure, even ancient secrets become fair game.

Not only will I have to tell Abel about my past, I might have to tell the world as well.

He thought the address might mean something to you.

An avenue of escape still exists—I do not have to answer this young man's call; I do not have to acknowledge the past. I could ignore Christopher Lewis and live the rest of my life as if he had never reached out to me. I would never have to tell my husband the sordid story of my previous life; I would never have to face a nosy pack of reporters.

I could simply say the address means nothing . . . now. I wouldn't exactly be telling the truth, but I wouldn't exactly be lying, either.

THE DEBT

I put the car in reverse, then glance over my shoulder. Christopher Lewis may be a thousand things, but he is a gentleman. From his carefully worded message, I know he will not hound me if I do not return his call.

But how can I ignore this man?

Crystal and Wes are standing and talking between their cars, but they pause to wave as I pull out. I never did sit for Crystal's interview, but she'll undoubtedly catch me later this week. She'll pull out her steno pad and ask a series of questions designed to elicit informative, pleasant, spiritual responses:

"Tell me about your salvation experience."

"How do you envision your role as a pastor's wife?"

"What is the greatest challenge facing Christian women today?"

In all the interviews I've given to Christian publications, no one has ever asked me to share my deepest fears . . . or my greatest sins. No one ever inquires about my life in the "before Christ" years; perhaps interviewers assume nothing that transpired back then could possibly matter to me now.

But can we pull the dark threads of our history without distorting the fabric of our lives? Surely a courageous woman would face up to her past and acknowledge the bleak days, even embrace them as part of the path that ultimately led her to acknowledge the goodness and sovereignty of God.

Unfortunately, my Bible college professors talked more

about striving for sanctification than dealing with the effects of sin.

I hand the parking stub to the gate attendant along with a five-dollar bill. He thanks me with a smile and a slight tip of the hat. He knows me as Emma Rose Howard, the Reverend's wife and a verifiable Good Woman.

He doesn't know me well.

I pull out of the parking lot, pause at the stop sign, then drive onto the main airport road. A billboard for a mobile phone company catches my eye—"Express Yourself!"

Ha! If only I could. I'd like nothing better than to announce and acknowledge my past, but I can't think only of myself. My husband and I lead a ministry that employs over three hundred people and influences thousands more. If my reputation is tainted, others will know. And possibly be hurt. And it would be better to be thrown into the sea with a millstone tied around my neck than to face the punishment in store for harming one of the young babes in Christ.

The car in my rearview mirror slants left and growls around me; the teenager at the wheel is obviously not satisfied to lag behind me on this two-lane road. I watch him roar ahead, then tap my thumb against the steering wheel. Maybe God's not satisfied with where I am in life . . . and the message waiting at the office is an invitation to swerve onto an uncharted path.

Why not turn the wheel and follow where the Lord leads? I'd be taking a risk, sure, but if God is leading, I shouldn't be afraid. After all, it's not like a gang of reporters is hounding me . . . but the press didn't care about Tammy Faye Bakker until scandal rocked the PTL ministry. Abel and I weren't on television in those days, but we couldn't help but notice how the press devoured details of that particular debacle. Mainstream newspapers reported on excesses ranging from the Bakkers' wardrobes to their air-conditioned doghouse, so that's when Abel and I decided we'd do our best to live moderately. Our church had grown to six thousand members by the time the Bakkers hit the news, and we had begun to suspect that television might be part of the Lord's plan for us.

We learned a lot from the PTL brouhaha—that's why Abel drives a Navigator while I favor a sedate Volvo sedan. We live in a nice home in a gated community, but our house is no nicer than our neighbors'. We have no dogs, therefore no doghouses, air-conditioned or otherwise, we're not into flashy jewelry, and we have no children . . .

My grip tightens on the steering wheel as I turn from the airport road into highway traffic. *We have no children . . .* legally. What will Abel say when he learns I have a son?

A huge white steeple stabs the sky as I point the Navigator up a hill. Sinai Church sits atop the mound of red rock for which it was named generations ago. The original building, a simple rectangular structure with a tin-clad steeple, served a mostly rural congregation from its completion in 1918 until May 1980, when Abel's father retired from its pulpit. That month twenty-five farming families voted to call my husband as pastor (two of the wives, I am told, dissented on account of Abel's marriage to a "Yankee from New York"), and so we arrived in the summer of 1980—newly wed, inexperienced, and eager to take on the world.

I pull into the church parking lot and wave at the security guard who has snapped to attention at the Navigator's approach. His sober expression melts into a grin when I lower the tinted window. "It's just me, Brian; the Reverend's out speaking."

He nods and waves me forward. "Good to see you, Emma Rose. Give the Reverend my congratulations on the prayer thing, will you?"

"I will." A wry smile lifts my mouth as I pull into Abel's reserved parking space. Though they are the salt of the earth, few of our local folks fully appreciate the honor Abel has just received, mainly because Abel always jokes about such events. This past Wednesday night at prayer meeting he mentioned that he had to go up to Washington to have breakfast with the president. As the crowd roared its approval, Abel sheepishly added that he was going to accept "an honor for the people of Sinai Church." That's how Abel sees it—it isn't his honor, but the ministry's. And all the glory belongs to God.

As I step out of the car, my gaze roves over a handsome white building that didn't even exist when Abel and I were first married. In the Lord's perfect timing, we arrived at the beginning of a building boom in the city. Wiltshire College had just abandoned its vocational curriculum and become a four-year liberal arts college; by 1990 it had tripled in size. The growing school attracted professors and businesses; farmers sold their land to developers who poured miles of concrete to support the shopping malls, gas stations, and grocery stores sprouting like wildflowers in a Kentucky meadow.

Fueled by Abel's determination and God's blessing, Sinai Church flourished. Abel made it a point to visit every single new professor and administrator at Wiltshire College; he bought mailing lists from the property appraiser and visited every newcomer in town. The church grew from a few families to over one hundred, then began to double every few months.

Now our complex sprawls over Sinai Hill. The original building, complete with tin steeple, has been preserved as a reception area for visitors, while our state-of-the-art sanctuary serves as a worship center and television studio. Our elevated platform is really a professional theater stage with footlights and trapdoors and curtains—all the accouterments of a regular theater.

I get out of the car, then grimace when I see a group of white-haired ladies in windbreakers and fanny packs posing beside the huge brick sign at the front of the property. They and the elderly gentleman snapping their picture are probably visiting Praise Partners, our name for the contributors who pledge twenty dollars a month to support our television ministry.

While I truly appreciate the sacrifices of our Praise Partners, this morning I don't have time to play hostess.

I duck my head, intending to make a run for the building, but I'm too slow. Before I take two steps, I hear: "Look! It's Emma Rose!"

If I ignore them, I'll hurt their feelings. If I stand and talk, I'll be trapped for at least fifteen minutes. Driving away is not an option; I need to get to my desk.

Time to exercise the diplomatic skills every pastor's wife hones to a fine edge.

Acknowledging our visitors with a broad wave, I begin to move up the hill with long strides. "Welcome to Sinai Church," I call over my shoulder. "Have a look around the grounds, and be sure to stop at the reception desk." I point toward the doorway labeled *Reception,* then smile when the visitors turn toward it like flowers seeking the sun.

While they are distracted, I hurry toward the unmarked door that leads directly to the executive offices.

Abel has always attracted single-minded, loyal people. He preaches the gospel, pure and straight, and makes no bones about Jesus being the only way to heaven. "Listen to the world and you'd think there are many ways to God," he says, "but Jesus himself said, 'I am the way, and no man comes to the Father but by me.' So it doesn't matter what Oprah or Dr. Phil or Deepak Chopra says. They don't have the keys to heaven; only Jesus holds the keys to life and death. And if he says he's the way, then he is."

In an age when everyone else is terribly concerned with political correctness, my husband's preaching is uncommonly blunt; perhaps that's the secret of his success. He doesn't need fireworks or celebrity guest stars to attract viewers. He manages very well with only a word from the Lord, a bit of humor, and a little music to warm people's hearts.

The music has been my responsibility ever since we married. I didn't even know I could sing until college—my parents certainly never encouraged me. My mother suffered from chronic migraines, so loud noises—including singing, transistor radios, and *American Bandstand*—were forbidden in our house.

I punch in the security code on the exterior lock, then slip through the doorway. Praise music immediately fills my ears, courtesy of the office intercom. I move down the carpeted hallway toward my office suite and hum along with the song playing over the office sound system.

I had never experienced the sheer beauty of vocal music until I joined the Calvary Bible College choir. My choir director singled me out one afternoon, and no one was more amazed than me to discover I had a strong alto voice. My awestruck roommate compared me to Karen Carpenter, but I didn't think my singing was any big deal until Abel told me he liked my songs. When I sang, he said, he could tell I was singing for the Lord.

I learned to play for the Lord, too. I suppose I have always been attuned to music, but in that first basic music class at college I learned there were names attached to the notes in my ear and they fitted together like black and white puzzle pieces on the piano. My piano teacher said my perfect pitch was a special gift from God, and it didn't take long before I could hear a song and reproduce it on the keyboard. I'm still not the best at reading music—there are kids in our church who read piano scores better than I do—but I seldom have to hear a song more than two or three times before I can play it.

Seeing music as worship completely changed my perspective about life and ministry. I had been thinking I had nothing to offer the world but my bad experiences, but through the avenue of music I could envision a future that involved far more than counseling troubled girls. I could sing, I could play, and I could help Abel. Everybody knew that preachers needed musicians; the two went together like salt and pepper.

Like the graceful swirls in a treble clef, my life took a new turn. Music became my means of ministry; Abel became my life. Now the Abel part often overshadows the music part, but I can still find myself swept away by the sheer beauty of a lyric or a melody. When I sing, "Oh love that will not let me go," I can't help but think about how far God's love has brought me . . . and how thankful I am that it holds me tight.

Sometimes I wonder if I even had a voice in the BC years. I know I didn't have a song.

Before turning into my office, I walk to the end of the hall and peer around the corner. Tanzel Ellers, the church receptionist, sits at her round desk before the main entrance to the office complex. Rumor has it that Tanzel is one of the two farmers' wives who voted against Abel coming to Sinai, but she's mostly all smiles these days.

"Morning, Emma Rose." An extra-cheery note resonates in her voice, probably because the tourists are now browsing the literature table against the wall.

"You take good care of those folks." I wave at the white-haired woman who has just turned to gape at me. "I'd love to have a cup of coffee with you all, but I'm going to be tied up in my office this afternoon."

The woman's eyes widen while her elbow prods the old man's ribs. "Look! She looks just like she does on TV!"

I shift my attention to Tanzel. "Anything these nice folks need, you'll see to it, right?"

She nods. "Of course."

I twiddle my fingers at the tourists, then retreat around the corner. I always feel a little guilty when I have to duck visitors because some people drive hours to visit the church they watch on TV every week. Every Sunday after services, Abel and I host a reception in the old sanctuary for anyone who wants to shake our hands or share a prayer request, but we're not set up to entertain people during the week.

I make my way down the carpeted hallway, keeping my head low in order to avoid having to personally greet secretaries for the Sunday school, education program, publications department, and physical plant office.

Another corner and I'm at the hall leading to the executive suites—home away from home for Abel, Josh, and me. I pause in the vestibule of Abel's office to greet Esther Mason, his grandmotherly secretary.

"Mornin', Esther. Have you heard from him yet?"

She heaves a frustrated sigh, then shakes her head. "The president of the businessmen's club has called twice. They're getting antsy."

"He should be there by now. He and Josh left the airport right before I did."

"Thank goodness. I hate it when I can't find him."

"I know what you mean."

Leaving her, I pass Josh's office, then stride into the soft pink suite reserved for me, Celene, and the women's ministry.

My hands are trembling when I lower my purse to Celene's desk, but she doesn't seem to notice.

I pull my gloves from my fingertips in an effort to hide my nervousness. "Anything exciting?"

She lifts a banded stack of envelopes from her in-box. "Not a blessed thing. But here's the morning mail—I've flagged the letters calling for a personal response."

My eyes dart toward the phone. "Any calls?"

"It's been pretty quiet since I talked to you. I put your messages on your desk."

I take the mail and thank her, then hesitate. "About that strange message . . ."

She looks up, her eyes wide.

"Let's keep that between us, okay? I'm going to tell Abel about it and let him decide if we need to alert security."

"No problem." She leans back in her chair, a sly grin brightening her face. "So—did you figure out who Christopher Lewis is? Could he be an old boyfriend?"

Something in me recoils at the question. "I have no old boyfriends."

Tsking, she shakes her head. "I don't understand you, Emma Rose. What were you before you married the Reverend, a nun? A woman like you should have had lots of old boyfriends."

I shake my head and walk through the open doorway, leaving her words to trail behind me. My windowless office is lit only by the tall lamp on the credenza. I drop my purse into an empty desk drawer, then pick up the tidy stack of pink messages in the center of the polished wood.

Like cream, the most significant message has risen to the

top. The "C" in the name *Christopher* has been traced several times, probably as Celene took the message and mulled over its significance.

Despite that revealing sign, I trust her completely. In the five years she has worked for me, Celene has never betrayed a confidence or committed an indiscretion. Christopher could have spilled his entire life story on the phone, and she wouldn't breathe a word of it unless I gave her permission.

Perhaps what I'm looking at *is* his life story. I read the date in Celene's loopy handwriting—January 6, 1976—and the address on Hillside Drive.

At this tangible reminder of my baby's birth date, cold, clear reality sweeps over me in a wave so powerful that my knees weaken. I sink into my chair, staring at the address where I was, in a very real sense, reborn.

The image of Mercy House materializes in my mind's eye—faint at first, then as vivid as a snapshot emerging in a tray of developer. When I close my eyes I can see Lortis June Moses, smell her honeysuckle perfume, and feel the crepey softness of her skin. Her sandpaper voice fills my ears: "There is a balm in Gilead . . . to heal the sin-sick soul."

Exhausted by the irresistible riptide of memory, after a long moment I reach for the phone and punch in the number on the pink slip. I hold my breath as I bring the phone to my ear, then my left hand, almost of its own accord, reaches over and disconnects the call.

I lean back, the receiver falling to my chest as I close my eyes against the sting of tears. I can't do this, not yet. Abel is my husband, my partner, my pastor. I can't spring this news on him as a *fait accompli;* it wouldn't be fair to involve him without warning.

Before I proceed . . . *if* I proceed . . . I must talk to Abel.

CHAPTER THREE

*E*ither by the grace of God or ingrained habit, I manage to tackle the business of the afternoon. After placing Christopher Lewis's message safely inside the Bible I keep at my desk, I sort through the other pink slips.

Abel has always delegated problems in the women's ministry to me. "I love women," he says, "and I married one. But I don't understand them, I don't think like one of them, and I sure don't know how to please them. Fortunately, my wife does."

Though I'm honored by my husband's trust, sometimes I'm not sure I do. Women—myself included—have a tendency to sprinkle blood from their wounds in wide circles instead of healing the hurt and applying a proper bandage. I am constantly encouraging our women to confront the source of their problems in a loving manner, but all too often that approach is a last resort instead of a first step.

One of my pink messages pertains to a call from Judy Rousey, who is upset because Rachel Williams criticized Judy's preschool program in a ladies' Bible study group. But instead of going to Rachel and asking how she could help solve her problem with the preschool program, Judy has written a letter to Abel, called me, and inflamed the entire preschool department staff.

I jot a note on my calendar to invite Judy and Rachel to a lunch meeting. We'll work it out over pasta and salad.

Edna Larson, a vice president of Women for a Christian America, wants to know if I'm available to speak at their national convention in July. Edna is too high-profile to risk offending, so instead of delegating the call to Celene, I will call personally to say I'm not sure about the date but will let her know within the week.

Sue Hargett, our high-school youth pastor's wife, wants to know if I can participate in what she calls an "immodest fashion show" for the teenage girls. "We're trying to make a point by showing the girls what not to wear," she tells me when I call. "We thought you'd make a great Lori Long Legs. You could wear a short skirt, you know, or shorts that are way too skimpy."

Grateful she can't see my face, I frown at my legs. The years have taken their toll, and my hose can't hide the faint blue map of varicose veins. "Um, I don't know, Sue . . ."

"We all change in the rest room right across from the chapel, so it's not like you'd have to walk around in your outfit. But I understand if you're busy. We just thought it'd be nice for the girls to see you in a different role."

Her unspoken message is coming through loud and clear—*it'd be nice for our girls to see you up close and in the flesh, not just on the platform.*

I accept her challenge and pencil the date on my calendar. "I'll be there. With a thick terrycloth robe to cover me as we run from the rest room to the chapel."

I hang up, then pencil "find a too-short skirt?" on my to-do list. Life at Sinai Church is never boring.

After responding to all my messages, I glance at my watch. Three o'clock. At least two more hours before I can talk to Abel.

I swivel my chair toward the narrow window at the side of my office. My brain knows I need to keep busy. I have responsibilities, and I ought to move on to something constructive like studying the lesson I'm supposed to teach for the Sunday morning new members' class, but my brain is spinning like a top around one fixed point: Christopher Lewis.

My son . . . and the gracious keeper of my secret.

Celene is intuitive, but she would never guess the relationship between me and the stranger who called. The entire world seems to know that Abel and I are childless, and I'd bet my last dollar that Celene and most of the church folk have joined Abel in believing I am the infertile partner in this marriage. In Scripture, after all, it's always the woman who is barren.

My husband—who has refused to submit to the procedures required for fertility testing—has accepted our childlessness as the Lord's will. He has always been honest about the heartbreak of the empty womb, freely mentioning our failure to conceive in sermons, interviews, and personal conversations. With a generosity born of ignorance, he says infertility is a shared problem, something that cannot be blamed on one partner or the other. If God chooses not to bless a couple with children, then the Lord clearly has other plans.

My gaze falls on a laminated plaque featuring an article from the front page of the *Washington Post*. The headline proclaims *Kentucky Pastor Wants to Sanitize TV for America's Children*.

I have read the first paragraph so many times I can quote it verbatim:

Abel Howard, fondly known as "the Reverend" to his extended flock, has joined with his wife, Emma Rose, to launch a crusade to clean up television, and, by extension, American society. When asked why he cares so devoutly about the nation's television viewing habits, Howard answered, "We care about television because

we care about the glassy-eyed, media-hypnotized children of America. My wife and I have no children of our
own. After dealing with that sorrow—through which
we realized that our desire for progeny is nothing compared to the incredible yearning God feels for his
errant children—we came to see that God intends our
offspring to be spiritual, not biological. For the sake of
our *spiritual* children—who range in age from one to
ninety-two—we want to bring this nation back to the
standards of decency and righteousness that once
exalted us as a people."

Abel has long forgotten about the pain of our empty bedrooms. The quest for spiritual children occupies his days and
nights and even his dreams, and my hopes have been swept up
in his quest for souls. I love the thought of bringing children
into the kingdom of God, but I can't deny that my empty
arms still ache when I walk through the brightly painted nurs-
ery classrooms.

Abel mourned for our unborn children and moved on;
sometimes I think he scheduled his grief in his appointment
book. My grief clings to me like a shadow; it lies next to me at
night, often waking me from sleep with soft groans. On those
nights I lie motionless in the thrall of moments alchemized
from forgotten time. In the moonlight pouring over our bed
I see the nurse holding my son over my breast. This time she

pauses, allowing me to count my baby's fingers and toes and study the sweet shape of his lips . . .

If I'm not careful, I'll drive myself crazy. I reach for my Bible, open it, and flip through the delicate pages until the pink message lies beneath my fingertips.

There it is again—the link to my son, my past.

I run my finger over the inked lines. What can you discern about a man from his name? *Christopher* sounds modern, elegant. More sophisticated than the Steves and Gregs and Mikes who teased me in grade school . . . and the pseudonymous Joes and Jacks who picked me up on the Lower East Side. One of those Joes or Jacks is Christopher's dad, but I have no way of knowing who fathered the child that ultimately saved me from life on the streets.

Christopher . . . the name sounds *good*. Lewis, obviously, comes from the family who adopted him. The agency never told me much about them, only that they were a Christian couple who lived somewhere in upstate New York and wanted a child. I have always imagined my boy growing up in flannel and sneakers, with a pony or a big dog at his side as he hikes through the Adirondack Mountains . . .

The image jars me. Goodness, how has he found his way to Kentucky? I bring the message closer and study the phone number—the area code and exchange are local.

Christopher Lewis did not call from New York, but from Wiltshire.

I bring my hand to my mouth as my stomach clenches.

Celene raps on the door, then opens it. "You didn't get lunch, Emma Rose. Do you want something to eat?"

I struggle to force words across my tongue. "Thanks, Celene, but I'm fine."

May God forgive the lie.

"Okay, then."

She closes the door; I lower the pink paper back to my Bible. Christopher Lewis would be twenty-eight now, a full-grown man. Perhaps he's married . . . maybe he has a child. Maybe the child is the reason for this call; Christopher might need to understand his genetic history because his baby needs a bone-marrow transplant or something.

I rake my hand through my hair. Or maybe I've watched too much television. But isn't that always the way it unfolds in movies? Adopted kids from happy families almost never search for their biological parents unless they need an organ transplant or suffer from some unusual genetic disease. Maybe Christopher is sick with some incurable illness, and I'll have to tell him he must have inherited it from his dad because I'm as healthy as a May morning. And then he'll ask who his father is, and I'll endure the excruciating agony of admitting I have no idea.

Because I was turning tricks to survive when my child was conceived. And I was seventeen. And so stoned most of the time that I couldn't even describe the men who picked me up, let alone remember their names. In those days I had no idea God had designed sex as a gift.

I bow my head and cover my face as a wave of agony rises from someplace below my breastbone and floods my face. I've been a minister's wife for nearly twenty-four years; I've been living this new life for twenty-eight. I walked the streets for no more than twenty-two months, so why have those days come back to haunt me?

God, what are you doing?

Abel says we should close our eyes to the past in order to keep sin at bay, yet something in me wants to throw open my arms and welcome this souvenir of my darkness. Is that per-verse . . . or only natural? Should I try to be human or godly?

I lower my head to the desk and close my eyes as memo-ries come flooding back.

Abel's upbringing and mine were about as alike as mus-tard and custard. While Abel played in the hills of Wiltshire, I grew up in Brocton, a small town in western New York state. My dad worked for the FBI; my mom lived for the bottle. Since we saw more of Dad's empty recliner than we did of him, Mom spent more time pouring herself drinks than car-ing about her only child.

Kids are resilient, they tell me, and I suppose I couldn't miss what I never had. As a kid I spent most of my time day-dreaming or reading. I was an A-plus student who found pleasure and affirmation in pleasing my teachers. If the summer of '74 had never come, I'd probably have graduated as salutatorian and gone to college on an academic scholarship.

But Joey Malone robbed twenty-four banks in the winter and spring of '74, and Dad was one of the federal agents sent out to track him down. Dad must have thought he'd hit the jackpot when he walked into a St. Louis tavern and discovered Malone bellied up to the bar. Witnesses said the lone agent tried to take Malone in, but Number Two on the FBI's most wanted list calmly shot Special Agent Tom Harbison in the chest, ordered a whiskey, and took the time to gulp it down before stepping over my father's body and striding out the front door.

After that, Mom wore the title *widow* like a veil, hiding in its gray shadows as she spurned public sympathy and drank even more. I kept thinking there ought to be a special word for kids who've lost their fathers, something more dignified than *poor thing,* which was all I heard from my neighbors and classmates.

Yet Ziggy Constantine, a brawny senior, whispered those words with a particular tenderness to which I eagerly responded. I didn't think Mom even cared about my dating until she came home early one night and found me and Ziggy making out on the living room couch. In a sodden rage she threw Ziggy out, then strode into my room, yanked my clothes from the closet, and flung them onto the front lawn.

Responding with the white-hot anger of a fifteen-year-old, I plucked a few things from the mess in the yard, tossed them into a gym bag, then strode back into the house long enough to grab every dollar, quarter, and dime I could find. After a confrontation at Ziggy's place, where I learned that seventeen-year-old boys are hard-wired to avoid any permanent responsibility suddenly thrust upon them, I took a bus to Manhattan. Time and poverty led me to the Lower East Side.

I wish my story were more unique. A thousand variations of my runaway experience have flashed across the nation's movie screens with both happy and tragic endings. In reality, my existence was far dirtier and hungrier than those depicted in most Hollywood dramas. I could have easily disappeared into the urban landscape, worn into nothingness like a piece of gum on the sidewalk, but God had other plans. My dreams of glamour and independence popped like a string of soap bubbles, and before two years had passed I found myself sick, pregnant for the second time, and too broke to pay for another abortion.

So I tried to kill myself. One morning I scored sleeping pills and a bottle of vodka from a pimp who worked Avenue B. Weeping over the misery of my life, I swallowed the first pill and pulled at the bottle, then swallowed the second pill and drank some more. I kept thinking death might hurt, so I wanted to be completely senseless when I took that last breath . . .

I woke up the next morning in an alley with rat bites on

my ankles and bits of gravel imbedded in my cheek. The pills had disappeared along with the bottle, and someone had pulled every last dime from my pockets.

I propped my arms on my knees and stared at the broken concrete. I was a waste of skin and bone; I couldn't even commit suicide properly. I had but one thing to give . . . and there were plenty of takers on Manhattan's Lower East Side.

A week later, I was on my way to score some drugs in Tompkins Square Park when I stopped for the light at Third Street and Avenue B. A graceless little restaurant occupied that corner, a place I'd never noticed. The paint had weathered out of the fading letters on the sign, so I could barely make out the name: Nola's Meat and Three.

I hardly ever ate when I was using, but something—maybe the baby—made me hungry. The aromas coming out of the open doorway called to me. For a long moment I stood motionless, breathing in the scents of baking bread and roasting beef. I don't know how long I stood rooted to the sizzling sidewalk, but before I could move a big woman came out, threw her arm around me with amazing tenderness, and led me inside. Two minutes later I was in a booth slurping up beef stew and gulping down biscuits that tasted like they'd been baked in heaven.

Nola Register settled into the seat across from me, her eyes beaming at me over a set of triple chins. She propped her head on her hand and watched me eat. She couldn't have been more than sixty, but her eyes looked a thousand years old. Two years before, I wouldn't have given Nola the time of day, no matter how much she fed me. Overweight and frowsy, she lumbered like a stevedore and smelled of yeast and perspiration. Something about the way her wiry hair jutted up like exclamation points made me nervous.

But her eyes shimmered with love and compassion. Those eyes caught me, embraced me, enslaved me. At that moment I was so hungry for love I'd have signed on as a potato peeler for life if she'd asked me to.

She had something far different in mind. "Honey," she finally said, "you're headed down a dead-end street. Whaddya say to a fresh start?"

I stared at Nola over a bowl of beef stew, a fountain welling behind my eyes. My vision blurred, and suddenly I couldn't speak over the sobs rising from my chest.

Nola stood up and came to sit beside me, then wrapped a meaty arm around my shoulders. "There, now," she whispered, rocking me in her embrace. "Everything's going to be all right."

Within twenty-four hours I was on a bus to Hudson Falls, a town in east-central New York; within another twenty-four hours I had been welcomed into the rectangular brick building known as Mercy House. Lortis June Moses, a woman with sharp cheekbones and silver ringlets curling on her forehead, ruled over my new home with a velvet fist. No messin', no men, and no Marlboros, Lortis told me in the front room. At Mercy House I'd find studyin', singin', and salvation—plenty to take the place of all my bad habits.

My stubborn pride rose up when Lortis June recited that speech, but within a week I discovered that the same firm love that animated Nola reigned in Lortis June.

At Mercy House I discovered a new way of life. Lortis June demonstrated that "Christian" was more than a box to check on a demographic survey. Being a Christian meant having a new birth, a new perspective, and a new life.

While volunteers helped me earn my GED, Lortis June helped me understand that God never intended me to be lost in my sin. I had been created for fellowship with God, she said, and my life would change if I decided to listen to God instead of ignoring him.

"I'm not saying your life will always be perfect," she told me. "But the trouble we Christians go through has been engineered for us, designed to bring us even closer to the Lord we love. So we can trust the trouble. We can even smile through the pain."

My love for the Lord grew as quickly as the baby swelling inside me. Within a month of arriving at Mercy House, I had chosen to give my life to God. Jesus and I enjoyed a kind of honeymoon phase until I had the baby.

After that, I didn't know what to do.

I had accomplished worthwhile things at Mercy House. I

passed the GED tests, received a high-school diploma, gave birth to a healthy baby boy, and found a loving home for him. I checked off every item on my life's "to-do" list but couldn't imagine what I was supposed to do next. I had no money for college and no means of financial support. Lortis June thought I might be able to get a partial scholarship from a Christian college, but even if I entered a work program, I'd still need financial help to complete a four-year degree. I began to think I might have to go back to Brocton and search for long-lost relatives—or Mom, God help me—but that idea appealed to me about as much as taking a voyage into the eternal night of the damned.

I was beginning to doubt Lortis June's promise that God had a plan for me when a letter arrived from Brocton. Displaying considerable ingenuity, my mother's lawyer had tracked me through the General Educational Development testing service.

My mother, he informed me, died nine months after I left home. The house had been in bad shape, but, acting under a power of attorney, he paid for repairs with the money left in her estate and sold the house within a few months. As my mother's only daughter, I had inherited the remaining estate, which amounted to just under fifty thousand dollars.

That night Lortis June sat with me in the tiny room we used for a chapel. The lawyer's letter weighted my hand, as heavy as the unshed tears in my heart. I had loved my mother with the unreasonable and unreasoning love a child feels for the center of her universe, but I had never known love from her. She had made no effort to find me.

Lortis June picked up my hand and pressed it between her work-worn palms. "The Lord moves in mysterious ways, honey." Her voice went soft with awe. "I can't pretend to know why this happened when it did, but I know you can trust our Jesus. Your mama is gone, but she's left you with what you need to get on with the rest of your life. God had a hand in that. He has a hand in everything that touches the lives of his children."

I stared at the letter in my lap. "Why couldn't God just make her love me? That would have been nicer than having money. She could have cleaned up and dried out, and then she would have helped me through school, and I could have worked to help her—"

"I've found it's best not to argue with the past." Lortis June patted my hand. "I just accept and move on. That's what you need to do."

So that's what I did. Accepted the money, went to college, met Abel Howard under a spreading oak tree. I found the love I'd been searching for and so much more. I began to forget the pain of having a mother who never even looked for me.

Blinking away bitter tears, I raise my hand to swipe the bangs from my eyes. For an instant I am startled to discover that my bangs are wispy, not the longer, heavier style I wore in college.

I am no longer a young woman. I am forty-five, old enough to be a grandmother. The paper in my open Bible may lead me to discover that I am.

The wonder of the message strikes me afresh—mostly because after Mom died, I never expected anyone to make an effort to find me.

But someone has.

CHAPTER FOUR

*U*nable to concentrate on anything more significant than the arrangement of books on my desk, I give up on work and drive home. I let myself into the house, turn off the alarm, drop the mail on the table in the study. Relieved of that small burden, I slip off my shoes and pad toward the bedroom Abel and I left only twenty-four hours ago.

When I packed for our overnight trip to Washington, our room had felt large and spacious, vibrant and elegant. Now the bedroom feels chilly and small, as if the walls have inched forward in our absence. The bed looms large in the center of the room; the other furniture cowers before it.

I drop my overnight bag onto the small bench at the foot-board and stare at the smooth satin comforter. I can almost see a gulley running down the center of the mattress, the beginning of the abyss that might develop before nightfall.

Tonight when I lie next to Abel, will he reach across the chasm to touch my hair as he usually does before he says good night? Or will my news prove too much to bear? I have known couples who gradually drifted apart; others are torn apart by infidelity and betrayal. Abel would never divorce me for something that occurred before we met, but my news might destroy his love. After all, he says love is a decision you make every day.

Will he decide to love me tomorrow?

The question hangs in the cool dark silence.

Desperate for something to do, I open my suitcase and pull out the rumpled suit I wore yesterday. I carry it into the bathroom, then drop it into the hamper dedicated to the dry cleaner. My toiletries kit gets shoved beneath the bathroom sink, my toothbrush clatters back into the china holder sitting beside the faucet.

Good grief, what is keeping Abel? I glance at the small clock on the marble vanity—it's five-fifteen, and Abel promised he'd leave the church by five. Our house is only ten minutes away, so I should hear the hum and creak of the garage door at any moment.

I'll stay busy, keep my mind occupied. I pull my lingerie

from the overnight case and drop it into the regular laundry hamper, then turn the case upside down and give it a shake to make sure I haven't missed anything. Satisfied, I push it to the top shelf in our walk-in closet, then step into the bathroom.

I'd love to soak my tension away in the whirlpool bath, but the tub is a disaster. Last month we discovered a leak in the water line leading to the tub; a plumber repaired the leak two days ago. But now we need a tile man to replace the tiles the plumber had to remove in order to access the plumbing. The tile job will be larger than we expected, because the tiles on our tub match the floor tiles, and the old tiles are no longer being manufactured. So we'll have to replace all the tub and floor tiles, which means I'll have to deal with home repairs for at least another week.

Sighing, I walk back into the bedroom. I should have called a tile guy today, but Abel and I have had more important things on our minds than bathtubs.

I sink to the edge of the bed and glance at the clock on my nightstand. Five-twenty. Abel is late, but that's nothing unusual. An urgent call could have come into the office at the last moment. But now he's too late for me to tell him my news—the deacons' dinner is at six, and something like this can't be sandwiched between appointments. I had wanted at *least* a half-hour to talk to Abel; I need time to gently break my news.

I wander back to the closet. Though I would give anything

to stay home to think about the day's revelation, nothing short of a heart attack can get me out of this banquet. If I don't go, Abel will be peppered with a thousand questions about where I am and if I am well.

At least I don't have to sing. I can sit quietly at the head table, paste on a pleasant smile, and mull over Christopher Lewis's call while my husband speaks. I'll just have to remember to laugh in all the appropriate places.

I put one hand on my hip and study my side of the crowded closet. What to wear? Nothing too flashy; these are local church people, many of whom will have come straight from work. Nothing too drab, either; they are proud of their pastor and his wife; they expect us to look like television personalities. A suit is too stiff; a flowered dress too domestic.

I finally settle on a tailored pantsuit with a delicately embroidered lapel. The embellishment elevates the outfit above the ordinary, but it's still about ten degrees shy of costume.

After changing, I step to the mirror to freshen my makeup. My shoulders tighten when a quick glance at the clock tells me it's five-thirty. I swipe another coat of mascara onto the tips of my lashes and realize that if Abel doesn't come through the door soon, we'll be lucky to make it to the dinner on time.

I brush my teeth, rinse with mouthwash, check the tips of my fingernails. I am applying another spritz of hair spray when I hear the electric hum of the garage door. It's five-forty. Abel will barely have time to change his shirt before we have to leave.

I wave the hair spray away from my face, then move into the bedroom. Abel enters a moment later. "Hey, hon." He pecks my cheek, then waves a yellow envelope before my eyes. "I found this by the front door."

It's a regular envelope, hand-lettered and addressed to "Mr. and Mrs. Abel Howard." There's nothing beneath our names, but someone has written a return address in the upper left corner: Cathleen Stock, 8374 Martingale Place, Wiltshire.

The woman lives next door, and the fact that there's no "Rev." in front of Abel's name tells me she doesn't know us at all.

Shrugging out of his coat, Abel gives me a broad smile. "Hey, you look great. Ready to go?"

I drop the envelope and sink into the leather recliner across from the bed. I had so hoped to be able to unload the burden I've been carrying all day, but there's no time.

Disappointment brings a lump to my throat: "I suppose so."

"I'll just be a minute." He strides by me, headed toward the bathroom. His voice echoes in the cavernous tiled space. "Did you bring in the mail?"

I hesitate before I answer. I did grab the mail, but I was so preoccupied I dropped everything on the desk without sorting through it. Most of our mail comes to us through the ministry; only personal bills come to the house, and those are all listed under the name of "E. R. Howard," the only designation we trust. For security reasons, we never open anything arriving at the house with our own names featured in the address.

The envelope in my hand, however, looks harmless enough. I slide my thumbnail under the seal. "The mail's on the desk in the study. Haven't had a chance to look at it."

"That's okay."

As Abel takes off his shirt, I open the folded page from the envelope. My neighbor has organized a progressive dinner for all willing residents of Martingale Place. The event is scheduled for February 22, 5:30 P.M. All families who want to participate should RSVP before February 15—

It's impossible, of course. We're just too busy for this sort of thing. I consult my mental calendar. The dinner is more than two weeks away, but the twenty-second is a Sunday . . . and there's no way we can attend on a Sunday evening. Even though my husband never preaches on Sunday night, preferring to give the other staff pastors an opportunity to speak, he wouldn't think of missing a service for a social activity.

Besides, Abel really likes to be "off" when he's home. It's the one place where no one asks his opinions about politics, theology, or whether or not the Church will endure any part of the Tribulation.

Abel steps out of the bathroom, buttoning a fresh white

shirt he's pulled from the closet. "Good day, hon?"

"Hmm." I press my lips together as I slip Cathleen's invitation beneath a coaster on my dresser. "An interesting day."

Abel grins. "Trouble in the women's ministry? I saw that letter from Judy Rousey. Sounds like she's got it in for Rachel Williams."

"I'm taking them both to lunch. We'll work it out."

I look him full in the face, hoping he'll see that Rachel and Judy are the last people in the world I want to talk about. If he looks intently enough, surely he'll see the secret lurking in my eyes and ask why my voice is pinched and tight.

But he's frowning at the buttons on his shirt. "I hate these things. They always make the buttons too small."

I don't answer, and my silence makes him look up. "What's wrong, Em—oh. You wanted to talk to me about something, right?"

The right question, but not the right attitude or the right time. I nod as the lump crowds my throat again, then I swallow. "It can wait. There's not enough time to get into it."

"You okay?" A faint thread of concern lines his voice as he tucks in his shirt. The question is sincere, but his eyes are distracted.

For an instant I am tempted to open my mouth and let everything in my heart spill out. Abel could be late to the dinner, couldn't he? And it wouldn't be the end of the world if he didn't show up. We have dozens of men on staff who could step in and take his place; several of the deacons are wonderful speakers. Other men miss meetings on account of family emergencies—well, I'm Abel's family, and tonight we have an emergency.

But my husband's thoughts are not with me; they have already focused on tonight's meeting. Tonight Abel has to speak to the men and women who actually do the work of the local church. Many of them are the aging pioneers who worked alongside us when we came to Sinai Church twenty-four years ago. He'll want this night to be relaxed and open; he'll speak from his heart and relax his guard. He won't want to miss this meeting, and if I tell him my news beforehand, walls will come up behind his eyes. Our people will see. They'll know something's on his mind. And they'll ask what it is.

I can't let my troubles intrude now.

"Later, gator." I stand and reach out to touch the soft wave falling over his ruddy brow. "I want to talk to you about something personal, but it'll keep."

The line of his mouth tightens. "You're not sick or anything?"

"I'm fine." I underline the words with all the sincerity at my disposal. "I just want to talk to you about an opportunity I'm thinking about pursuing. I'd like your opinion before I proceed."

Relief floods his features. He buckles his belt, then heads back into our cavernous closet.

"What color are you wearing?" he calls, and I am slammed by the awareness that he stood right in front of me without really seeing . . . anything.

"Black." I move to the bathroom doorway and lean against the casing. "Nice to know you still pay attention to how I look."

"You always look beautiful, Em."

He steps out of the closet again, a red tie looped around his neck, then plucks a black sports coat from a hanger on the back of the door. "Ready?"

I nod, suddenly too weary for words. I had hoped to share this burden by nightfall. The thought of carrying it alone for two or three hours more makes my shoulders ache.

The banquet is a cookie-cutter copy of dozens of others I have attended in the years of my marriage. I am seated at the head table with Abel at my left and Jane Swenson, wife of the chairman of the deacons, at my right. Jane is at least eighty years old and a dear saint, but she spends the entire evening filling my ear with complaints about the "unruly hellions" our middle-grade youth pastor escorts into the worship center every week.

"Up and down, down and up; during the service they are like little rats," she says between bites of chicken breast and green beans. "Honestly, what happened to good manners? I know those kids aren't allowed to run around in school, so why does that youth pastor let them run around during worship?"

I scan the crowd for the pastor under discussion. "I'm sure he's trying to teach them," I tell Jane. "I think we should be grateful the kids are in church at all."

Chewing in the deliberate and cautious manner I have come to associate with the aged, Jane shakes her head. "I don't see what good church is doing 'em if they won't sit and listen to the sermon."

Squinting between sprays of fern that jut from the oversized bouquet before the lectern, I finally spot Jake Simons, pastor to our middle-grades department, sitting at a table with his wife and several deacons. I hope his dinner companions aren't giving him a hard time about kids wandering through the sanctuary during worship.

As we finish our cheesecake, John Swenson stands to introduce Abel, though no introductions are necessary. My husband is greeted by enthusiastic applause as he takes his place behind the lectern, and for the next half-hour the audience is enthralled by his plans for the future—a new campaign to clean up television, a program to monitor the votes of politicians on Capitol Hill, and the publication of tracts designed for spiritually-ignorant folks like the Hollywood producer who wrote our ministry and asked for information on the gospel.

"I'm sure this fellow is still as lost as Atlantis," Abel says, grinning, "but the light of God has begun to shine upon his heart. And when the light of God shines, my friends, sin is rooted out, souls are convicted, and people come to Christ. And that is what our church is all about!"

Thunderous applause fills the room at each thump of Abel's lectern, and I know these people are thrilled to be getting a sneak peek at what God is planning to do through their church and their prophet. Looking at them, I can't help but think of the ancient Romans, who sacrificed much to train their gladiators in the field. They see Abel as Wiltshire's warrior, its captain, and their shepherd.

And he is only too happy to rise to the challenge.

He concludes his remarks with thanks for the work they do to support the church, followed by a heartfelt prayer of blessing for the men who minister to the body of believers and the women who support them. When he finally says "amen," chairs all over the room scrape across the carpet and women dive to retrieve their handbags.

Jane Swenson leans over to give me a warm hug. I return it, but something in me resists the urge to kiss her wrinkled cheek. If I had wandered into Sinai Church in my younger days, she'd probably have resented my attendance at services. I didn't know how to sit still for worship. Because my parents never took me to church, the only religious images in my mind were clips from old movies—people lighting candles, confessing to priests, and wearing somber colors while singing hymns in hard wooden pews.

As Abel steps out from behind the head table, an impromptu line of deacons and their wives forms as they come forward to speak to him personally. Ordinarily I would stand by his side or slip away in my car, but tonight we arrived in one vehicle so I can't go home now. Neither can I stand beside him—my face feels as if it is made from tissue paper and might shred with one sharp smile.

So I walk into the hallway and retreat to the ladies' lounge. No one lingers on the cushioned benches in the elegant front room, but a quick glance at the line of pale pink stalls assures me I am not alone. After visiting the wall of mirrors to check my makeup—a habit borne out of regular TV appearances— I settle onto a bench and open my purse as if I have some urgent business with its contents.

A moment later Eunice Hood, one of the deacons' wives, comes out of the stall, splashes her hands at the sink, then blows her nose. She pulls a bit of tissue from her purse and dabs at a smear of mascara beneath her eyes, then slips through the front lounge with barely a glance at my bent head. She looks as though she's been crying, but I haven't the energy to ask her if something's wrong.

As the door closes, I prop my elbow on my knee and let my shoulders slump. If not for fear of discovery, I would curl up on this bench and weep myself, for while my husband was speaking of the future, I could think only of the past.

What is God doing to me? My life has been devoted to the

advancement of the kingdom of God, yet for some unknown reason the Lord has allowed my past to rear its ugly head. Why? And why now?

I love my husband dearly, but even though he is generous and understanding, he may not understand Christopher Lewis. Abel knows about the world, but he has a hard time accepting sin and weakness in those he trusts. More than once he has quietly asked deacons to resign because of their involvement with alcohol, pornography, or adultery.

What will he do when he learns that my past includes all those things . . . and worse?

Tears brim at my eyes. I dash them away, but still my eyes sting. My mascara will be running soon, and the rims of my eyes might already be red and swollen . . .

Please, God, keep the deacons' wives at a safe distance.

In the ballroom, Abel has at least another half-hour of handshaking to perform. Each deacon present will want to personally assure "the Reverend" of his support, and more than a few will lean close to whisper words of "concern"— better translated "complaint"—into Abel's ear. But though he is bone-tired, Abel will nod, smile sincerely, and thank the gentlemen for their concern.

Later, of course, he will proceed exactly as he feels the Lord wants him to proceed. There's a fine art in leading a church—the pastor is the shepherd, Abel says, and while the sheep may love to bleat and baa and balk, the shepherd is responsible to the One who owns the sheep. Wise is the shepherd who listens to the counsel of elders, but a pastor is ultimately responsible to God alone.

I lean against the wall and close my eyes, resigning myself to a long wait. Abel loves to preach about sheep—though they are not the brightest animals on earth, he says they can be amazingly brave and assertive. They will do almost anything to follow the shepherd they have learned to trust.

It would be uncharitable, I suppose, to remind Abel that not all his sheep trust him. When people bombard our offices with petty concerns that have nothing whatsoever to do with the purpose of ministry, I am tempted to return their notes and letters with one word written across the page in bold, red ink: "BAAA."

Good grief, what is wrong with me? I'm not usually so cynical. I love our church members dearly. For years they have supported us with their prayers, and the week after my emergency appendectomy they absolutely flooded our house with flowers and food. They are wonderful, giving people . . . but most of them share a mind-set that would have trouble accepting my current situation.

I lift my eyes to the ceiling. *Forgive me, Lord, for feeling so skeptical about the people you have called Abel to lead.* A good shepherd does not hate the flock, but protects the lambs, rescues the wayward ones, and leads the sheep beside still waters.

I would give almost anything for a rest beside still waters

right now. I need my shepherd, my husband, but the bleating flock will not leave him alone.

For half an hour I wait, filling the time with a meticulous purging of my purse. After tossing away the last unnecessary receipt, scrap of cellophane, and paper clip, I check my watch, then stand, smooth my slacks, and adjust my jacket. With my organized purse on my shoulder, I walk toward the ballroom wearing a smile that feels only two sizes too small.

Abel has whittled the line down to one deacon. This last fellow, a young man who recently joined Sinai Church, is babbling about how excited he is to be involved in a ministry where God is moving, miracles are happening, and people are making a difference in the world.

After catching my eye, Abel grasps his shoulder, shakes his hand, and sends him off to bed with a heartfelt word of blessing. As the young deacon walks toward the exit, I take Abel's arm like a mother who needs to drag her reluctant young son away from the playground.

"Come on." I lead him toward the rear exit where we parked. "Let's go home."

And as we go, I realize that events have forced me to share my news in the last hour of our day. Perhaps this is how it should be. If Abel must know my deepest secret, it seems appropriate that he learn of it in our most intimate space.

While Abel showers, I sink to my vanity stool and peer at my reflection in the mirror. I've already dressed for bed and washed my face, so the eyes staring back at me are bald and bare. Faint smudges of weariness appear in the half-circles below my eyes, and all color has vanished from my cheeks.

I look like a woman whose energy went down the drain with her makeup. I am bone-tired from carrying this secret, and I will not carry it another hour. I need my husband to understand that Christopher Lewis could be my son . . . and if he is, I want to meet him.

I'm not exactly sure when I came to that decision. I spent most of the day dreading Abel's reaction. The reasons for that anxiety, however, reach beyond his discovery of my sin. Now that I am about to look my husband in the eye and open my heart, I think I have been dreading his reaction because I want to meet my son.

Abel didn't talk much on the drive home, but his silence didn't bother me. In my newlywed days I used to think that Abel's silences sprang from his unhappiness with something I'd said or done; now I know he needs a few moments to mentally flip the switch from being "on" to "off."

My husband is a great preacher, but he's also a wonderful man. Away from the public eye, he can be funny and warm and witty. He could have made a great living selling anything from computers to cars, but he answered the call of God and has never looked back. I've never had second thoughts, either.

I married him for better or worse, and after that brief period of "worse" in which we adjusted to each other and I adjusted to sharing my husband with the demands of a growing church, things got better.

Something tells me we may be headed for another bad patch—maybe the worst yet.

A cloud of steam rises from behind the frosted shower doors while a baritone voice belts out "Oye Como Va"—Abel's in a good mood if he's singing that Santana tune. He would never sing a rock song in public—especially if he had no idea what the words mean—but I think the act of venturing into unknown rock-and-roll makes him feel a little wild and dangerous.

I pick up a brush and run it through my short hair. Children would have been good for Abel; they would have loosened him up. And he would have been a great father. Sometimes I wonder if our ministry would have taken a different form if we'd had children. If Abel had to make time for T-ball games and soccer matches, if he had to attend father-daughter banquets and spend time at the mall, would his vision have centered more around home and family issues? Or would his ministry be exactly the same, forcing me to handle all the child-rearing responsibilities alone?

I drop the hairbrush, wary of debating a moot point. God knew we would not have children; he does not make mistakes when he calls men and women to ministries. He called Abel to his work; he called me to Abel.

Still, I can't help wondering about what might have
been . . . if we'd been a little more flexible. I would have
been willing to investigate adoption, but when Abel never
mentioned it, I couldn't find the courage to approach the
topic. I couldn't imagine sitting before an adoption counselor and admitting that I wanted to adopt a baby even
though I'd given one away.

So I will never know what it's like to parent a child. I have
acknowledged and accepted that truth many times over the
years because I don't want to become bitter. I don't think I'm
resentful . . . and I don't think resentment is driving my desire
to meet Christopher Lewis.

The sound of running water ceases, and I'm startled by
the sudden silence. The moment of revelation moves closer,
and my heart begins to thump.

I've spent most of the afternoon and night imagining
Abel's reaction. I'm sure he will be stunned. Even if at some
point he grasped the depravity of my prior life, we have lived
in a sanitized Christian bubble for so many years that the reality of my past will be shocking, perhaps even revolting.

He might flare into anger—directed at me or Christopher
Lewis. More than twenty years of ministry have taught me
that people often become angry when God changes the
settings of their lives. Abel will probably be suspicious of
Christopher . . . and he will definitely be annoyed. Though he
would be the last person on earth to reveal his frustration in

public, unexpected, unscheduled urgencies have always irritated my husband.

I look up as the shower door opens with a metallic pop. Abel has wrapped his damp towel about his waist, and he gives me a smile as he moves to the sink where his toothbrush waits.

At forty-five, Abel is a handsome man. Though his waist measures two inches more than it did when we married, he has not gone paunchy around the middle like other preachers I have met. He does not work out—he likes to quote the apostle Paul, who proclaimed that physical exercise profits little—but he is nearly always moving at the speed of sound, mentally if not physically.

He arches a brow as he works the brush over his teeth. "Wha diff fayne venson haf oof ay?"

From my library of prerecorded wifely responses, I summon a laugh. "Translation, please?"

He spits into the sink, rinses, then pats his mouth with a hand towel. "I said, 'What did Jane Swenson have to say tonight?' I saw her carrying on about something."

I lift one shoulder in a shrug. "She's upset because the young people tend to wander around in the service. She blames Jake, of course."

Abel laughs as he finger combs his auburn hair. "As if Jake could control them! The problem begins when parents don't bring their children to church. The kids wandering the sanctuary are the ones whose folks are home in pajamas, so the problem is only going to get worse. But the kids are in church—that's something."

"That's what I told her."

"I knew you'd say the right thing." He comes toward me, bends to drop a kiss on the top of my head, then moves out of the bathroom. I close my eyes, listening to the gentle slide of his bureau drawer. He will pull on pajama bottoms, then he will pick up the television remote and power on the TV so he can watch the news until eleven-thirty.

Unfortunately, I must interrupt his routine.

I stand and walk into the bedroom, where the situation has unfolded exactly as I imagined it. FOX News is blaring from the small set on a table, the remote lies at Abel's side, and he sits with his back against the headboard, a copy of our denominational newspaper in his hands.

Ordinarily I would lift the comforter and crawl in next to him, but now that feels . . . presumptuous.

"Abel?"

He doesn't answer, so I sit beside him, pick up the remote, and punch the power button. The TV goes black, followed an instant later by the crinkle of Abel's paper.

He peers at me over a bent corner, his face twisted into a human question mark. "What's going on?"

I lean toward him, supporting myself with one trembling arm. "We need to talk, remember? I don't think I can put it off any longer."

His eyes fill with the realization that I am not joking. Immediately the entire newspaper falls into his lap. "What do we need to talk about?"

I look away, unable to bear the brightness of his eyes. "Give me a minute, will you?" My voice is strangled again; a boulder has risen from the base of my throat to block my speech. I wait for it to dissolve, but Abel has never been content to allow anyone to hesitate if he could fill in the missing word.

"Are you sure you're not sick? Did you discover a lump or something?"

I shake my head, half-irritated by his probing. "I'm fine."

"Then what in heaven's name—"

"I got a phone call today." That much came out easily. Our phones ring a hundred times every day with people calling from all over the world.

Abel receives this news calmly and leans back against the headboard. "Who called?"

"I'm not absolutely positive . . . but I think he's my son."

My husband takes a wincing little breath. "Your . . . You had a *baby*?"

My heart thumps against my rib cage as I realize the significance of his question. For years Abel has consoled himself with the private belief that our infertility is my fault. I have unwittingly delivered news that could rattle his self-esteem, injure his masculinity, and even undermine his role in our marriage.

"Yes, but it was many years ago. Long before I met you . . . and before I met the Lord."

Abel's mouth changes just enough to bristle the reddish whiskers on his cheek, but he says nothing. So I rush to fill the silence with stories and facts he never wanted to hear. Using quicker, blunter words than I would have chosen if I weren't so frustrated, I tell the story of my past. I finish with news of Christopher Lewis, who has called my office at the church and wishes to speak to me . . . but only if I want to contact him.

Abel does not speak the entire time I am talking, but the words "church" and "office" seem to snap him out of his daze. He waits until I finish, then reaches for his newspaper.

"Ignore the message." His answer is automatic; so is his return to his reading. "Your past is done, gone, wiped clean by the blood of Jesus. It no longer exists."

He speaks these last words to the printed page, having lifted it as a barrier between us. I recognize his action for the defensive posture it is, but I'm not in the mood to humor him.

I reach for the paper and swipe it down, crushing the pages against Abel's lap. "Christopher Lewis exists, Abel. And if what I suspect is true, I am his mother."

A tremor touches his lips. "You are the biological source of his life. The woman who adopted him is his mother."

Though I know it's true, the answer stings.

"Finding me can't have been easy, and he only wants to

speak to me. He's here in Wiltshire, so he has come a long way and worked hard to search me out—"

"If you ignore him, he'll go away. If he has any considera-tion at all, he'll respect your need for privacy and leave us alone."

I draw a deep breath. Abel hasn't had time to think things through; he hasn't carried this knowledge around all day like a seed in the recesses of his heart. I have, and in the hours of waiting and fretting and fuming, a strong desire has taken root. With the desire came an idea—it may be an unfair slap at my son's character, but it is one sure way to convince Abel that I should call Christopher Lewis.

I look at my husband with a slanted brow. "*Will* he leave us alone?"

Abel's flat expression gives way to pained concentration. "What do you mean?"

"What if he doesn't?" I point to the crumpled newspaper in a calculatingly careless gesture. "What if he goes to the press with his story? He could, you know. He's obviously found something to link me with his history. He could track down that reporter who's always giving you so much trouble—"

Abel lifts a finger, cutting me off, as his eyes fire with speculation. Leaning forward with his elbows on his knees, he is no longer the perturbed husband, but a worried televange-list and national religious leader.

"I suppose," he finally says, not looking at me, "you'll have to call him. Sound him out. Admit nothing, but discern what his intentions are." His face clouds as irritation sharpens his tone. "For heaven's sake, what if he's planning to extort money from the ministry? This is not going to become a scandal, Em. I won't let him taint our reputation. Not a word of this story can get out."

For a moment he looks at me as if he's convinced Christopher Lewis and I have conspired to inflict harm upon his life's work. That look cuts me deeply, but I am resolved to see this through.

"It'll be okay. I have a good feeling about this." Retreating from Abel's hot eyes, I stand and move to the doorway, then press the light switch. Shadows engulf the room, but even in the darkness I can feel Abel's burning stare.

I move to my side of the bed and lift the comforter, then slide under it and turn toward the wall. "Do you want to listen?" I toss the question over my shoulder. "We could call him together, on the speakerphone."

"Heavens, no." His resentment is like a third body in our bed, a hulking, glowering presence.

The trust I've nurtured through twenty-four years of circumspect living has vanished along with the lights.

CHAPTER FIVE

*T*he rising sun floods our bedroom with a gray and watery light. I'm usually the first one out of bed, but the double doors leading into the bathroom are framed in a yellow glow, and the sound of running water breaks the stillness of the morning.

Abel never rises early unless he's had a restless night. When he sleeps soundly, nothing short of two alarm clocks and my nudging his shoulder will rouse him.

So . . . my news impacted him severely, as I feared it would.

I turn over and close my eyes, but sleep has fled with the

dawn. A thousand thoughts buzz through my brain, but the loudest and most persistent is *Today I might speak to my son.*

I know I should approach this phone call with caution and trepidation. Abel wants me to be wary, alert, and on the defensive. If Christopher asks for anything more than casual contact, especially if he solicits money, I should hang up and resolve to put him out of my mind. I entrusted my child to God twenty-eight years ago; I can certainly trust the Lord to take care of him from today forward. This young man is not my responsibility; he is not part of my present life.

But he might be bone of my bone and blood of my blood. If he is who I think he is, this stranger and I were intimately acquainted for nine months. We are bound together in a way Abel and I will never be.

Father God . . . what are you doing?

Suddenly I find myself hoping that Christopher Lewis *is* my son, that he has tackled mountains of paperwork, conquered the devils of red tape, and traveled hundreds of miles to find the woman who gave him life.

Pulling the comforter over my head, I stare into the darkness. "Please, Lord, let it be him."

Celene moves automatically toward the break room off the hallway when she sees me coming. "Coffee, Emma Rose?"

"Please."

My heart sinks when I see my office door standing open. But this is Friday, and the women who work in the executive offices always have devotions in my office on Friday mornings. Monday through Thursday they troop down the hall to the cafeteria, where one of the staff pastors leads them in prayer and shares a devotional thought; on Fridays, the task falls into my lap.

I usually enjoy this time of sharing. The ladies feel free to be themselves in my company; they talk about things they would never mention if a man were present. Celene has told us her sister is battling breast cancer; Esther Mason, Abel's secretary, is worried about her son's marriage. Crystal Donaldson, who's still single, is struggling to live a chaste life in a world where most men expect sex on a first date. These women open their hearts in the sanctuary of my private office, but today I find myself hoping they will be brief, then I am instantly smitten by guilt.

Wrong, so wrong. I need to be attentive to these women. They've come to rely on me, and I can't let them down.

I go to my desk and drop my purse into the drawer, then open my Bible and see the edge of the pink message slip peeking from its hiding place in the Psalms. I resist the urge to read the message again; one of the ladies might notice it. Besides, I have memorized the phone number.

From the moment I got out of bed I've been resisting the

urge to pick up the phone. Caution ultimately prevented me. Abel wouldn't want me to call from our home phone— Christopher Lewis, whoever he is, might trap our unlisted number from caller ID. If he proved to be a crank, we'd have to change the number again.

Besides, who wants to have a once-in-a-lifetime conversation before their first cup of coffee?

Crystal raps on my open door with a knuckle, then smiles when I gesture for her to come in.

"We never did have a chance to talk yesterday," she reminds me. "And I still have a few questions I'd like to ask for the article I'm doing."

I glance at my appointment calendar. "Can I get back to you next Monday?"

"Celene said you had a light schedule this week."

"I do—I did, but something's come up. I tell you what— drop a list of questions by Celene's desk. I'll answer them as soon as I can, and Celene can send my replies by e-mail."

Crystal nods, but disappointment flares in her eyes. She was hoping for more than written answers, but right now I'm not sure I want anyone reporting on my mannerisms, my mood, or my facial expressions. I've been burned by reporters far more skilled than Crystal—a writer for the *New York Times* visited our ministry last year and declared that I delivered my Sunday school lessons in a manner that was "quite competent, but completely perfunctory."

The criticism stung. My fleshly response was to wonder aloud if *she* could teach the same material for twenty-four years without falling into a routine, then the Spirit convicted me about my attitude and I resolved to find new approaches to teaching.

Not only had the reporter skewered me, but she'd also found fault with our worship praise team ("a group of 'Friends' clones"), our children's facility ("the church does Disney"), and our parking lot attendants ("too country club").

The most hurtful item was a picture a *Times* photographer snapped of one of our young people. Wearing a leather jacket with "I am crucified with Christ" emblazoned across the back, the young man had his picture taken while he was lifting his hands in worship. Combined with the message on his jacket, the photo seemed to imply our members literally imagined themselves crucified.

The *Times*, Abel said, tried to portray us as some kind of cult, which we definitely are not. After that disaster, he decreed that we'd allow no more secular reporters free access to the church campus. Formal interviews, fine; unrestricted freedom, no way. Members of the media reported things they couldn't explain or understand because they had no spiritual knowledge.

The arrival of Celene and Esther jars me from my memory-induced haze. I stand as they take seats on the sofa against the far wall, then nod to three other secretaries who shuffle into the room.

My smile fades as I turn away on a pretext of moving my desk chair into their circle. Nothing is as it should be this morning, everything feels slightly off-kilter. I feel the change sparking my blood; can they not see that I am pregnant with a secret? But no, they are wrapped in routine.

When my chair has bridged the gap between my desk and the guest chairs, I sit down and cross my legs in a silence broken only by the swish of my pantyhose. I am about to read from my open Bible when Josh Bartol sweeps in and drops a group of stapled pages into my lap.

"The Reverend would like you to read that," he says.

I find myself holding a two-page, typed letter, topped by one of the forms our correspondence department uses to route the dozens of letters our ministry receives each day. One of the readers in our mail department has checked the box next to "For Reverend Howard" and drawn three exclamation marks next to Abel's name.

Josh slips his hands into his pockets. "The Reverend is extremely upset about this. I think we're going to investigate and maybe call a press conference later in the week."

I glance at the letter. It's from a viewer in Atlanta who was browsing in a Books & More bookstore and discovered a book called *Your Wife or Mine?*

"This book is nothing more than a how-to guide for wife swapping," Lester Keit has written. "I was horrified, as any God-fearing man would be. I took the book to the store manager, asked him why he would sell such trash, and he said he had a perfect right to sell anything he liked. I know you can't do everything, Reverend Howard," Mr. Keit finished, "but you have tremendous influence, so I thought I should bring this to your attention. If anyone can help turn the tide of immorality in this country, Christians can. But we need you to rally the troops."

I can't stop a grimace. "Yuck."

"You're right, it's awful and disgusting." Josh opens his mouth as if he would say more, then looks around and takes a hasty half-step back. "The Reverend's going to use this, I think. We'll probably be leading a boycott of those bookstores."

I lower the letter. "Didn't one of these stores just open in Wiltshire?"

He nods. "Right across from the Wal-Mart on East Highway."

Celene leans toward the letter. "What's it about?"

"Nothing that need concern us right now." I slip the pages beneath my Bible and smile around the circle of women. "Shall we get started?"

Josh backs out of the room. "Have Celene shoot a copy of the letter, then return it to my office, will you? We're trying to call Mr. Keit for some follow-up, then we'll decide what direction we're going to go with it."

I exhale heavily as Josh exits, then flip through the pages of my Bible, searching for a marked passage. I have been leading women's devotions and Bible studies since the early days of my marriage; sometimes I think I could speak extemporaneously about anything from Absolution to Zechariah.

I pause when a highlighted passage in 2 Corinthians catches my eye. Perfect.

"'Therefore, come out from them and separate yourselves from them,' says the Lord," I read. "'Don't touch their filthy things, and I will welcome you. And I will be your Father, and you will be my sons and daughters,' says the Lord Almighty. Because we have these promises, dear friends, let us cleanse ourselves from everything that can defile our body or spirit. And let us work toward complete purity because we fear God."

I lower my Bible and look at the earnest faces of the coworkers around me. They are good women, every one of them, and they could earn more working in almost any other office in town. But because they love God and believe in Abel's vision, they have devoted themselves to this ministry.

Despite my heightened nerves, I feel a sudden rush of gratitude. I haven't felt so many strong emotions since my hormonal pregnancy days.

"Paul was warning the people of Corinth about spiritual contamination," I tell them. "He knew how easy it is for the world to corrupt our minds and thoughts. So he is reminding us to stay out of the world and avoid anything that would sully our minds."

I give Crystal a special smile. "But you already know this,

or you wouldn't be working here. The Reverend is striving hard to clean up television, movies, and"—I pull out the letter on my lap—"it looks like we're going to try to do something new to clean up our nation's immoral mind-set. We are the light of the world, but we can't do any good if we walk around with dirty lampshades. Light can't shine through an unclean vessel. So let's make sure we keep our hearts and minds pure and fit for the Master's use."

The room has been quiet, but when I close my eyes to pray, an almost tangible hush fills the circle where we've gathered.

"Father, I thank you for every woman in this room. I pray you would bless them in their work, that you would give them purity of mind and heart, and that you would touch our spirits every time we even *think* of straying from the things that are holy and pure and good. Keep us clean, dear Lord. Keep us holy. Keep us separate from the world so we can be completely blameless and fit for work in your kingdom."

A soft chorus of "amens" flutters around the room as I open my eyes. I was hoping my short prayer would end the session, but when I look up I see a small frown of disappointment on Esther's face.

"Everything okay with you, Esther?"

"My son." She pinches the bridge of her nose and closes her eyes. "He and his wife are still separated. I've been praying so hard—"

"And we'll all keep praying with you. We'll pray every time we think of you today."

I am anxious to clear the room, but I can't give these dear women short shrift. "Any other prayer requests we should know about?"

Celene waves her hand. "My sister has another chemo treatment this week."

"Okay. We'll keep praying."

Crystal gives me a bewildered look.

"I know it feels a little backward to take prayer requests after I've officially prayed," I tell the group, "but the Bible does tell us to pray without ceasing. Today when you think of Esther and Celene, please remember to breathe a prayer for their loved ones."

I wait another second, then stand. "Forgive me, ladies, but it looks like it's going to be a busy morning. Next time I promise we'll have more time for sharing."

They rise and file out, their understanding smiles softening my guilt. Celene is the last to leave. She hesitates in the doorway and asks if I need anything.

I shake my head. "I'm fine."

She lifts a brow. "Don't you want me to make a copy of that letter and return the original to Josh?"

For an instant my mind goes blank, then I remember the stapled pages in my hand. "Right, of course. But hold the copy at your desk, will you? I'd like to be alone for a while."

With a dozen questions in her eyes, Celene comes forward and takes the letter, then closes the door and leaves me alone.

I sink into my chair and prop my head on my hand. My watch tells me it's eight-twenty-six, which might still be too early to call.

But I have to speak to Christopher Lewis soon. I can't seem to function with thoughts of him running through my brain, and too many people are depending on me. I can't avoid my responsibilities for long.

I decide to call at nine A.M.

For a long while I sit with my hands folded on the desk, my thoughts chasing each other round and round in my head. The minutes stretch themselves thin as nine o'clock flutters ahead of my fingers like a summer butterfly.

Guilt rises up to accuse me in the silence. I've been short with the women, I rushed through a devotion, and I think I might have cheated to arrive at this moment. Abel doesn't want me to call Christopher Lewis. I used my influence to manipulate him just as Eve influenced Adam to take a bite of that forbidden fruit . . .

I regret my failings, but if this were Eden and that telephone forbidden, I would still lift the receiver and place this call.

I've just gained a new appreciation for the power of temptation.

The clock on the wall, a gift from the Glory Girls Sunday school class, chimes the hour.

I watch my hand pick up the phone; my fingers punch in the number. I bring the receiver to my ear and listen as the local number rings in some building probably less than a twenty-minute drive from where I'm sitting.

I consider the three possible outcomes of this effort—he will not answer, I will get a machine, or I will reach Christopher Lewis. If he doesn't answer, I will call again this afternoon; perhaps I can find time between the Missionary Union luncheon and Abel's monthly conference call to our Praise Partner state reps. If a machine takes the call, I will not leave a message . . . unless I get the machine three times, which may mean he is screening his calls.

As the phone rings a second time, another thought occurs—what if a woman picks up? He may be in Wiltshire with his wife, he may live with a roommate, he may live with—I shudder—a girlfriend. I cannot assume he is a godly Christian man; I have no way of knowing what values he holds. I know what Abel would like him to be—decent, Christian, and discreet—while more than anything I want Christopher Lewis to be . . . my son. I want him to be godly and strong and healthy ᵕ handsome, but most of all I want him to be *mine*.

ᵕe rings a third time. If he's still sleeping, he will

be annoyed if I let the phone ring again; if he's been in the shower, he'll be irritated if I hang up too soon. My heart thumps in an odd rhythm as the fingers of my right hand inch toward the phone. I should disconnect the call; if he hasn't picked up by now, he's not in. And I don't want to summon him from the shower or the garage; when we connect I want him to be calm and rested and prepared for whatever this conversation might bring—

"Hello?"

The sudden clarity of a male voice startles my thoughts into silence.

I hear nothing but the hum of the telephone line, then his voice drops. "Emma Rose Howard?"

His words are like a slug to the center of my breastbone. Somehow I gather enough breath to speak. "Christopher Lewis?"

"That's me."

"I received . . . your message yesterday."

"Thank God. I know this hasn't been an easy decision for you."

The silence between us vibrates with tension, so I utter the first thing that pops into my head, which happens to be a completely inane remark: "How can I help you, Mr. Lewis?"

Warm, melodic laughter rumbles over the phone line. I am bathed in it, and tears—of embarrassment?—spring to my eyes.

"I'm s-sorry," I stammer. "I don't know why I said that. Habit, probably."

"Don't worry about it." He laughs again. "I'm just glad my message made sense to you."

I pull the pink slip from my Bible. "You were born on January 6, 1976?"

"Yes."

"The Hillside address was written on your birth certificate?"

"Not on the form itself, but in the margin, like a nurse's afterthought. And not my amended birth certificate, mind you, but the original."

I close my eyes as truth sweeps over me with the force of a rushing train. "How did you manage it? The records were sealed."

"That's not really important, is it? I have friends who have friends in high places. But what I wanted to say is . . . well, I wanted to say hello. I wanted to thank you for what you did for me. And let you know that I'd really like to meet you . . . if that's okay with you."

A blush rises from my collar and heats my neck. I swivel my chair away from the desk and stare at the wall behind me.

He continues, his voice like music in my ear. "I'm sure you want to proceed with caution, so let me assure you that I'm not asking for money or a job or anything like that. I don't intend to harm you in any way. I . . . just want to know you. I've come a long way to find you."

"Are you sick?" The question slips from my tongue before I can cloak it in softer words. I don't know much about legal matters, but if a young man had leukemia or some other genetic disease, his lawyer might be able to obtain a court order and open sealed adoption records.

He chuckles. "I don't need anything from you, Emma Rose, nothing at all. If you're willing, though, I'd appreciate the gift of your time. I hope you can understand . . . that I've always yearned to know you."

And I you. The words leap to my lips, hover there for a moment, then pass into vapor without being spoken. I can't unlock my heart without knowing more about his motivations . . . and not without seeing his face. It's still entirely possible that this man is someone who stumbled across my son's birth certificate and wants to wreak havoc in our ministry. If Christopher Lewis is my son, I'll be able to read the truth in his face.

I draw a deep breath, then swallow. "I'll have to discuss this with my husband. Abel's a public figure, you see, and he's very careful about anything that might . . . well, he's careful to keep our private lives private."

"I know all about you, Emma Rose—do you mind if I call you that?"

I wince as a twinge of unease tightens the back of my neck. Now he sounds like a stalker.

"Call me Emma." My heart is drumming against the sides

of my rib cage, but I try to maintain a steady voice. "People who knew me in the before-television years call me Emma."

"Really?" Laughter creeps back into his voice. "I guess I qualify, then. Well, as I was saying, I know who you are and I'm familiar with your ministry. I think it's great, in fact. I don't intend to embarrass you in any way. I'd just like to meet you, to know you better. But if that's asking too much, I can go back to New York."

I shove my wariness aside. "It's not asking too much."

How could it be, when I have yearned for the same thing? If I had spent months trying to locate him, I wouldn't give up easily.

A hopeful note fills his voice. "We can meet, then?"

"I need to talk to my husband first. He may want to meet you, too."

"I'd be delighted."

I close my eyes, knowing that *delighted* is the last word Abel would use to describe his feelings about this reunion.

I turn to look at my calendar. "All right, then. Will you be at this number? Are you here in Wiltshire?"

"Yes. I'll be working in the area for a while."

"So is this the best number to reach you?"

"It's a pay phone, but you can call any time, day or night. Someone should be around to get me or take a message."

"All right, then." I take a deep breath. I know this conversation needs to end, but, fraud or not, I'm reluctant to let him go. "I hope this works out, Christopher. I have so much to ask you."

He laughs again. "Anything you want to know, I'll tell you. I'm pretty much an open book."

"Good." My voice wavers. "I'll call again, probably tomorrow. I'm not sure I'll have an opportunity to speak to Abel until later in the day."

"Tomorrow, then."

"Good-bye . . . Christopher."

I hang up the phone, then cover my face with my hands, torn between laughter and tears. If what he said was true, the sin in my past has produced a mature, considerate man who wants to know me.

For so many years I have smiled in silence while Abel told the world that God did not bless us with children so we might bear spiritual offspring. We have borne spiritual children, hundreds of them, but now I have a son.

A man with my genes, perhaps my eyes, someone into whose face I can look and see a shadow of myself. Until yesterday, I had buried my baby so deep in the vault of memory that thoughts of him could rise and stretch only in my dreams.

I pull my desk calendar toward me and pencil his phone number on Saturday's page. I will call him tomorrow, and I will try to arrange a meeting. Until then, it's going to be hard to keep this news to myself.

I lean back in my chair and rub my stomach in a slow circle, recalling the ache in the lower back, the sensation of fullness, the flutter of life in a pregnant belly. Now these feelings flow not from a baby, but from anticipation. In a few hours I will look upon the boy I surrendered so long ago, the child I had abandoned all hope of ever knowing.

CHAPTER SIX

*E*ventually my sense of wonder fades and I find my thoughts returning to the world around me. I spring to my feet and leave my office, moving past Celene without explanation. I stride down the hall to Abel's suite, give Esther a nod and a quick smile, then step into my husband's inner office.

Josh is leaning across Abel's desk when I enter; both men are intent upon a sheet of paper in Abel's hand. My husband looks up as I approach.

"I didn't think it could get any worse." He frowns at the page as if it were a bad smell. "I asked Esther to do a search for that wife-swapping book at several other Books & More bookstores, and it's either available or can be ordered from every one of them. When Josh asked a division manager why they carried such filth, he said they were doing all they could to promote the free expression of ideas."

"I didn't talk to the CEO," Josh adds, his expression a trifle woebegone. "The quote came from the southeastern sales manager. We're hoping to get some good material from the head honcho later today."

Abel leans back in his chair. "I imagine they're circling the wagons now, trying to put together a statement for the press. They know we're interested in the story, and they know we have the capability of reaching forty million households with our message. It'll be interesting to see how this situation shakes out."

"It's a great cause." Josh is fairly glowing with excitement. "I love the political ramifications. Though we're bound to hear from the free-speech liberals, it'll be worth the risk of disturbing a Sunday service with a handful of protesters."

"Oh, I believe in free speech." Abel pressed his hands together and leaned back in his chair. "It's free speech that allows us to broadcast on Sunday mornings, and we can't forget that. But free speech doesn't give you the right to yell 'fire' in a crowded theater, either, and that's the approach we need to take. Speech that's hurtful—speech that injures the very fabric of our society—need not be given free rein in this country."

Any other day I would have perched on the edge of a chair and listened to every detail; today I want to clear the room and speak of something no one else can hear.

I sink into a chair and give Josh a pointed look. "Would you mind if I spoke to Abel alone for a few minutes?"

For an instant his eyes widen, then he recovers. "Sure. Um . . . just let me gather my notes, and I'll be out of your way."

As he fumbles for papers on the desk, I let my gaze rove over Abel's cluttered office. The bookshelf against the wall is crowded with commentaries and bestsellers about Christian living; the far corner contains a filing cabinet filled with particularly poignant personal letters he has received over the years. My husband's passion for sheep is evident in the wall art, the ceramic sculpture on the bookcase, and the collection of toothpick-and-cotton-ball lambs the children make for him every Christmas. The little fuzzy creations are scattered over the bookshelves like an errant herd.

An embroidered sampler hangs crookedly near the window, and I make a mental note to straighten it before leaving. I stitched the project myself, covering the tiny fabric squares with Abel's life verse, Genesis 4:2: "And Abel was a keeper of sheep."

After gathering his notes, Josh leaves, but not before tossing his boss a questioning look. Abel ignores it, but a cloud settles on his brow as the door closes.

He folds his hands. "Let me guess; you called that young man?"

"I did—and Abel, I think he's my son. I won't know until I see him, but all the pieces fit. Somehow he gained access to the adoption records and his original birth certificate."

"If he could do it, anyone could. So this guy could be a phony."

"But he could be telling the absolute truth."

Abel picks up a pencil and twiddles it between his fingers. "So . . . what does he want?"

"He says he wants to meet me. That's all."

Abel's warning look puts an immediate damper on my rising spirits. "That's what he says now. After you meet him, he'll want a relationship, then he'll want a job. Next thing you know, he'll want to move into the house—"

"I don't think so, Abel." I pause, drawing strength from an unfounded but strong conviction that my son could not be less than sincere. "He said he didn't want anything from me."

"And you believe him?"

"Why shouldn't I?"

Abel snorts as he exhales. "Sometimes, Em, you can be unbelievably naive. This man—whom you've never even seen—has managed to find out about your past. Maybe he ran into someone who knew you from your life on the streets; maybe he's someone you picked up."

Against my will, rage rises in my cheeks. "I can't believe you said that."

"Sorry." He lifts his hands in a gesture of surrender. He's not playing fair, and he knows it.

"Emma," he begins again, speaking in the patient voice I've heard him use with little children and aged ladies, "you need to be cautious. This man will play you like a fiddle if you're not careful. I agreed you should call him in order to protect the ministry—"

"You made your reasons abundantly clear."

"—and you say he doesn't want anything from us. Fine. So thank him for his time and tell him he needs to move on with his life."

"It's not that simple, Abel. I'm his mother."

For the first time since I entered the room, my husband looks directly into my eyes. "He has a mother; the woman who adopted him did all the hard work."

"Maybe she didn't. Maybe that's why he's looking for me." The comment bubbles up from some place deep within me. I know child rearing involves years of difficult, strenuous, heartrending work, but so does surrendering a child. After the initial agony, you wonder and pray and watch every kid who walks by to see if he even faintly resembles the baby who nestled in your womb . . .

"Don't get crazy on me, Em." Abel's voice softens. "I can imagine what you must be feeling, but this is one time you can't let your heart rule your head. This young man says he wants a meeting—if you go, I've a strong hunch he'll be wanting something else by the time you get ready to leave."

I rub my temple and exhale slowly. "I don't think this is about money."

"Of course it is! Does he know who you are?"

"Once he found the birth certificate, I'm sure it didn't take long to trace my steps."

"Does he know what you are?"

I consider the question. Christopher says he knows all about me. If he has watched *Prayer and Praise* for any length of time, he knows I'm a Christian, a pastor's wife, and a musician. He must know that Abel and I have taken a strong stand against immorality on television, in film, and in politics. He probably knows about Abel's crusades to clean up America; he might even know about the occasions we've had scores of activists marching around Sinai Church because Abel dared to protest Gay Pride Day at Disney World or profanity on television.

He has to know that our ministry takes in millions of dollars each year.

I give Abel a brief, distracted glance and force a smile. "What are you saying?"

"I'm saying," he leans toward me, "that this man is probably out to blackmail us. He knows we stand for righteousness and purity, but he is evidence of your scandalous past. He is part of the darkness from which you've been freed. You've been walking in the light for so long you have forgotten what people are capable of."

Indignation flares within me. "I know more than you think, Abel." I stand, one hand clenching against my palm. "I know more about darkness and pain than you ever will."

Leaving him speechless, I turn on the ball of my foot and retreat.

Twenty minutes later I'm back in my office. I'm supposed to be writing my monthly column for *Purity,* but I have turned away from the computer to sketch faces on a legal pad— angular faces, round faces, square faces, faces with my own pointed chin. Which face is Christopher's?

I have been trying to work, but Abel's parting words still ring in my ears. He thinks he can understand sin and its corruption by reading books and news reports, but though he's as human as any man I know, depravity has never touched my husband with its sorrowful consequences. No man but Jesus was ever born without sin, but sometimes I think Abel was born with only the barest sprinkling.

My husband has been a believer practically since preschool, having been born into a Christian family that could have written a book on holy living. His father had just entered the ministry when Abel came into the world. Abel prayed the sinner's prayer before he could read and went under the baptismal waters before he could ride a bike.

"I was young, but my experience was real," he told me the night of our first date. "I fell in love with Jesus when I was only a kid, and I've never seen any reason not to follow him. Sure, I went through the usual kid troubles, but because my parents and the church members were watching out for me, I never really wandered from the straight and narrow. Jesus yanks hard on my chain whenever I'm tempted to stray."

He shrugged as he related his testimony, and I remember thinking he was like the prodigal's elder brother, steadfast and tough and faithful. It didn't hurt that his shoulders looked broad and strong in the soft streetlights lining the road that led to the girls' dorm. I had burdens to carry in those days, and Abel seemed the sort of man who could help me bear up under any struggle.

Abel's shoulders are still broad and muscular, but is it fair to ask him to carry a burden from my past?

Not knowing what else to do, I pick up the phone and punch in a number that will be burned into my memory until my dying day. I haven't dialed this number in at least three years, but I hope the woman who owns it is still alive, well, and willing to talk to me.

Lortis June Moses is a second mother to me. In 1976 she

served as "housemother" to fourteen girls at Mercy House; the last time I spoke to her she was still living there, but no longer managing the residence. She'd been in her early fifties when I passed through the home, so she has to be at least eighty now . . .

Please, Lord, let her be there.

A young, professional voice answers the phone. "Mercy House."

"Hello." My voice is clotted, so I pause to clear my throat. "I'm looking for Lortis June Moses. Is she still around?"

The woman on the phone laughs. "I don't think we could pry her out of here with a crowbar. Would you like me to connect you with her room?"

"Please."

My chair creaks as I lean back and marvel at Lortis June's longevity. She had been a widow when I met her—a young widow, actually, but at seventeen, I thought Lortis June positively ancient. She ran a clean house, well-organized and punctual, and within ten minutes of meeting her we girls knew what would (clean beds, clean nails, clean language) and would not (messy beds, dirty nails, crude language) be tolerated. But despite her rigorous standards, Lortis June always managed to exude warmth and compassion. She welcomed us into Mercy House without asking questions, accepting us as we were . . . and I had to be one of the most messed-up girls to ever cross her threshold.

In my first three weeks, Lortis June worked with the physician to help my body rid itself of drugs. She sat with me all night, guarding the door so I couldn't slip out to prowl the streets in search of whatever pills would help me get through another day. She sat across from me in the study hall, making sure I had books, paper, and pencils; she sat on the edge of my bed and held me as I wept the pain of rejection away.

And like Nola Register, Lortis June loved to talk about Jesus. Nola had convinced me I was a wreck and needed a savior; Lortis June demonstrated how a person could live a victorious life in Christ. If I had never read Galatians 5:22, I would recognize fruits of the Spirit because in Lortis June I saw love, joy, peace, patience, goodness, gentleness, self-control . . . and mercy. Measureless mercy.

"Hello?" The voice at the other end is creaky with age, but I recognize it immediately.

"Lortis June? It's Emma Howard."

A second passes, then she cackles. "Land's sakes, child, I thought you'd forgotten all about me!"

"I'm sorry, I should call more often."

She laughs again. "Where are you, honey?"

"Still in Kentucky—we've been in Kentucky over twenty years."

"How's your husband?"

"Fine."

"And your walk with the Lord?"

Lortis June's blunt approach to spiritual issues never fails to startle me. Even Abel has learned to be fairly diplomatic in his conversational approach.

Smiling, I accept her challenge. "I'm good. Lately I've been asking the Lord to reveal himself in new ways, and I think he is. The ministry is thriving; we're seeing hundreds of people come to Christ. Yesterday Abel was honored by the president at the National Prayer Breakfast in Washington."

"The president of the prayer breakfast?"

"The President of the United States, Lortis June. Abel got to shake his hand."

"That's wonderful, honey. Hang on a minute, will you, while I turn down that blasted television."

I hear the phone clunk against something hard, then several seconds pass before the sound of the television ceases. Lortis June must be moving more slowly these days, but I'm impressed she's still living independently.

The phone clunks again. "Now, then—where were we?"

Despite the pressures weighing on my mind, I remember my manners. "How are you? I was surprised to hear you're still at the home."

"Where else am I going to go? Besides, girls these days need someone to talk to; they're even more mixed up than you were." The words fall without rancor or blame; she calls life the way she sees it. "But you didn't phone to ask about me. What's on your mind, child?"

I swallow hard as an unexpected crest of emotion rises within me. "Do you remember . . . my baby?"

"Land, that I do. I have his picture right here by the phone."

Lortis June, who had gone with me to the hospital, insisted that I be given a photo of my baby. When I left Mercy House, I wanted to give her something important. That photo was the only valuable thing I possessed.

"Prettiest baby boy I've ever seen," she says, her voice soft. "I've kept his picture safe in a little silver frame. Are you . . . missing him?"

"He called me, Lortis June. Somehow he's tracked me down, and I spoke with him this morning. He says he wants to meet me."

"Land sakes alive."

"I don't know what to do."

"Lord, have mercy."

Silence rolls over the phone line, and I tense at the sound of it. Words seldom fail Lortis June.

"Well," she speaks slowly, "if God allowed him to find you, a meeting might be his will. How do you feel about it?"

I lift my gaze to the ceiling, where small tails of dust move in the breath of the heating duct. "I feel . . . elated. Terrified. Disloyal. And unbelievably guilty."

"You don't have to feel guilty about planning an adoption for that baby. If you had taken him with you when you left . . .

well, I'm not sure you could have made it, child. You were carrying the weight of the world in those days."

"I don't feel guilty for the adoption. I feel guilty for not telling my husband about it. He never wanted to know, but yesterday I had to tell him about the baby . . . and everything else. I felt better after telling him, but he didn't exactly want to hear any of it."

Silence, then: "How'd he take it?"

"I think he's in denial." My thoughts drift to the memory of Abel hunched over his desk, his eyes fixed on reports about Books & More bookstores. "Looking at him, you'd think he wasn't giving my news a second thought, but I know Abel. When something bothers him, he heads off full steam in another direction."

"He's a godly man, Emma. I hear him preach every week, and I can't find any fault in what he says."

"That's the problem—Abel has hardly any faults at all." I offer this confidence with a whimper. "Oh, he's not perfect— he leaves his socks on the floor and forgets to check with me before scheduling things. But he lives what he preaches, no doubt about that."

"Well, that's what—" Lortis June's words are lost in a coughing fit.

My tension level rises. "You okay? Should you be seeing a doctor for that?"

She clears her throat, then cackles another laugh. "Honey, when you're eighty-one and breathing on your own, you're doing fine. Don't worry about me; this is just a cold. The Lord is going to keep me on earth as long as I'm useful, and there are lots of places to be useful 'round here."

"So." Gently, I draw her back to the topic at hand. "What should I do, Lortis June? Abel's not wild about me meeting this young man—he's afraid he has ulterior motives."

"Emma." A faint note of reproach underlines her voice. "Think about it. If you had found his name, would you call him?"

Would I? Maybe not at first. I wouldn't call if he were too young, or even still living at home. I probably wouldn't even call in his college years, because young adults are so impressionable. But if I carried the information around long enough, the desire to know him would simmer in my subconscious . . . as it has for all these years.

"Yes, I'd call. If only to hear his voice and know he was all right."

"He must have the same desires. So pray about it, then follow the Spirit's leading. Meet the young man, fill your heart with his face, and let the Lord guide you from there."

"Are you sure? A wife is supposed to respect her husband's opinion, and Abel thinks this is crazy—"

"Abel may not be thinking clearly at this point. Talk to him, see if you can help him see things the way you do. And tell me this—did you love that little boy when you released him way back then?"

"Of course I did."

"Do you love him now?"

The question slices like a scalpel, opening a chamber in my heart that has been sealed for years. Raw feeling pours out, emotions that flood my soul and threaten to choke off my speech.

Love is a decision you make every day.

"Yes," I manage to reply through a current of tears. "I love him."

"Then go to him, child. Your Abel will understand. Keep your eyes open so you can see what the Lord intends to do through this. Be as wise as a serpent and harmless as a dove, but go to him."

I thank her, promise to call more often, and hang up. And as I stare at the framed photos of Abel and me atop my credenza, I realize that I called Lortis June because she's at the top of my list of people who walk with God. Abel's on that list, too, but in the last few days our connection has weakened somehow . . .

And in Lortis June's presence, I never felt anything but love.

After giving a speech across town at the Missionary Union luncheon, I drive back to the church and hurry to my office.

Celene hands me a stack of messages as I pass her desk; I flip through them and shake my head when I realize that so many issues I thought important a few days ago now seem like trivial annoyances.

Christopher has not called. I didn't expect him to, but something in me had hoped he would.

I can't wait to speak to him again.

I ask Celene to hold my calls, close the door, and pick up the phone. After punching in Christopher's number, I slide my appointment book closer. I don't have much free time this weekend, but I'd move heaven and earth and any number of appointments to make this meeting happen.

He answers on the second ring. "Hello?"

"Christopher? It's Emma."

"Hello!" His voice rasps with joy.

At the sound of his excitement I have to blink away tears. "I'd-love-to-meet-you." The words come out in a rush, borne on an impulse I don't want to weaken by second thought.

"Great!" Again, joy vibrates in his voice. "I've been praying you'd want to come."

I nod because I can't speak.

"When are you free?" he asks.

My gaze falls upon the calendar, filled with appointments I'd happily cancel if necessary.

"You tell me what's best for you," I say. "I can move things around to suit your schedule."

"Will your husband come, too?"

Part of my brain registers his thoughtfulness; another part shrinks from the thought of Abel's involvement. I suddenly realize I want to savor this pleasure alone. Abel wasn't part of my life when Christopher was born, so why does he need to be part of this reunion?

Am I being selfish . . . or am I afraid to bring the two men together?

"I'm not sure Abel is free," I answer, glad that this much is true. "He is almost always booked, even on weekends. But if you'll tell me when and where you'd like to meet, I'll do my best to be there."

"Wonderful." His voice has taken on an almost-dreamy quality. "Well, I know your days are full, so how about an evening?"

Again, evidence of supreme thoughtfulness. Most evenings I'm out with Abel on one of his speaking engagements, but Christopher wouldn't know that. And I could easily beg out of one of Abel's fund raising dinners.

"An evening would be fine."

"Great." He hesitates. "Aw, shoot, I can't wait. How about tomorrow night? Can you make it?"

I open my mouth to agree, then glance at the calendar. Tomorrow is Saturday, and Saturday nights are sacrosanct at Sinai Church. Abel has held a contemporary worship service every Saturday night for the past twenty years. I've seen him drag himself out of bed with a fever just so he can trudge into the pulpit and proclaim that nothing short of emergency surgery can keep him from joining God's people at the appointed time for worship.

There's no way on God's green earth Abel will agree to meet Christopher Lewis on a Saturday night. But I have just finished promising that I'd come, so I will.

I close my eyes. "Tomorrow night it is. What time?"

"Nine o'clock? I know that's late, but—"

"Nine o'clock is perfect." The service is finished by nine, so maybe Abel can come after he's completed his ritual of shaking the hand of every last person who wants to talk to him. This might be ideal—I can meet Christopher in private, then Abel can join us and see that this young man poses no threat. "Where shall I meet you?"

"How about O'Shays? It's on Fourth Street."

For an instant I'm startled by the unfamiliar name, then I realize that this, too, is good. Abel wouldn't want Christopher coming to the house for this first meeting, and after services our church members tend to flock to Denny's and Village Inn. I'm less likely to run into people I know at an out-of-the-way place downtown, so I won't have to stop and explain this private meeting with a young man.

I write *O'Shays* in my appointment book. "I'll find it. And I'll be there at nine."

"Thanks."

"Um, Christopher"—I tap my pencil on the page—"how will I know you?"

His laughter is warm and rich and tickles my ear. "Considering the few people likely to be in O'Shays at that hour, how can you think we won't know each other?"

He's still chuckling when I tell him good-bye.

CHAPTER SEVEN

$\mathcal{M}$y thoughts are swarming like bees when I enter the conference room, late, for Abel's monthly call to the state Praise Partner representatives. All fifteen pastors of Sinai Church are seated in chairs around the long table, their attention focused on the black phone facing Abel. Their staff secretaries sit behind them with pens and steno pads at hand.

From her seat behind Abel, Esther Mason presses a finger to her lips as I enter. Abel is speaking in the stentorian tones he usually reserves for his sermons, so I've arrived in the middle of his monthly report.

I sink into an empty chair next to Josh and cross my arms,

trying to remember the items on the agenda for this meeting. Any other day I would be able to recite Abel's schedule forward and backward; today my brain feels like Swiss cheese.

I listen for a moment, then pull a pencil from behind my ear and scrawl, *What's on the agenda?* across my notepad. I elbow Josh, who reads my note, then smiles a grim little grin and leans to whisper in my ear.

"We managed to get forty-two of the fifty state reps on the line, so the Reverend's going to bring up the bookstore matter."

Of course.

Abel is now telling the state reps—pastors who have affiliated themselves with our ministry goals—about the book he has discovered in Books & More bookstores. "Wife swapping," he says, placing his palms on the table as he leans over the speakerphone, "is a disgrace and a threat to the institution of marriage. People who think this is fun, that it's harmless, are ignoring the thousands of impressionable young lives who will forever be scarred by people who place their personal, perverted pleasure above the sanctity of marriage. The American public has hit a new low in standards of decency. Television has taken us from *Temptation Island* to *Momentary Marriage,* and this book about so-called 'swinging' is a natural result of the garbage that's being piped into our living rooms every night.

"We're going to talk to the officials at the national office of Books & More bookstores. If they don't agree to pull this offensive title, we're going to mount our own media campaign. We're going to interview adults whose marriages were destroyed by this kind of lifestyle; we're going to interview children whose lives were scarred by parents who cared more for worshiping at the altar of hedonism than raising healthy, happy children. We have to act now, brothers, and we have to act with strength and determination. The fabric of this nation is eroding faster than we can shore it up."

Abel pauses to take a breath, but his address has been so succinct, so smooth, that the room erupts in spontaneous applause. Hearing whoops and garbled "amens" from the telephone speaker, I applaud with the others and nod at the staffers who look at me with eyes that say, *He's really going to give it to them this time!*

Drawing a deep breath, Abel pulls a handkerchief from his pocket, mops his brow, then releases the deep, three-noted laugh that has become his trademark.

"Well, friends," he grins at the speakerphone, "I'm glad to know we're united on this one. I wish I had the time to speak to each of you personally, but if you need me, please don't hesitate to call. One of us will get back to you right away."

I look at Josh, who is busy making notes on a legal pad. Unless it's a particularly urgent situation, he will field calls from the state reps. There's no way my husband can get his work done if he's on the phone all day.

"Before I close, I want to thank each of you for all your

hard work." Abel smiles around the room, assuring each person present that he's grateful to us as well as the pastors on the phone. "It may be an uphill battle, but our victory is assured. One day soon, the Lord will be exalted, the devil will be defeated, and we will gain the ultimate victory!"

The room applauds again. Just as the sound begins to fade, Josh leans forward and disconnects the call. Abel pushes back his chair, thanks his staff for attending, then retreats through a back door.

Drawn by the invisible thread that links us, I slip into the hall and hurry to Abel's office. We meet in the hallway.

"Hi there, hon." He opens the door and holds it for me. "What'd you think?"

"What I heard was great." I precede him into the room, then drop into the leather guest chair in front of his desk.

"I was a little disappointed in the turnout." He sinks onto the sofa, his hands at his sides, and for a moment he looks like a little boy who has just lost a championship baseball game.

I lean forward, propping my elbows on my knees. "Josh said you had forty-two reps on the line. That's good, isn't it?"

"I was hoping for all fifty. We'll need one hundred percent involvement if we're going to pull off this boycott on the national level. We're planning to launch a media blitz with a press conference on Sunday the fifteenth. We were hoping to have our reps do the same thing in their states, but forty-two won't cut it. Our California rep was AWOL, also the guy from New York."

"Maybe Josh can call them and get them to sign on?"

Abel frowns. "Not sure it'd do any good. That California guy was gung-ho a year ago, but I've a feeling the blush has worn off the rose. Some people just can't stay committed. If they don't see personal success coming their way, they back away and look around for a more illustrious cause to support."

Closing his eyes, he drops his head to the back of the sofa. Through the closed door that leads to Esther's office, I hear movement and the sound of voices.

"Hon, before Esther and Josh come in, I'd like to ask you something."

An expression of resignation flickers over his face, but his eyes do not open. "Hmm?"

"It's about Christopher Lewis. He wants to meet me . . . and I said yes. He invited you, too, if you want to come."

His eyes twitch behind his closed lids. "My schedule is packed, Em. With this new campaign—"

"I told him you were busy." Mingled relief and shame flow through me. "I told him I'd probably come alone."

One blue eye opens. "Are you sure about this?"

"I want to meet him."

The eyelid lowers. When he speaks, his voice is flat. "When?"

"Tomorrow night, after church. I'm meeting him at a little restaurant downtown, some place called O'Shays."

Abel's eyes suddenly blaze into mine. "You're kidding."

"What do you mean?"

"O'Shays is a bar, Emma. Everybody knows that."

I stiffen, offended by the scowl darkening his brow. "I'm sure it's a restaurant. They might serve alcohol, but so does nearly every other restaurant in this town."

"It's a bar."

"How do you know?" I realize I'm challenging my husband, but his attitude is testing the limits of my tolerance. "You've never been there, have you?"

"I don't need to visit a pigsty to know it's filled with slop. I've heard talk about O'Shays. It's a bar, one of the seediest in town. It's probably not even safe for you to be alone downtown late at night."

I straighten in my chair. "I really don't think Christopher would pick a bar for our first meeting. Besides, nine o'clock is not the middle of the night. I'll go, I'll meet him, I'll come home. Simple."

Abel lowers his chin like a bull contemplating a charge, then shakes his head. "I don't like it."

My reservoir of patience, which has been heated by the emotional boiler of the past twenty-four hours, completely evaporates.

"Abel, have I ever asked you for anything as important as

this? I have given my life to serve you and God and the people of this church. Now I'm asking you for one thing—let me meet this young man. I'll go quietly, I'll be discreet, but I'm begging you, don't deny me this opportunity. Please, honey— if you love me, you'll let me go."

He closes his eyes as if he can't bear to witness my foolishness, but he does not protest again.

CHAPTER EIGHT

*A*bel and I try to keep Saturdays free for ourselves—after all, Saturday is the Sabbath, and it's impossible for a minister's family to rest on Sunday. We usually sleep late, then go out for a late breakfast at Denny's. Without fail, though, in the restaurant Abel will encounter someone from church and have to put on his "pastor hat" for half the morning.

Today, however, I have too much energy to sleep. I rise with the sun and slip out of bed, then turn off the alarm and step outside to fetch the newspaper. A glittering veneer of ice coats our winter-bare shrubs, and I find myself believing Punxsutawney Phil's prediction of six more weeks of winter.

Back inside the warmth of the house, I wipe my slippers on the entry rug and find myself eying the foyer with the judicious eye of a newcomer. If I were to bring Christopher to the house, what would his first impression lead him to think of us?

My eye roves over the white floor tiles, the gilded foyer table, and the elaborate grandfather clock just inside the door. The dining room, which is off to the immediate right, features a chandelier dripping with cut glass and purple pendants. My prized crystal lines the shelves in the china closet; a silver tea set rests on the antique buffet.

Beyond the foyer, our living room opens to wide windows with a view of the golf course. The leather sofas are comfortable, the antiques completely serviceable, the art traditional . . . yet this is not a welcoming house.

I feel the truth like an electric tingle in my bloodstream. Not one personal item lies within my view, not a single family photo or memento. There are no keys carelessly tossed on the foyer table, no shoes kicked off by the door. No toys in the hall, no scuffmarks on the tile, not even a doggie toy beneath the table.

This doesn't look like a home, it looks like a carefully dusted, perfectly preserved museum.

A wave of self-pity threatens to engulf me, but I push it back and head toward the kitchen. I've done my best to create a comfortable home, but I can't help it if we're rarely here. We are at the church Sunday through Friday, and we're often away from home on weeknights. If Abel isn't speaking here in Wiltshire, he's taking the jet to speak for a Praise Partners fund raiser somewhere or he's preaching at a revival.

When we are home, we hardly ever have guests at the house. We scarcely know our neighbors, and we've made it a habit to meet with church people at the church. Abel says a man needs a haven away from the ministry, so our home has always been our private place . . . maybe *too* private.

I drop the newspaper on the kitchen island, then move to the coffeemaker and press the power on. While it hisses and sputters, I check to be sure there's coffee in the filter, then pour fresh water into the top.

Is it possible we've become too secluded? Frowning, I lower the empty decanter beneath the spout and wait for the fragrant flow. Abel says a minister shouldn't have close friends, because it breeds jealousy and competition within the church. My experience tends to agree with his, and while I am friendly to everyone, I couldn't say that I have any truly close friends even among our staff. If an intimate friend is someone to whom you can confide your darkest secrets, then I have no intimate friends . . . except the Lord. Abel is my closest companion, and at the moment he's scarcely speaking to me. He hasn't forbidden me to see Christopher, but he hasn't given me his blessing, either. I'd bet my bottom dollar (if preachers' wives were allowed to bet) that he's praying I'll become convicted and not go to O'Shays tonight.

As the coffee brews, I cross my arms and look out my kitchen window. My next-door neighbor, Cathleen Somebody-or-other, is training a puppy on a patch of lawn between our houses. Her dog, a long-legged gangly creature, is tiptoeing over the frosted grass as if he's not quite sure about the wisdom of walking outside on such a cold morning.

I can't help smiling, and something in me hopes Cathleen will look my way so I can wave. She'd probably faint if I did—I don't think we've said more than ten words since the morning she brought me a plate of cookies to welcome us to the neighborhood. She and her husband live alone, I think, but a steady stream of cars pulls in and out of her driveway. One night—it must have been somebody's birthday—I counted four different families who came to visit, three of them with small children. Like an eavesdropper, I sipped my coffee on the front porch and listened to the happy squeals of kids and adults at play.

I can't believe I'm envying a woman I hardly know.

I don't think Cathleen and her husband go to church—ours or anyone else's—and several times I've been tempted to go over there and invite her to Sunday services at Sinai. I don't go, though, because in my deepest heart I know what her reaction will be. She will blink in surprise, then smile and thank me for the invitation. She might even promise to think about it, but she won't come.

She needs Jesus . . . but she probably isn't aware of her need. So what can we offer that she wants and doesn't already have?

Parking spaces in downtown Wiltshire are easy to find at night. Like most mid-sized cities, our downtown has fallen upon hard times as stores have moved out to the suburbs. The only really active businesses here are the Greyhound Bus station, the Kentucky Bank and Trust, and Elmer's Hardware, in which you can obtain whatever thingamajig you need along with free advice on everything from plumbing to politics.

Making my way toward the maze of one-way streets, I try to remember the last time I ventured downtown—probably three years ago, when two of our young people were arrested for breaking and entering one of the local liquor stores. I visited the jail with the youth pastor's wife because she was too terrified to go downtown alone.

As I make my way through the heart of the city I feel a thrill of fear—darkness presses liquidly against the car windows, and for a moment I feel as if I'm piloting a submarine through an ocean of ink. But iron streetlights in the heart of town pour cones of yellow light over the sidewalks and storefronts, and an occasional neon sign glows through the gloom.

Stopping at a blinking traffic signal, I am surprised to see that several businesses still survive on these pitted asphalt streets. After proceeding through the intersection, I pass several antique stores, a consignment shop for women's clothing, a homeless shelter, and the Christian Science Reading Room, where a bright halogen bulb burns over the barred steel door.

Few people are about. Two young boys slide in and out of the shadows as they ride their skateboards over the cracked concrete. A woman hurries through the lamplight, her purse over her shoulder and both hands holding tight to the strap.

I travel down two blocks of Fourth Street before I spot O'Shays. The narrow structure stands in a thin wash of moonlight, its single window cluttered with neon signs. I put on my signal to park in front of the building, but the saving grace of second thought restrains me.

From what I can tell, Abel might be right about this being a bar. And since the back of my car is clearly marked with a Jesus fish, I should probably park several feet away to avoid the appearance of impropriety.

I circle the block again and park short of my destination. As I turn the key in the ignition, I can't help but grimace at my assumptions. I'd been thinking that O'Shays would be nearly empty because nine o'clock was late for a downtown restaurant to be open. Christopher implied it would be empty, too, but for entirely different reasons. If this bar is like the others I've known, the Saturday night party crowd won't arrive until after eleven.

Too late for commerce and too early for nightlife, at eight-fifty-five I step out of my car, lock the door with the remote, and gingerly make my way over the cracked sidewalks. Chilled by the wind, I draw up inside my coat like a turtle. Abel's warnings echo in my ears, but desperation drives me forward. *My son* wants to meet me, and I would not miss this opportunity for the world.

I have so many questions. I want to know how Christopher grew up, what his adoptive parents are like, what he's doing and where he's living. Most of all (though these are questions I probably won't have the courage to ask), I want to know if he thought of me as he grew up . . . and if the flesh-and-blood woman he's finally meeting lives up to the image he has carried in his heart.

Did his adoptive mother speak of me with love? Did she speak of me at all? It would probably serve me right if she told Christopher he sprouted in a cabbage patch. Heaven knows I probably deserve one cabbage-patch story for every time I remembered my son, then banished the memory before Abel could read the longing in my eyes.

My long stride breaks when I glance toward the shadowed walls and see a newspaper-covered bum stretched over the sidewalk. Wiltshire isn't a place where you see this kind of thing, and for a moment I feel as though I have somehow been transported to New York or New Orleans. But no, this is downtown Wiltshire, and I have just passed the cobbler's shop where I used to take Abel's shoes.

I edge toward the curb as a sudden chill climbs the ladder of my spine. I look for a policeman—surely it's against the law to sleep on the street—but there are no blue-and-white sedans in sight, nothing but streetlights and shadows and leafless trees swaying in the wind.

Panic roots me to the spot. What if this man is dead? I glance toward the body again and am struck by the stiffness of the man's curled fingers. Is that evidence of rigor mortis? I should call 911 . . .

I am just about to dig for my cell phone when the man moves. I step back as he pushes himself up from the ground. The newspaper over his head falls away, exposing a face shaped into lines and pockets of sagging flesh that are more suggestive of overindulgence than age. A quilted plaid blanket around his shoulders falls away as he props himself against the wall.

His head bobs, his gray gaze meets mine. For an instant his eyes narrow, then he seems to remember who and where he is—

"Hey, lady," he thrusts out that pallid hand, "got a dollar?"

Shaking my head, I hurry down the block. I've been where that man is; I know how the game is played. If I give him a dollar, he'll spend it on alcohol or dope. If he really wants help, he could go to the shelter on Second Street or even to the YMCA in Lexington. Street people know where to go—I always did.

I halt on the sidewalk when I spot the peeling marker above the O'Shays entrance. A glowing Budweiser sign hangs in the door, and a matching clock in the window assures me they are open. Through the glass I see a polished wooden bar and a dark-haired man standing behind it.

I don't understand why my son would choose this place for our first meeting—maybe because it's quiet at this time of night—but it's too late to back out now.

At least the place looks clean. And if they sell something as simple as sandwiches, I can truthfully tell Abel that O'Shays is a restaurant.

I lift my chin and tuck my purse more securely under my arm. I won't let the fact that they serve alcohol bother me. After all, Abel and I enjoy eating at the country club, and that dining room has a bar tucked into a side room.

Pressing my lips together, I open the door and move forward. A bell above the door jangles a welcome and my heels make tapping sounds as I cross the black-and-white-tiled floor, but only the bartender looks up at my approach. A woman sits at the far end of the bar, her head bent low, and a couple of men occupy one of the booths that line the left side of the room.

The joint isn't exactly jumping.

Giving the bartender a shaky smile, I walk slowly past the booths, only to find all the tables strewn with dirty ashtrays and unwashed glasses.

"Sorry about the mess over there," the bartender calls. "Haven't cleaned up after the after-work crowd yet. But you can have a seat at the bar."

I am about to pretend I have come seeking a rest room when the bartender leans toward me and lowers his voice. "You look a little lost, lady. Do you need help?"

"Um," I edge closer to the polished brass railing, "I'm supposed to meet someone here."

I hold my breath, half-afraid that this tall, dark-haired young man will grin and confess that he is Christopher, but he only plucks an empty glass from the soldierly row behind him. "Can I get you something while you wait?"

I'm not at all sure of the etiquette a Christian woman should use in a place like this, but I seem to remember my mother assuring me that ladies did not ever sit unescorted at a bar. But she was a drunk thirty years ago, so maybe things have changed.

The buxomy blonde occupying the bend of the bar doesn't seem to mind being alone. With one hand she supports her head, with the other she manages to hold her cigarette and absently stroke the rim of her glass. Her eyes are wide and unfocused, as if her thoughts are a thousand miles away.

I slide onto one of the stools and smooth my skirt. "Thanks." I smile at the bartender and set my purse in my lap. "I'll just wait here a few minutes."

"No problem." He winks at me. "But don't you want something to wet your whistle?"

I look at the woman and the amber-colored liquid in her

glass. I'm not sure what she's drinking, but I can smell the alcohol from two stools away.

Some odors you never forget.

I meet the bartender's gaze. "I'd love a pot of hot tea. English Breakfast, if you have it."

Mr. Bartender lifts a brow. "Tea?"

"Yes, please, whatever brand you can find."

He shakes his head slightly, then turns. "That'll take a few minutes. We don't get much call for tea."

I sit on the stool, perspiring inside my coat, but I am too self-conscious to rise and slip it off. I don't want to look like I'm staying if Christopher doesn't show. My watch tells me it is five past nine, so punctuality is not one of his virtues. That's all right; tonight I can forgive a case of tardiness. If he's as nervous as I am, he's probably pacing down the block someplace, working up the nerve to come in.

The bartender brings me a mug of hot water and a dusty packet of Lipton tea. It's not what I'd call first-class service, but it'll do.

I pull off my gloves, then unwrap the tea bag. "Do you have a menu?"

His brow lifts again, and suddenly it occurs to me that he might know my face from TV. I don't know how much Christian television he watches, but this *is* the Bible Belt.

I give him one of my brightest smiles. "I thought I might get something to eat."

"Right."

"Thank you." While he walks to the end of the bar, I drop the tea bag into the hot water. Thin streamers of darkness swirl in the mug, then I hear the clunk of something hitting the bar.

The bartender has dropped a bowl of salted peanuts next to my elbow.

Wincing, I look up at him. "You don't have a menu, do you?"

The corner of his mouth lifts in a half-smile, exposing tobacco-stained teeth. "Heck fire, lady, you're a bona fide genius. You want food, that's what we got. If you get really hungry, I might be able to find a box of goldfish crackers somewheres."

I do not answer, but pull my tea bag from the mug then drop it, still dripping, onto the bar. Since bartenders in movies seem to take supreme joy in wiping the counter, I've just given him a way to make himself deliriously happy.

Gall burns the back of my throat as I sip my tea. Abel was right about one thing—the most important meeting of my life is about to take place in a tavern. I haven't stepped inside a bar in . . . well, I can't remember the last time. I drank plenty when I was living on the streets, but because I was underage, I mostly imbibed from long neck bottles my friends handed me. Once or twice I walked into a bar with a john to pick up a bottle, but even then I knew well-bred ladies didn't sit unescorted at bars, even if they were sipping nothing stronger than tea.

I lower my gaze. What must Christopher have been think-ing when he picked this dump for our first meeting? Perhaps Abel was right, and this is all a cruel fraud. Some reporter must have sniffed out my past and pretended to be my long-lost son. Now he's probably waiting outside to snap a picture of Abel Howard's bleary-eyed wife staggering out of a dilapi-dated tavern—

"You been stood up, sweetie?"

The throaty voice belongs to the cigarette-smoking blonde. During my momentary pity party, she has slid from her stool to the empty seat next to me, accompanied by the overpowering aroma of cheap perfume. When I glance at her, I see that she is advertising a décolletage Mae West would have envied.

Lush is the word my mind automatically supplies.

Reluctantly, I look through the lacy tendrils of her ciga-rette smoke. "I beg your pardon?"

"I said"—her sour breath bathes my face—"did some guy stand you up?"

"Some guy?" My brittle laugh is more like a cry of pain. "It's beginning to look that way."

She takes a sip of her drink, which has come along for the ride, then lowers her glass. Her eyes cross as she looks at me. "Fuggedaboudim."

It takes me a minute to translate. "Oh," I say, not knowing how else to reply.

She rakes her talons through her mane. "I could tell you was all dressed up for somebody."

I run my hand over my skirt. I spent nearly half an hour trying to choose an outfit that would look nice without looking gaudy. I didn't want to appear sexy, and I certainly didn't want to seem maternal. I just wanted to look . . . respectable. Nice. Pretty enough that my son would feel proud of me.

The woman finishes her drink, then drops the glass to the bar. Using the empty glass as an ashtray, she flutters her mascara-caked lashes and casts me a sidelong look. "I think I know you. You been in here before?"

I shake my head. "First time."

"Then you go to Charley's, over on Sixth."

I force a smile. "I doubt we've ever met."

She wags a finger at me, then pulls a fresh cigarette from her glittery purse. "I never forget a face, and you've got a nice one. Too nice to be left sitting here all alone."

I sip my tea. It's bitter and needs sugar, but something tells me any sugar packets this bartender might have are buried behind a ten-year-old box of goldfish crackers.

"Hey, Jim." The blonde waves her unlit cigarette at the bartender. "You asleep at your post?"

Annoyance struggles with resignation on the bartender's face as he comes over and lights her cigarette. She inhales, then tips her head back, closes her eyes, and exhales twin streamers through her nose like some ancient movie actress.

Rolling his eyes, Jim moves away.

"Hey." Her lashes lift at the sound of his footsteps. "You forgot to bring me a refill."

"You've had enough, Shirley."

"I'm not drivin', I'm walkin'. Ain't no law against walking home with a few drinks in ya."

"I don't think you'll make it home if you keep knocking them back."

I glance behind me, hoping that by some miracle the dirty tables have cleaned themselves so I can retreat from this conversation. The tables are still filthy, and no wonder. Jim hasn't left the bar since I arrived.

I glance at my watch. I'll wait until nine-fifteen, no later, then I'll slip out. I'll walk with my purse shielding my face in case there's a photographer lurking about.

Shirley taps a length of ash into her empty glass, then props one hand on her thigh and looks at me. "So—who is this bum that stood you up?"

"He's not a bum." Surprising, how easily I defend a man I've never met. I look toward the bartender, hoping he'll rescue me from Shirley's attention. "He's . . . my son. I think."

Her jaw drops in exaggerated amusement. "You *think* he's your son? Whaddhe do to get you so mad at him?"

Engulfed by frustration, I look away, hoping to insulate

myself against the woman's attempts at conversation. I should ignore her; experience has taught me it's impossible to reason with a drunk.

"I had a son once," Shirley continues, apparently unaware that I have dropped out of the conversation. "Real cute little boy. Dark hair, dark eyes, lots of curls—and smart, too. Real smart. Took after his daddy, I think, 'cause I ain't never been smart."

She reaches for her glass and tips it back, then sputters as she spits out the ash. "Aw, man!" Dropping the tumbler, she leans both elbows on the bar. "Land's sakes, Jim! You've got me drinking dirt down here! Howsabout somethin' else?"

While her attention is diverted, I stand and slip out of my coat. If Jim's not going to clean up, I might as well lend a hand. The pastor's wife in me can't stand to sit and watch when there is work to be done.

I select the least cluttered table and begin to clear it. I have just moved a pair of lipstick-smeared glasses from a table to the bar when the bell above the door jangles. This time, Jim, Shirley, and I turn to see a young man enter, a tall and slender fellow with dark hair, blue eyes, a firm chin . . . and my mother's nose.

My hand flies to my chest; my heart pounds beneath my palm. The newcomer's eyes seem to take in the long and narrow room with one glance, then his eyes fix on me. A long, slow smile brightens his face as he strides forward.

Do I hug him? Shake his hand?

For a moment I stand in terror of this intimate stranger, then his arms are around me, lifting me from the floor, and we are laughing together.

Thank you, Father, for finally allowing me to embrace my son.

CHAPTER NINE

A wellspring of emotions bubbles up the instant I recognize the man who was once my baby. When I look at Christopher, I am struck by an overwhelming impulse to cover him with kisses and count his fingers and toes.

I can't do that, of course. He is a grown man, dignified and distinctive. Though I know he is not yet thirty, faint creases outline his mouth and eyes, muting his youth with strength. He is wearing jeans and a sweater beneath a nice black leather jacket. The coat could be expensive; it could be a cheap imitation. I don't know much about trendy men's clothing, and at the moment, I don't care.

From beside the bar, I hear Shirley's crusty voice: "*Chris? Chris is your son?*"

"Yes." I laugh as my eyes connect with his. "I'm sure he is."

Ten minutes later we are sitting across from each other in a booth, oblivious to Shirley's droning and Jim's comments from behind the bar. Christopher is sipping a glass of ginger ale; my mug sits before me, the tea now cold and dark. Other people have begun to trickle in—a few men at the bar are talking about sports, a cluster of college kids has crowded into booths near the front door.

I don't care about any of them. The only words registering in my brain are Christopher's, the only face that matters is his. My doubts and reservations fled the moment he came through the door.

"I was beginning to worry," I tell him, unwilling to look away from his beautiful face. "I had almost convinced myself your call was some reporter's attempt to ferret out my sordid past."

He grimaces, and I immediately regret my choice of words.

"Sorry. I didn't mean to imply you are something I could ever be ashamed of—unless—well, I don't know what I mean. But I am thrilled, Christopher, to finally meet you. I never dared to dream of this day, yet here you are."

"Call me Chris, please." He reaches across the table and catches my fingers. His skin is warm and supple, his hand strong and full of promise. When I look down, I see a young man's hand entwined around a middle-aged woman's . . . yet it all seems so incredibly *right*.

Looking up, I blink in a moment of lightheadedness. "You have my mother's nose."

He laughs. "I think I have your eyes."

"You think so?" I squint at him in the dim light, trying to discover my features in his face. "I can't tell. Probably because I never really look at myself—not in an analytical sense, anyway. I'm always checking my makeup, but I never really study my face . . . as you can probably tell from my bedraggled appearance."

"You're lovely." His words bring a flush to my cheeks, and the realization that I'm blushing like a schoolgirl sends even more heat into my face.

I lower my gaze, unable to look into those probing blue eyes. He is answering all my questions, addressing needs I couldn't even begin to express, and we've only been sitting together a few minutes.

"I want to know all about you." I squeeze his hand, then release it. "I want to know about your family, if you're married, what you're doing with your life."

"I want to know about you, too. But you can have the first question."

He leans back, slouching against the wall of the booth, and suddenly I am grateful he chose this odd little place. It's getting noisy, but no one will eavesdrop here, nor will anyone chase us out until we have exhausted this opportunity.

"Are you married?" I ask.

He grins. "Not yet."

"Any prospects?"

"None on the horizon. I was almost engaged once, but the young lady wasn't comfortable with my vagabond existence."

I nod in an attempt to remain open and nonjudgmental. What does he mean? I suppose he could be anything from a sports recruiter to a full-time hobo . . .

No, he's too nicely dressed to be a bum.

I fish for an answer. "So . . . you travel a lot in your work?"

"I listen for the voice of God and I go where he sends me."

I close my eyes as an ocean of gratitude threatens to spill out through my lashes. "Your parents kept their promise, then. They said they would bring you up in a Christian home."

He smiles almost shyly through wispy dark bangs. "They're wonderful people who genuinely love the Lord. I was their only child, so they made sure I had everything I needed. They taught me about God from an early age."

"I'm so relieved. I was trusting God when I allowed the agency to place you, but I was such a baby Christian in those days. I didn't have a lot of experience with trust."

"Seems appropriate, though, doesn't it? A baby Christian placing her baby in God's hands?"

My heart turns over when he smiles. "So . . ." I struggle to maintain control of my voice. "What brings you to Wiltshire? I always assumed you grew up in New York State."

"I did. But after college I developed this incredible yearning to know you. My dad has connections in high places, so he was able to get the adoption records opened." He lowers his voice. "I don't know how he did it, and I didn't ask. But one year at Christmas I open this box, and in it I find my original birth certificate."

"That was . . . a long time ago?"

"Yeah—I think I was twenty at the time. I waited, seeking God, waiting for the right time to approach you. I'd watch you and your husband on TV . . . sometimes I got a little crazy with wanting to know you."

I can't speak. Each word that falls from his lips is like a pearl falling into my open hand, and I am desperate to catch each one.

He rubs his hand across his face, and I can hear the faint rasp of the stubble on his cheek. "Finally God gave me the freedom to come. I arrived in Wiltshire about six weeks ago, and have been working here, waiting until the time was right . . ."

When his voice trails away, I realize this meeting means as much to him as it does to me.

Seeing the shimmer of tears in his eyes, I steer the conversation toward a less emotional topic. "What sort of work are you doing?"

Please, Lord, for Abel's sake let him be gainfully employed.

"I'm a minister." A small smile ruffles his lips, then his eyes grow serious. "There are so many needs here, have you noticed?"

I gape at him in pleased surprise, knowing Abel will be hard-pressed to complain about a fellow preacher. "Why, that's wonderful! What church are you working with? Abel knows every pastor in the area, so we probably—"

"I'm doing parachurch work, nondenominational. I minister to people where I find them."

I tilt my head, uncertain how to interpret his answer. "Well . . . it's wonderful that you've received the call. Tell me about it—did God call you in seminary? Or were you only a child?"

Something that might have been humor flits into his blue eyes.

"We're all called, Emma. The moment we surrender our lives to Jesus we are called to follow him. And he leads us down paths that are as different as our personalities."

For a moment I wonder if he has gone to a real seminary—it's as if he's speaking Hebrew while I'm conversing in Greek.

"Yes, yes, I know we're all supposed to serve God. But the call to pastoral ministry—surely that was different for you."

He shakes his head. "Afraid not."

"So . . . you were never called to be a pastor?"

He glances at the ceiling, then lowers his gaze and smiles at his glass. "I was called to minister as a follower of Christ, Emma. I've been called to obey."

"But"—A chilly breeze of disappointment frosts my smile—"we're all called to do that."

"But how many of us actually follow through?"

For an instant I wonder if he is chiding me for something, but his face is clear and honest, his eyes shining in simple sincerity.

Somehow, somewhere, someone failed to teach this boy about ministry in the real world.

"The call of a pastor is a unique thing," I explain, folding my hands. "Abel was sixteen when he heard the call, and he knew his life would always be different. He stopped going to parties and school dances, he began to search for a good Christian college, he started listening to the great preachers. From that moment on, he knew what his life's work would be."

Christopher nods. "I know what my life's work will be, too."

"What?"

"Following Christ."

I bite back a sigh of pure exasperation. "God calls us to tasks. There's that verse about how God outfits the church by giving us pastors and teachers and evangelists and prophets—"

"You're absolutely right," Chris answers. "But tell me—is every Sunday school teacher at your church on staff?"

I shake my head. "Of course not."

"Yet their gift is as God-given as the pastor's. So why is one calling more sacred than another? No, Emma—we are all called to follow Christ. He has given us special gifts, and he expects us to use them as we move through the world. I used to think that being a Christian meant doing my religious duty—now I know that only God knows what my duty is from minute to minute. My job is to follow and obey."

I stare at him as my thoughts turn to my college days. My professors praised the "preacher boys" and held them up to us as examples. We women were told that God called men to ministry, and women to men.

If what Chris is saying is true . . .

The sound of breaking glass shatters my thought processes. Behind the bar, Jim is cursing his clumsiness.

When I look at my son again, I am grateful for the interruption. Somehow we have entered a debate, and a debate is the last thing I want.

I manage a weak laugh. "Do you argue with everyone you meet?"

His eyes flash above an impenitent grin. "I've never been shy about explaining the truth. I thought we were having an interesting discussion."

I lift a brow and look down at my teacup.

"Listen," Chris leans forward and grips my hand again. "I really didn't come here to talk about myself. I know I said I didn't come to demand anything of you, but there are so many things I want to know."

I smile, enchanted by the beautiful boy beaming from within the man. "What can I tell you?"

He looks down, then squeezes my fingertips. "Did you know my father well?"

I am grateful for his lowered eyes, and at this moment I would give every cent in my bank account if I could buy a purified personal history. For an instant I even consider lying . . . but I will not be false with my son. Not even to spare him pain.

"No," I whisper, wondering if he will drop my hand and walk out in disgust. "I'd give anything if I could tell you a different story, but I wasn't a Christian in those days. I wasn't even a good person. I was seventeen, a prostitute working the Lower East Side, when I got pregnant with you. I don't even know who your father was."

I brace myself for his reaction, but when his eyes lift to meet mine, I see no condemnation in them, only soft concern.

"That must have been a horrible time for you."

"I was horrible—lost, on drugs, pregnant, and broke. You were my second pregnancy . . . and you wouldn't have been born if I'd had money for an abortion. Of course, if I'd had the money, I'd probably be dead now. The pregnancy got me off the streets and into Mercy House, and that's where Jesus turned my life around. So in a way, Chris, God used you to bring me to the Savior."

His eyes, which are clear and lovely and deep, swim as he encases my hand in both his own. "So tell me about your life now."

I don't really want to talk about myself, but he's come so far it would be cruel to deny him.

I shrug. "My life is an open book. What folks see on television is pretty much the way I am. Abel and I keep busy with the church and television ministry. The church is a huge task in itself—with ten thousand members, we visit the sick, put out fires, teach, lead—all the usual things you'd expect. We have a dedicated staff and a wonderful group of deacons who help with the day-to-day feeding of the church, but still, pastoring is a big job. As far as the TV program goes—I sing, Abel preaches, and together we do what we can to clean up our little corner of the world and point people to Jesus."

"I've seen you on TV," he says, smiling, "but I want to know what you do *outside* the church. What fills your world, Emma?"

I stare at him, suddenly speechless. What else does he expect me to do?

"We have n-no children," I stammer. "So our lives revolve around the ministry."

A tinge of sadness fills his eyes. "I'm sorry, I don't mean to pry. My mother is always saying I ask too many questions."

I'm about to assure him that I don't mind, but he speaks first.

"Does it bother you if I refer to my mom?"

I prop my chin on my hand and meet his direct gaze. "I'll be forever grateful to your mother. She did what I couldn't possibly have done."

The line of his shoulders relaxes. "She's a good lady. I think you'd like her."

I accept this as an answered prayer. For years I have prayed he would be loved and cherished . . .

"What's your favorite food?"

I blink. "Food? I . . . don't really have a favorite. I eat whatever's in front of me."

"But if you had to choose."

"Well, I . . ." I rub my brow. "Okay, I like pizza. And I hardly ever get it."

Leaning back, Chris whoops with delight. "Me, too! I love pizza; I'd eat it five nights a week if I could. Mom always thought it was an adolescent fixation, but I haven't outgrown it at all."

My heart warms as the light of understanding dawns. Despite our differing viewpoints, surely genetics binds us in other ways.

"Favorite music?" I ask.

"Country in the car," he says, "but classical when I'm thinking. Sarah Brightman is the best."

I tug at my collar and shove my disappointment aside. I hate to tell him I don't know the slightest thing about country music, and I have no clue who Sarah Brightman is. Abel and I listen to Christian praise music at the office. At home we favor the TV, which is usually tuned to FOX News or CNN.

I open my hand as if I'm counting off items on a grocery list. "Favorite color?"

"Blue."

I cock my finger toward him. "Touché. Periwinkle blue for me. Love that shade."

"Favorite dessert?" he counters.

"Oh, that's easy. Key lime pie."

"That is too cool!" He slaps the table for emphasis. "I *love* Key lime pie. I'd probably rank carrot cake as my number one favorite, but key lime is right up there."

"I like carrot cake." My gaze falls to the glass of ginger ale on the table. "Favorite drink?"

"Sweetened iced tea," he answers. "The way they make it down here. I've got an aunt who puts a cup and a half of sugar into every pitcher. It's like syrup, but it's delicious."

"Uh-huh." My gaze darts to the bar, where Jim and Shirley have bent their heads in conversation. "Do you drink . . . alcohol?"

He tilts his head to meet my gaze. "Would it bother you if I did?"

I'm stunned by the question, but I shrug to hide my disappointment. "Abel and I are teetotalers, of course. And even if the church didn't expect us to abstain, my history serves as a warning. My mother was a drunk. I was following right in her footsteps, so alcohol holds nothing but bad memories for me."

A faint glint of humor appears in his eyes. "I noticed the tea. Bet Jim gave you an odd look when you ordered it."

I glance at the bartender, whom Chris obviously knows by name. "You come here often?"

"Once or twice a week."

"And when you come here—" I hesitate, hating the needling tone that has crept into my voice. This is probably not the time or place to bring this up; I don't want our first meeting to be tainted by anything negative. But this might be the only time I see him, and he needs to know how alcohol killed my mother and nearly killed me.

Wrapping myself in maternal concern, I meet his gaze. "When you come here, Chris, do you drink?"

His eyes are glowing with the clear, deep blue that burns in the heart of a flame. "Coming here bothered you, didn't it?"

I am about to shrug and feign nonchalance, then I remember my commitment to total honesty. "Yes, it did. If anyone other than you had asked, I wouldn't have come. As it was, I only agreed to come because I assumed this was a restaurant."

He lowers his head, but not before I see a grin tug at his mouth. "There are people here, Emma. I go where the people are."

"There are people everywhere," I counter. "Even at church. If you want fellowship, you should visit a more appropriate place."

"But if I want to minister . . . what better place than this?"

It is a reasonable answer, but for some reason it stings.

"Tell me," he says after a long moment, "if you didn't have your cell phone and your car broke down in front of this place, would you come inside to call for help?"

"Well . . . yes, if I had to. It'd be an emergency and it'd only take a minute."

"So, you'd set your standards aside to rescue a car? Yet how much more valuable is a person than your wheels? It is perfectly right to do good in a bar. God wants us to be merciful; he doesn't care about the little sacrifices we make to show others we're spiritual."

Only when I realize I am gaping at him do I snap my mouth shut. In my mental filing cabinet I have over a dozen homilies on the importance of avoiding every appearance of evil, but the sheer authority in Chris's answer has left me speechless.

I'm the pastor's wife, I'm the elder Christian, I'm the *mother*, for heaven's sake. So why can't I come back with a proper reply?

Drawing a deep breath, I decide to try another approach. "I admire your sincerity, Chris, but you can't honestly expect me to say it's okay for church people to spend time in places like this. Some of our people are alcoholics; some of them are too weak to resist temptation—"

He lifts his hand, cutting me off. "I'm not saying you should send those who are weak in the faith. But I have been a Christian for years, and so have you. I can be tempted"—a flush brightens his face—"but drunkenness has never appealed to me."

He picks up the napkin that had been beneath his glass and idly wipes the table. "Listen, we didn't come here to argue. I asked you to come because I want to know you. I'd love to hear about your childhood, where you grew up . . . anything you want to share."

Grateful for the change of topic, I settle back and unwind the tangled threads of my memory, reciting every story I can remember. I tell him about how I'd been proud to be the daughter of an honest-to-goodness FBI agent, about Dad teaching me things like how a real agent always offers his credentials with his left hand so his right hand is free to draw a gun.

I tell him that I didn't have a particularly happy childhood—Mom was always in her room with a headache and/or hangover; Dad was always at work or out with his buddies. Without siblings to play with, I spent my time with books, which made me a bit of a social outcast at school.

"In fifth grade, though, one of the really popular girls seemed to notice me after I answered a question in class. She turned right around and smiled at me, then made a point of hanging around with me on the playground. I couldn't believe it—I thought I had finally found a friend—until she told me her youth group was having a 'pack the pew' contest and she'd win a prize if she had the most people in her church pew that weekend. I told her I couldn't go, and after begging for a few minutes, she turned and walked away. She never spoke to me again."

I lower my gaze to the tabletop—even now, the memory of her rejection hurts.

"I'm sorry," Chris says, his voice soft. "Kids can be cruel."

I force a laugh. "My childhood wasn't completely miserable. There were some good times."

I dredge up memories I haven't unearthed in years, blow the dust off a few gems that startle me with their brilliance. Yes, things were bad after Dad died, but I knew good times, too. Laughter bubbles into my voice as I tell Chris about a mysterious admirer who once slipped an anonymous note through the vents in my eighth-grade locker.

"What'd the note say?"

My cheeks burn as I lift my eyes to meet his. "Isn't that odd? I remember every word. It said, 'I just wanted you to know someone admires you very much.'"

Christopher is examining my face with considerable concentration. "Did you ever find out who sent it?"

"No. But I never forgot it. It was . . . a gift."

I am surprised to realize that life before Abel was not

completely miserable. And while I tell the good stories, Chris sips his ginger ale, laughing when I laugh, smiling when I smile. He is suddenly my best friend and confidant, the only person to whom I have ever completely opened the doors of my past.

He does not flinch when I tell him about the dark years—about my mother's descent into alcoholism, the horrible fights that culminated in my being kicked out of the house, all the terrible things I did to numb my pain and survive on the streets.

And then I tell him about Nola, who rescued me, and Lortis June, who led me to Jesus. "Without those two women," I say, looking into my boy's beautiful eyes, "neither of us would be here tonight."

"They showed you love . . . just like the person who sent that anonymous note."

His insight startles me into silence. I knew so little love when I was growing up . . . no wonder I hungered for it.

He is the first to glance at his watch. "It's very late," he says, "and I don't want your husband to hate me for keeping you out all night. I think it's time for me to walk you to your car."

A frisson of horror snakes down my spine when I look at the time—twelve-thirty A.M. I must have assumed this working-class bar would empty out when the hour grew late, but it's Saturday night and the place is far more crowded than when I entered at nine. Jim now has a helper behind the bar, Shirley the Lush is draped over some man who is ogling her cleavage and buying her beers; the college kids at the front tables are fizzing with laughter for no apparent reason.

But I need to get home. Abel will be worried about me.

"Before we go—" Opening my purse, I frantically dig through the contents, setting my compact, pen, Altoids, cell phone, car keys, change purse, and wallet on the table before I find my packet of business cards. I slide one free, then pick up the pen.

"This reaches my cell phone," I tell him, writing the number on the back of the card. "If you need anything, don't hesitate to call."

Christopher—*my son*—takes the card, thanks me, and slides it into the pocket of his jeans.

We stand and I slip into my coat. That's when I notice that Chris has a folded *People* magazine tucked into his jacket pocket.

"You read *People*?" I ask.

He snaps his fingers. "I knew I forgot something. Favorite magazine?"

I'm a little bewildered, but I play along. "*Purity* magazine, of course."

A wide grin spreads across his face. "I like *People*. It gives me something to talk about when I meet . . . well, people."

My astonishment must be evident on my face, because Chris laughs. "Don't you read *People*?"

I take a half-step back. "Not even in the doctor's office. It just seems so . . . worldly."

"Oh, Emma." A spark of some indefinable emotion lights his eyes. "Tell me—what was the cover article in *Purity* magazine last month?"

I don't hesitate. "We featured a debate on the pre-millennial versus post-millennial Rapture. It was very well done."

"Ah." Chris waves his hand toward the row of men and women perched at the bar. "And if you were to take a poll tonight, how many of these folks would have an opinion on that topic?"

I cross my arms and bite the inside of my cheek. He's making fun of me now—gentle fun, but still . . .

"Watch this." He plucks the *People* from his pocket, slides it beneath my folded arm, then turns to face the bar. Lifting his hands, he clears his throat. "Ladies and gentlemen, may I have your attention?"

After a moment of shuffling, the roar in the bar fades. Through the blue haze of cigarette smoke I see the college kids smirking at Chris while the old men at the bar watch with befuddled expressions.

"I'm taking an impromptu poll," Chris says, "about *Boy Meets Girl*. Which woman should Martin choose? The sweet one or the hottie?"

Lowering my head, I bring one hand up to cover my face. I'm stunned, absolutely mortified, but as I look down I see the cover of the magazine in my arms: "Charlotte or Moria?" the headline reads. "Which one offers true love?"

I wouldn't have believed it possible, but Chris's question ignites a discussion unlike anything I've ever heard in Sinai Church. The young ones begin to chant Moria's name, while the old men at the bar begin to argue over whether Charlotte is genuinely nice or too good to be true. Chris stands there, grinning, while the comments fly thick and fast, then he turns and winks at me.

"See what I mean?"

"I still don't see what good—"

"I could ask that same question to almost anyone I meet on the street, and from that we could get into a discussion of what true love—God's love—is all about. It's easy to talk to people when you know what's on their minds."

I sigh. I've never raised a son, but I'm beginning to understand why the mothers of adolescents in my ladies' fellowship group wear looks of exhaustion.

"This has been wonderful, Chris, but I need to get home."

His grin fades to concern. "Sorry—let me walk you out."

He follows behind me as I precede him through the narrow aisle between the bar and the crowded booths. At one point one of the men at the bar swivels and blocks my path with his foot. "Hey," he says, leering drunkenly, "where ya goin', pretty lady?"

Instinctively, I clutch my purse to my chest. Chris steps up, one hand falling protectively on my shoulder, and something in his gaze makes the drunk lower his foot and turn away.

I can't help but shudder as we continue toward the door. The alcoholic stench of the man's breath brought back memories not even time can erase, and again I find myself questioning why Chris picked this, of all places.

"Sorry about that," he murmurs. "But don't let guys like him rattle you. I've learned not to be surprised when sinners sin."

With one hand on my shoulder, Chris guides me through the crowd. Outside, I point to my car in the distance and we walk toward it, but Chris's step slows as we pass the sleeping bum on the sidewalk.

I hurry by, unlock the car, and get in. As I close the door, Chris catches up, then places both hands on the roof and bows his head. His words are muffled by the closed window, but I hear him say something about "angels" and "protect her."

He's praying for me.

Then he brings his fingertips to his lips, presses the kiss to my window, and steps back, releasing me to drive away.

I am loath to start the engine, but even this night has to end. And Chris is right—Abel is bound to be worried. Staying longer would not be wise or considerate.

I start the car, put it in reverse, and carefully pull out of the parking space. Just before driving away, however, I look for Chris to give him one last wave, but he is no longer watching me.

He is bent over the homeless man, helping him to his feet. My eyes sting as I reluctantly drive away.

It is one A.M.—officially Sunday morning—when I finally creep through the garage door and reset the security system. A thousand thoughts churn in my mind as I move through the shadowy kitchen; my heart brims with so many feelings that one little upset is likely to cause an emotional meltdown.

Fortunately, the sink is clean, there are no half-empty dishes on the counter, and the message board by the phone bears only one post-it note: *Em—plumber called tile guy. Will drop off stuff Sunday P.M. and start work Monday morning— 7:30.*

Thank heaven—one less thing for my to-do list.

I pause by the sink, arrested by the sight of a reflected woman in the window. Abel is asleep, her eyes tell me. So why didn't you stay with your son?

I should have. I had not driven a half-mile before I found myself wanting to see him again. We spent most of the night talking about me; I need another night to learn more about him.

Years ago I gave him life; tonight I answered his questions. When I surrendered my right to raise him, I know I surrendered my right to be involved in his life. Yet this brief encounter has whetted an appetite that can't be satisfied in the space of a few hours.

"Go away," I tell my reflection.

I snap off the tiny lamp burning in the window above the sink, then go to the study to check for any urgent messages that might have come in while I was out. The answering machine is empty, so I drop my purse into a chair, then slip through the hallway and into the darkness of our bedroom. Abel has left a lamp burning in the bathroom. In the rectangle of light shining through the doorway I see him, a series of mounds beneath our satin comforter. His soft snoring accompanies the electric hum of the ceiling fan over the bed.

I tiptoe into the bathroom, pull the door closed behind me, and grab a nightgown from a drawer in the closet. After brushing my teeth and running a brush through my hair (which smells of smoke, but Abel might not notice before I have a chance to shower), I creep into our bedroom and slide into bed.

I have just settled onto my side when the mountain next to me shifts. Staring into a sudden silence, I wait for him to speak.

"Well?" His tone is sharp.

Thank goodness, Abel is willing to listen. I push myself into a sitting position and face my husband in the darkness.

"I met him, Abel. He's a very nice young man, a Christian and a minister. I think you'd like him."

"What sort of minister invites a lady to meet him in a bar? I can smell the stink of the place from here."

"Oh, you cannot!"

"I can."

I reach over and turn on the bedside lamp so Abel can see I am the same woman who left him only a few hours ago.

"The place was smoky, I'll admit. But Chris didn't drink, and neither did I."

Abel props himself on his pillows, then folds his hands across his chest. "So—is your curiosity satisfied?"

I know what he wants to hear. My sweet, wary husband desperately wants to return to a time when he believed his wife's most serious failing was occasionally stumbling over the lyrics of a song she was supposed to have memorized.

I pull a pillow into my arms. "Meeting him was a thrill, of course. But he's only working here for a while, Abel, and I spent most of the night talking about myself. I didn't suggest another meeting, but if he calls again I'd love to spend more time with him. I'd like you to meet him, too."

My husband's hands slide up his arms and lock at his elbows. "I'm not sure that's a good idea."

Leaning forward, I brush his cheek with my lips. "I love you, darling. I know you love me. And you can trust me in this—with all my heart I believe Christopher Lewis means us no harm."

"You can't even be sure he's your son."

"I'm sure—he has my mother's nose. I can't explain it, but the moment he came through the door, I knew we were connected. All at once I felt as though I'd spent my entire life searching for him . . . without realizing what I was doing. I know that sounds crazy and sort of mystical, but that's just what I felt."

Abel exhales and closes his eyes. I wait a moment for his response, then I tug gently on a tuft of hair near his temple.

"Do you want to hear all about it? I'll tell you anything you want to know."

"I've a big day tomorrow, and so do you." His features have hardened in disapproval. "We've already let this thing intrude into the Lord's Day. Now we need to sleep."

I hear the rebuke in his statement, feel the snap of guilt he intends.

"Good night, then." I pull away and switch off the lamp, then lie back against my pillows. And though my husband's rebuke and pointed disinterest have drawn tears, Abel's reaction cannot diminish my joy.

After a while, his snoring once again keeps time to the whirling ceiling fan. I fall asleep thinking of the young man who listens every day for the call of God . . . and found me in the process.

CHAPTER TEN

*W*hen I wake the next morning—forty-five minutes later than usual—the house is as silent as death.

I presume Abel has already left for church. He attends a
prayer meeting with the deacons each Sunday morning at
seven, but he usually wakes me with a kiss before he leaves. As
I slide out of the sheets and hurry into the bathroom, I can't
help but wonder if Abel forgot to wake me because he was preoccupied . . . or chose not to wake me because he was upset.

I can't take shortcuts in the shower because my hair smells
of cigarettes ("Smoking won't send you to hell," Abel always
says, "but it'll sure make you smell like you've been there"),

and I'm so distracted by thoughts of my son and my husband that I find myself squirting conditioner into my palm before I've applied the shampoo.

Out of the shower, I grab a towel, then hurry to the closet. I'm not sure what our calendar holds for the day, but Abel rarely leaves a Sunday afternoon unplanned. So I choose an outfit that will work for most anything—a gray wool skirt, a soft sweater, and a navy blazer.

I take five minutes to dab and dash on makeup; ten minutes to blow my short hair into the soft look appropriate for a woman my age. I'm out the door half an hour after waking.

After battling the long line of traffic leading into the church parking lot, I pull into my reserved space, wave my thanks to the attendants who escorted me to my spot, and hurry into the worship center.

Our first service begins at eight o'clock. I usually run through my song in the choir room before the program begins, but today there's no time for rehearsal. I slip into my chair beside the piano, then pick up the beige-colored phone that connects me directly to Mike Thomas, our sound engineer. After wishing me a cheery good morning, he asks what I plan to sing.

Guilt slaps at my soul. One of my college professors was forever saying that God blessed our endeavors according to our preparation, but I've had no time to prepare this morning. I can only hope God will honor the time I spent learning this song several years ago.

"How about 'How Great Thou Art'?" I ask. "You have the track handy, or should I do it at the piano?"

"No track," Mike says. "So we'll go with the piano. I'll have someone down to set up the mike in a minute."

I lower the phone and lean back in my chair. I ought to be relieved. I think I could sing that beloved old song in my sleep, but I hate feeling rushed on a Sunday morning. Worship services should be approached thoughtfully, reverently, and with great care.

A thin adolescent kid with spiked hair and glasses comes stomping up the platform steps, a microphone stand in his hand. "Mornin', Emma Rose," he says, setting the mike stand by the piano bench. He adjusts the angle of the cordless microphone in the clip. "This good for you?"

I nod. "Thanks."

He stomps back down the stairs as the choir comes through the double doors at the back of the choir loft. The sound in the crowded sanctuary rises at the choir's approach—almost as if worshipers are racing to finish the last of their conversations. The place is buzzing by the time Kenyon Glazier, our minister of music, climbs into the pulpit and lifts his arms.

"Welcome to Sinai Church! Let's stand and praise the Lord together!"

I rise with the others as we begin to sing "Crown Him with Many Crowns." The three camera operators swing into position, the organist makes the pipes sing, the orchestra swells the rafters with glorious brass and strings. Our local fifteen-year-old piano prodigy—a girl whose name escapes me—pounds the keys of the Steinway. They ought to hire her to play full-time, but then there'd be no reason for Emma Rose Howard to sit on the platform.

In the midst of the song, Abel emerges from a side door, Josh trailing in his wake. Josh slides into an aisle seat in the front pew; Abel climbs the steps to the platform, smiling broadly at the choir members. Finally he turns to face the crowd, his Bible pressed to his chest and his eyes closed, as Kenyon directs the ending of the song with a dramatic flourish.

Twenty minutes later—after the welcome, announcements, choir special, and Praise Partners report—the ushers march forward to take the offering. Seeing them approach, Abel climbs into the elevated pulpit.

"It is good to see you all here today." Standing in the curve of his bulletproof perch, Abel grips the dark wooden trim and beams a smile over the congregation. "I know this church is important to you, as well it should be. When you accepted Christ, you accepted the responsibility to build your life around this church and its Savior."

I want to know what you do outside the church.

Christopher's voice speaks from my memory, startling me with its clarity. My hand rises to finger the string of pearls at my neck as I peer past the piano at the congregation. I'm not sure what I expect to see, but his voice was so crisp I wouldn't have been surprised to find him crouching behind my chair.

When Abel begins to pray, I bow my head and stand, then slide silently onto the piano bench. Moments of dead air are not allowed in a service at Sinai Church; even the ushers are aware of the need to keep things moving for the sake of the television audience. As soon as Abel says "amen," I will begin to play, and I will continue singing until the last offering plate has been safely handed to the accounting committee chairman at the back of the church.

I am well into the first chorus of my solo before I turn to look out at the congregation. The television monitor sits on the floor by the first pew, and through my peripheral vision I can see that the director has called for a closeup. My entire head fills the screen, and the effect is so disconcerting that I shift my eyes to the right, sliding my gaze over the folks sitting down front. No matter where I look, from the corner of my eye I see the unblinking lens of a TV camera trained on me.

I have just begun the second verse when my eyes encounter a sight that sends shock coursing through my body like a jolt of electricity. In the fourth or fifth row, enveloped by the discreet space strangers maintain between each other, Christopher is sitting with his eyes closed. His dark head is bobbing to the gentle pulse of the song, and his mouth is moving with mine.

Sudden tears blur my vision. I lower my gaze and see my

hands on the keyboard, but they are like the hands of a stranger. I find myself grasping for the notes of a song I could have played blindfolded, but now I can't even remember what key I'm singing in and I'm terrified to play notes that will be completely, utterly wrong.

My ears are ringing so loudly I can't hear the song in my head; my fingers have forgotten how to play. I have no idea what comes next. I lift my foot off the piano pedal, muffling the last chord, and silence pours from the open lid of the Steinway.

Every person in the congregation has tensed. I can feel the pressure of hundreds of pairs of eyes; I know they are wondering why I've stopped. The cameras are staring, too—wide, curious, and intimately personal.

I cannot play. I'm not sure I can sing. But I can at least speak.

"And when I think," I whisper, lowering my trembling hands to my lap, "that God, his Son not sparing, sent him to die, I scarce can take it in."

A woman in the choir begins to sob.

"That on the cross," I close my eyes against the shame of this failure, "my burden gladly bearing . . . he bled and died to take away my sin."

Kenyon Glazier, who is sitting close enough to see that my hands are trembling, rises to his feet. Covering my breakdown with style and grace, he moves into the pulpit and soon the entire church is singing the chorus a capella, rattling the windows with an emotional chorus of "How Great Thou Art."

When the last note has died away, I slip from the piano bench and take my seat. Aware of the camera, I am careful to compose my face into peaceful, settled lines. Inwardly, though, I am roiling in a sea of turbulent emotion. While I am thrilled Christopher came to church, I am drowning in humiliation because I offered less than my best to the Lord. I have made a mistake not only in front of a national television audience, but in front of my son.

Far worse than my personal mortification is the knowledge that some people will think I lost control of my emotions because I was overcome by my love for God.

I have never felt like such a hypocrite.

CHAPTER ELEVEN

*O*n Monday morning, I sit at the kitchen counter and sip my coffee. Abel has already gone to the office, and I'm a little amazed that his departure has left me feeling grateful and at peace.

We moved through Sunday in a cautious state of truce, neither of us speaking of my son unless absolutely necessary. At lunch I truthfully explained my lapse at the keyboard by admitting I'd been thrown by the sight of Christopher in the congregation. Abel received this news silently, then asked me to pass the dinner rolls.

Neither of us mentioned Chris again. I kept my cell phone

within reach in case he should call, but our Sunday afternoon faded into Sunday evening without a word from my son.

I check my watch, then take another sip of coffee. I will be late for work today. The tile installer was supposed to arrive at seven-thirty, but it's now eight-fifteen and his pickup truck has just pulled up to the curb.

I answer the door in my stocking feet.

"Tile man," he says, glancing at the gleaming tiles in the foyer. "You want I should take off my shoes?"

I shake my head. "Don't worry about it."

The tile guy—I'm not sure I caught his name—is an older man with a grizzled white beard and ponytail to match. Beneath his denim overcoat he wears stained white pants and a white T-shirt.

I lift my hand in a "follow me" gesture and lead him through the bedroom into the bathroom. "I'll leave you to it, then." I point to the tub. "Sorry it's such a mess."

The man grunts.

"I, um, have to go to work now. If you go out for lunch, will you lock up? You can call me, and I'll come back to let you in—I work about ten minutes from here."

The man grunts again, then squats to examine the scarred plywood frame around the tub. "I don't go out for lunch."

"Well." I clasp my hands together. "Okay. I'll leave you alone so you can get started."

My practical side makes me reluctant to leave anyone in

the house when both Abel and I are gone, but I suppose that's why most construction workers are bonded and insured. I slip into my shoes and grab my purse, eager to get out of the tile installer's way.

When I reach the church office, I can tell something's in the air. By this time devotions are usually done and the secretaries are at their desks, but the place has a deserted look when I come through the front door. Tanzel has even left the reception desk unattended.

I discover why when I pass the short hallway leading into Abel's office. Josh has gathered all the women around Esther's desk, and he's distributing paperwork. I pause in the doorway to catch up on what I've missed.

"Your job, if you choose to accept it," Josh gibes, handing Celene a sheet of paper, "is to call all the Books & More bookstores on your list and ask if they're willing to order the wife-swapping book. We suspect you're going to get a positive answer; if so, you can hang up. What we're looking for is a bookstore manager who'll go against company policy. If you find someone who refuses to order that trash; let me know right away. That's the guy we want to interview on-camera."

The secretaries accept their assignments and move away. Celene makes a face when her eyes meet mine. "Nebraska." She waves her page. "I was hoping to talk to people in someplace warm like Hawaii."

"I'll trade you." Crystal Donaldson, who's been pulled

from her magazine duties, is holding several stapled sheets by the corner. "I've got three and a half pages of Books & More stores in California. I'm gonna be on the phone all day."

Grinning, Celene clutches her single sheet to her chest. "Maybe Nebraska isn't so bad after all."

I follow Celene down the hall to our offices and pause at her desk. "Sorry I'm late—had to let the tile guy into the house. Anything for me this morning?"

"As a matter of fact, yes." She shuffles papers on her desk, then offers me a memo with *From the Desk of Josh Bartol* stamped across the top. "Josh says the Reverend wants you to interview some folks whose marriages broke up on account of a swinging lifestyle. We can use previously published quotes, but they'd really like to find a few people who'll talk on camera."

"Got it."

"And Crystal dropped off a list of questions for you. Something about an interview for the magazine?"

"Um . . . hold on to those for me, will you? I doubt I'll have time to get to them today."

"Okay—and there's this." Without further comment Celene hands me a response card—one of the hundreds of forms we make available for our parishioners to fill out and drop into the comment box as they leave the Sunday service. Usually the cards contain prayer requests, notes about shut-ins who need a pastoral visit, or complaints about the music being too soft, too loud, too contemporary, or too traditional. Someone has folded this one, however, and written my name across the top in chunky letters.

I open the card. The name and address are blank, but in the comment section, a bold and masculine hand has written: "Your music blessed me. Chris."

Thanking Celene with a smile, I move into my office and pull my chair toward the desk. This is a Monday like a hundred other Mondays, yet even with a stranger in my house and a load of work on my desk, I suddenly feel as happy as a new millionaire.

Chris wasn't embarrassed by my meltdown. He understood. And he took the time to let me know I did okay.

I prop my elbows on the desk and cover my face with my hands. "Father," I close my eyes, "thank you for making something beautiful out of my mistakes. Thank you for leading Chris to church yesterday. But this morning, you're going to have to help me concentrate. Open my eyes to the things you'd have me see, lead me to the people you'd have me interview. May this work count for the kingdom, may our efforts matter in the light of eternity."

I've prayed this prayer a hundred times, but as I sit and attempt to quiet my spirit, a series of images flashes across the backs of my eyelids—I see Shirley the Lush, the homeless man on the sidewalk, and Chris, his blue eyes crinkling into nets as he smiles.

"Concentration, Lord," I repeat, breathing harder. "Not daydreams. Please, help me focus."

"Emma Rose?"

I lower my hands. Celene stands in the doorway, a manila folder in her hand. "Josh dropped these letters off for you. We have an entire file of folks who've written us about marital infidelity. He thought this would be a good place for you to start."

Of course, I should have thought of checking the correspondence files. Televangelists receive thousands of letters every week, most of them supportive. But along with checks for five, ten, and fifty dollars, people also write to us about problems ranging from explosive tempers to shopping addictions. When letters began to pour in during our first year on the air, Abel asked several Christian counselors to create form letters that could be adjusted slightly and sent as personal replies to viewers, complete with a freshly inked Abel Howard autograph provided by SigTech 4000, a top-of-the-line signature machine. Most of these replies address the problem in general terms, then urge the correspondent to seek help from a local Christian counselor. After the reply has been sent, workers in our mail department carefully file the original letters by topic.

The file in Celene's hand is bulging.

I stand to take it from her. "So many letters about swinging? I had no idea."

She snorts softly. "The file is more general than that, but

this is only one year's worth of letters from people whose spouses had an affair. We got a slew of them when that reality show about temptation aired, remember? Infidelity was a hot topic back then."

How could I forget? I thought Abel was going to burst a blood vessel last year when a national network aired *Tahiti Temptation,* a reality show where contestants wagered on the faithfulness of married couples thrust into alluring situations.

I take the file and lower it to the center of my desk. "Before I get into this, I think I need a cup of coffee."

She smiles. "Want me to bring it to you?"

"I'll get it myself. But you can lead the way if you need one, too."

"Heavens, yes. I've a hunch the Reverend's about to drag us through the mud again. I get a slimy feeling just reading about all this stuff."

As I step around the desk, I think about how uncomfortable I felt with Shirley the Lush breathing brandy down my neck.

"More than you realize," I tell Celene. "I know what you mean."

By four-thirty, I feel as wrung out as a ten-year-old washcloth. I've spent the greater part of the afternoon on the phone with women whose names I pulled from the correspondence file. While most of them were delighted to hear from Emma Rose Howard, few of them wanted to talk about the issues that spurred them to write us in the first place. Even after I promised anonymity, most of them dragged their feet.

I can't blame them; I know only too well the pain of dredging up the past. But in the last few days I have also learned that from pain can come healing, restoration, and profound joy.

So I persevere. We only need two or three volunteers, so after I jot down the third willing woman's name, I drop my pen and press my fingertips against my eyelids, grateful to be done but silently regretting that Abel has chosen this particular crusade.

Marital infidelity is a messy business, nearly as distasteful as pedophilia and homosexuality. Two years ago our ministry launched a boycott against Disney World because the head honchos at Disney decided to offer gay and lesbian employees insurance benefits usually reserved for legal spouses. We also protested the Gay and Lesbian Day held each year at Disney World in Orlando.

That campaign drew tremendous heat from believers and unbelievers alike. Even the Christian community fractured into camps, and the most outspoken of them sent representatives to Wiltshire to advertise their positions. One Sunday, representatives from the leather-clad Dykes on Bikes paraded up and down the north side of Sinai Street while the "True Believers" marched on the south side. I was dumbfounded to discover that the "True Believers," who professed to love the same Jesus I do, were holding signs predicting hell for "queers" and anyone who reads anything other than the King James Version of the Bible.

Our church people walked up the hill in silence that day, sobered by the reality of the twisted world around us. Our TV director sent the cameras outside to catch shots of the north and south sides screaming at each other, and somehow God used the entire mess. More people than usual walked the aisle that day, and our incoming mail rose fifty-two percent in the week following the airing of that program.

But the trouble didn't end after that memorable Sunday. Abel kept preaching against Disney, and as a result we were vilified in the press and even ridiculed by a late-night television comedian. I didn't see that particular show, but the NBC guy tried to portray me as a wannabe Tammy Faye Bakker. The joke fell flat, Josh informed me, probably because Tammy Faye and I are as different as salt and pepper.

By the time that campaign ended, Disney World had not changed its employment practices, the Gay and Lesbian Day continued to be held each year (Disney had never actually sponsored it), and our contributions had increased sixty-four percent.

Though Abel was privately disappointed that the boycott

did not effect a change at Disney, he was quick to point out that God did use our efforts. We gained viewers and contributors, so the gospel reached more people than ever, new people committed themselves to supporting God's work, and we had additional funds with which to continue our ministry.

I think Abel is hoping for even greater success with the campaign against Books & More bookstores. Whether or not he keeps *Your Wife or Mine?* out of those bookstores is not nearly as important as spotlighting the importance of marital fidelity, picking up new viewers, and exposing hundreds of new people to the gospel of Jesus Christ.

He hasn't shared all the details with me, but Celene tells me Josh outlined the master strategy in a staff meeting this morning. Abel is planning to publicly launch a campaign to boycott Books & More bookstores in a huge press conference to be held Sunday afternoon, right after the eleven A.M. service. He will promote the boycott in every *Prayer and Praise* program airing in the month of March, and between now and the beginning of April, Abel will grant dozens of interviews about the impact of Christian shoppers on the national economy.

In addition to the media onslaught, our viewers will be inundated with letters—at least one per week, each of them professionally designed by our direct marketing company and written in black ink with rivers of red underlining and truckloads of exclamation points. Those letters, sent to anyone who has ever written us, will bring in contributions with which we can buy more airtime to reach even more souls. Nothing will be wasted—even letters that are never delivered will be returned to us with a U.S. Postal Service change-of-address sticker, enabling us to update those all-important names on our mailing list.

"Direct mail is not inappropriate for ministry." Abel's voice rises from my memory. "We are using the tools of the world, in some cases even using the world's money, to further the cause of Jesus Christ. This is business for all the right reasons."

I am pondering the dollar value of a single name and address when I hear Mozart playing from within the depths of my purse. I dig for my cell phone. Few people have this number—only Abel, Celene, Josh, and now, Chris.

I know who's on the line even before I look at the caller ID.

"Hello?"

"Emma?" His voice sounds as breathless as mine.

"Chris!" The room swirls around me in a mad moment of panic—after all, I gave him this number for emergencies. "Is everything okay?"

"Everything's fine. I . . . just wanted to call."

I lean back in my chair as the room settles into proper perspective. My son has decided to call me. Nothing could be more natural.

"Did you have a good day?" I ask.

"Yeah." I hear a smile in his voice. "Very good. I'd love to tell you all about it in person if . . . well, if you have the time. And if you want to see me again."

"I would *love* to see you."

"Great." He chuckles, and I know I have never heard a more beautiful sound. "I don't want to keep you out late again, so are you free tomorrow morning?"

I glance at my calendar. I'm supposed to lead a ladies' Bible study in the chapel from nine to eleven, but Louise Hammel would love to cover for me. She's a natural teacher.

"I can get free."

"That's cool. Listen, I was trying to think of a way to show you the kind of ministry I do, and I think I've figured it out."

I laugh. "Don't tell me you hired a television crew to follow you around."

"Hey, that's close! But I only have a camera. So today I shot some pictures of the people the Lord has laid on my heart, and I'd love to show them to you. I dropped them off at a photo shop downtown, and I was thinking you could meet me there when they open tomorrow morning. I'll pick up my pictures, then we can walk to this little diner next door and have breakfast. My treat."

"You don't have to treat me."

He laughs again. "It's the least I can do. And I promise the diner is nice. No drunks, no smoke. Just eggs and grits and a wisecracking waitress named Annie."

Is there anyone in town he hasn't met? My gaze falls on the photo of Abel on my desk; for a moment I can see Chris's features reflected in the glass. "Sounds wonderful."

"It's Jackson's Photo on Sixth Street, and it opens at eight-thirty. Can you be there that early?"

"Wouldn't miss it. By the way, Chris?"

"Yeah?"

"I got your note . . . and thanks."

"I meant it."

We say good-bye, and as I hang up the phone I realize I'm experiencing the same fluttery feeling I used to get at the prospect of seeing Abel after a long day of classes. The situation is vastly different, but the emotion is the same.

I've fallen in love with my son, and I can't wait to see him again. I'd love for Abel to meet him, too, but he joins the Wiltshire Pastors Association for prayer and breakfast every Tuesday morning, and I know he won't want to miss the meeting.

I drop my cell phone back into my purse and make a note to have Celene call Louise about the change in plans.

CHAPTER TWELVE

Six o'clock finds me and Abel at the kitchen bar eating dinner from takeout containers. Rarely do we eat at home, and even more rarely do I cook.

Abel is scarfing down his order of grilled shrimp and pasta because he's due back at the church in less than an hour. Esther had to schedule a counseling session with a Sunday school teacher accused of teaching incorrect theology, and though my husband would rather be planning his press conference, he will not forsake this duty. Abel, keeper of the sheep, does not hesitate to rebuke a wanderer when necessary.

I am picking at a dish of grilled shrimp and vegetables, my

thoughts a thousand miles away. Tucked beneath the cabinet in front of us, a mini-television tuned to a twenty-four-hour news channel provides background noise while we sit in our separateness.

I'm longing to tell Abel about my upcoming meeting with Chris, but the grim line of his jaw assures me he's not in the mood to discuss my newfound son.

He lifts his head, however, when the ticker for breaking news scrolls across the bottom of the screen. The camera cuts to a somber reporter standing outside a lovely home behind a manicured lawn. "We have just heard," the reporter announces as a photograph of a smiling black man appears in the upper right corner of the television, "that Joseph Greenly, newly appointed head football coach for the Cincinnati Bengals, was gunned down in the driveway of the residence behind me. A telephone tip attributes the shooting to the World Church of the Aryan Brotherhood, and police are scouring this neighborhood for clues. People here have been stunned by this cowardly act."

Abel punches the remote, lowering the volume. "I hate hearing that kind of news. Those racists give all churches a bad name."

I cannot tear my eyes away from the silent television. The screen is now featuring a family photograph—Greenly, his wife, and four stairstep children, all young and adorable. The picture dissolves to a shot of what must be the Bengals locker room, where a group of players from all races have come together to mourn the loss of a talented coach and a good man.

The image of the children floats before my eyes. I have a son, too, and at this moment I can't imagine the pain of having a family member ripped from my life.

Abel waves his hand before my eyes. "You home in there?"

I focus on him. "Sure."

"Were you able to get some names for the interviews?"

I use my fork to spear a strip of green pepper. "I found three women who are willing to go on-camera. Two of them are here in Kentucky."

"No men?"

"Men aren't as willing to talk about infidelity, Abel. I was lucky to find the women."

He squeezes my elbow. "You do great work, Em. I'm sure nobody but you could have talked those women into cooperating."

Maybe I understood something of their pain. The words are so sharp for a moment I worry that I've spoken aloud.

Five days ago I told Abel about my past, but I gave him the condensed version. I have never shared the depths of my agony. I have never known the pain of infidelity, but I've known abandonment, fear, loneliness, starvation, illness, misery, and loss. He can imagine what I must have endured, but empathy is not one of Abel's gifts. Already I can tell he has tried to put my revelation out of his mind and move on with his life. He will throw himself into this bookstore boycott, directing all his attention and zeal toward uplifting fidelity in American marriages . . . while he ignores the growing rift in his own.

I stab another bite of grilled vegetables. "I heard from Christopher today."

Abel keeps chewing, then swallows. "Whatever for?"

"He wants me to learn about the ministry he's doing. So I'm meeting him in the morning for breakfast."

He pulls the tail from a shrimp with remarkable vehemence. "I don't understand how you can just go out and *do* ministry. What is he, a street corner preacher?"

I speak in the lightest voice I can manage. "That's why he wants me to see for myself. I'm not sure I understand, either, but I'm sure there are as many different ways to reach people as there are people."

Abel's gaze shifts to some interior field of vision I can't imagine.

"I asked Louise Hammel to take my Bible study group," I continue, my cheeks burning under his simmering disapproval. "I wouldn't shirk my responsibilities, Abel."

He says nothing for a moment, then drops his fork. With his gaze fixed to the silent television, he says, "'If you love your father or mother more than you love me, you are not worthy of being mine; or if you love your son or daughter more than me, you are not worthy of being mine.'"

For an instant I wonder why he thinks that quip is funny, then the truth hits me between the eyes—he's quoting *Scripture*. For the first time in our marriage, my husband is preaching at me.

Wavering between guilt and anger, I stare at him. "Abel Harrison Howard. How dare you insinuate that I love Christopher more than God."

He tilts his head. "Who are you putting first tomorrow morning? God or your son?"

"I hardly think missing one lesson is tantamount to idolatry." Unable to believe what I'm hearing, I swivel in my chair and face him directly. "I don't know how to make you understand, Abel. I know this is confusing to you; I know you can't relate. I have found the son I thought I had lost forever, but I'd love to share the experience with you. Come with me, meet him, see what a special young man he is—"

"I can't." He shifts his gaze as words fly from his lips like shrapnel. "I won't. I had nothing to do with your past, and I won't let you drag me into it now. A minister of the gospel should remain above reproach; he should avoid every appearance of evil and especially the taint of scandal."

My cheeks are burning, but I can't speak.

Abel picks up a glass of water. "If you won't avoid this man for your own sake, you should avoid him for the sake of the ministry. This is still a relatively small town, Emma, and someone is going to see you with this kid. Bad enough that he took you to a bar, but how can you go to breakfast with a man who is not your husband? The meeting may be perfectly innocent, but our enemies in the press would love to crucify us with speculation about that relationship. One photograph— just one—could cause us to lose donors. And I don't think you want me to go public with the full explanation."

His words resonate in the kitchen, clattering harshly among the pans hanging from the pot rack. As reluctant as I am to consider his viewpoint, my mind's eye conjures up the photo Abel fears. I hate to admit it, but he's right—in an unguarded moment I might lean toward Christopher or place my hand on his shoulder. How would that look to an outsider?

For so many years I have been careful not to give anyone reason to criticize—I don't buy cooking sherry because people will think I'm drinking, I don't linger in the magazine aisle of the grocery store because *Soap Opera Digest* and *Cosmopolitan* are stacked right next to *Good Housekeeping*, I don't entertain men at our home unless Abel or Celene is also in the house. We don't subscribe to HBO because it carries programming that qualifies as soft porn; I have never joined any community women's clubs because I might be invited to a party where drinks might be served.

I don't even say "darn" because it sounds too much like something else.

I turned my back on the old life and have worked so hard to be good in my new life. I have trained myself to obey the biblical admonition to walk circumspectly, yet all those years of discipline have fallen away in the light of my miracle son.

Abel is right, of course. I must be more careful.

My cheeks are burning as I lower my head and pick up my fork. "I'm sorry, Abel, if I've caused you any distress. I'll be careful, I promise. Tomorrow I'll tell Chris that any future meetings should be in a more private place. If he's going to stay in town awhile, maybe we could introduce him in a service so people will know who he is. We don't have to say he's my son, but we could say he's a minister visiting town for a few weeks—"

Abel's face flushes. "We are *not* putting an untested, self-proclaimed preacher on the platform!"

For a moment I can only stare at my dinner, then the missing pieces fall into place. It's not Christopher's presence in church Abel minds; after all, my son's forehead is not branded with a scarlet letter proclaiming him a prostitute's child. Chris could come to church alone any time and Abel wouldn't complain.

But if he appears with me . . . that's what my husband can't tolerate. Abel is afraid of my past and maybe even of my blazing love for my son. He's afraid of Christopher's freedom and my response to it.

I lower my fork as understanding dawns. I have never seen this kind of vulnerability in my husband.

After slipping off my barstool, I move to his side then

comb his hair away from his forehead with my fingertips. "I love you, Abel, in a far different way than I love Christopher. And I will do whatever I must to be a good wife, but you can't deny me the opportunity to know my son. I've spent the last twenty-something years denying him, and I will not deny him again. Besides, he'll be leaving eventually. He told me he lives a vagabond existence."

"Can't you see?" Abel's voice is hoarse, as if forced through a tight throat. "He's calling you to relationship, Emma. He wants your heart."

"And he has it . . . as do you." The realization strikes me as I pronounce the words. "Chris was born out of my sin, but he is innocent of it. And I cannot help but love him even more for seeking me out."

I press a kiss to my husband's cheek, then move into the living room, giving Abel space to gather his composure before he must leave to solve yet another of the ministry's problems.

Sleep eludes me that night even after Abel returns from his counseling session, undresses, and climbs into bed. Within ten minutes of eleven he is snoring softly; I am wide awake.

I set aside the devotional book I have been reading and swing my feet to the floor. The study lies on the other side of our bathroom, but as I walk through the darkness I stub my toe on a bag of powdered grout the tile man has left next to the tub.

Muffling my cry of pain, I limp the length of the bathroom. I have scarcely looked at the work the tile guy did today—one glance assured me the tiles around the tub were in place, so I assume he'll do the floor tomorrow—but right now my mind is occupied with more important things. Still limping, I slip through the narrow door leading into our study.

Outside the wide window, the streets of our gated community lie silent and still. A full moon in the east splashes our lawn with silver and black, and after a moment I see the nighttime security guard glide past in his electric golf cart.

Eleven o'clock and all is well in this sheltered village.

Bracing myself against the bookshelves, I switch on the lamp, then let my gaze glide over the spines of leather volumes. Our library holds an entire shelf of Bibles, probably more than three dozen, because publishers send us copies of their new editions every year at Christmas.

I take a random volume from the stack and notice that the publisher has embossed our names on the cover: Abel and Emma Rose Howard. The coupling of our names feels inappropriate—how can you share something as personal as a Bible? The one I use most—which currently sits on my office desk—is underlined, highlighted, and scrawled with marginal notes.

I open the Bible and riffle the thin leaves, hearing the faint snap and crack of pages still bound together by a strip of gilt edging.

A book is such a powerful thing. The one I hold in my hand has changed men and nations. Within this one volume, I am holding a record of the world's history and its future. Even men and women who choose not to believe it cannot dispute its influence.

What gives books the power to change the hearts and minds of readers? I have no trouble understanding why the Bible is powerful; the Spirit of God moves upon people as they read and he is the One who effects change. But what powers energized *Uncle Tom's Cabin, Mein Kampf,* and *Silent Spring?* Did Harriet Beecher Stowe, Adolf Hitler, and Rachel Carson realize how their words would change history?

I sink onto the settee in the office, holding the Bible on my palm as I consider Abel's latest crusade. He is moving against a single book that endorses an immoral practice, but could he be doing more harm than good? How many people would never know about *Your Wife or Mine?* if Abel doesn't mention it on TV throughout the next four weeks?

Christians are infamous for jumping into crusades against imagined evils. Among the many files in our correspondence department are folders marked "Procter and Gamble Hoax" and "Madalyn Murray O'Hair." Over the years we have received hundreds of letters about Procter and Gamble being a satanic organization (they're not) and Madalyn Murray O'Hair petitioning the FCC to take Christian programming off the air (she didn't). Add to those hoaxes countless letters about a boy named Brian Warner becoming Marilyn Manson because members of a church youth group shunned him (not true) and photocopied petitions from people protesting the "Second Coming Project," an attempt to clone Jesus (also untrue), and I can see why the folks in our correspondence department have grown wary and skeptical.

I can't blame them. Last year when another pastor launched an environmentalist crusade by asking "What would Jesus drive?" we found ourselves lumped in with other evangelists and pilloried in the press. Weeks later, we received a flurry of petitions to restore prayer in public schools despite the fact that our current president has done more to secure religious freedom on public-school campuses than any administration in a decade.

I rub my temple, where a nagging headache has begun to announce its presence. How can I criticize other people for inflaming public opinion when we are doing the same thing?

At least Abel is careful to check out rumors before responding to them. He objects only to situations that are offensive in the eyes of God. He is absolutely right when he says this book about wife swapping can cause great harm and marital infidelity is destroying the fabric of decent society.

But it's not the only sin running rampant through

America. There's abortion, and murder, and racism . . .

I sit at the computer and slide the mouse across the desk to wake up the hibernating monitor. Thanks to a cable modem, we are constantly on-line. It's a simple matter to open the browser and type in the URL for Books&More.com.

I type *Your Wife or Mine?* into a search field, and within a minute the book appears on my screen, complete with reviews. The first review praises the book in glowing terms and oozes with gratitude that someone is finally writing about swingers with understanding and compassion.

Well . . . that's a red flag. But not all of the reviews are complimentary, and the description of the book itself gives me pause. According to the blurb, the author is not promoting the swinging lifestyle, but exploring the mind-sets and morals of those involved in the practice. The book sounds more like an academic study than promotional propaganda, but perhaps the description is misleading.

On a whim, I go to Amazon.com and type in the same title. Yes, there it is—with only two reviews, one approving, one critical. I keep typing and clicking. The book is not listed at Barnes&Noble.com, but addall.com lists over thirty on-line bookstores where the title can be purchased.

So why aren't we protesting *all* these bookstores?

The pressure in my head increases. I click back to our Internet home page and stare at the breaking headlines. News of the murdered NFL coach flashes at the top of the screen

206

with an update—police have tracked a suspect to a truck stop and surrounded the facility. They are hoping the alleged shooter will surrender without harming any of the people inside.

A headline scrawls beneath the main story: "Neighbor Says Suspect Is White Supremacist."

Something clicks in my brain as a memory from high school surfaces. I navigate back to the bookstore pages, where I type in the words "White Supremacist." At least seven titles appear. Next, I do a search for *The Anarchist Cookbook.* There it is, a slim volume of recipes for bombs, complete with a high sales ranking, nearly two hundred reader reviews, and a letter from the author.

I lean forward to read the fine print. The author has posted a note explaining that he wrote the book as a nineteen-year-old at the height of the Vietnam War. The work was copyrighted in the name of the publisher, and when the author matured, married, and became a Christian, the publisher ignored his pleas to have the book taken out of print.

A few more clicks on related titles bring me to a volume on how to manufacture and disperse poisonous substances, including nerve gases, anthrax, ricin, and botulin toxin. A note informs me that a Japanese cult uses this book as their lab manual.

I click on other topics, searching my memory for names I have heard in the news. At nearly all the on-line bookstores I find books by noted white supremacists, black revolutionaries, and leading practitioners of Wicca. I have no trouble finding copies of *The Protocols of the Elders of Zion*, the libelous book used by Hitler's regime as justification for murdering over six million Jews, and *The Satanic Bible*.

Seeking relief, I type in the URL of an on-line Christian bookstore, but after perusing the titles I discover that Abel and I disagree with several philosophies represented on the cybershelves. There are books about prosperity theology (*Pray and Grow Rich!*), volumes both supporting and decrying Harry Potter (how can both be correct?), and biographies of preachers who cared more for expanding their earthly kingdoms than advancing the kingdom of God.

Leaning back in my chair, I stare at the glowing computer monitor. If we were to lambaste every book with which we disagreed, we'd wear ourselves out . . . and look as much like intolerant hatemongers as the racists who murdered that unfortunate football coach. If we were to boycott every bookstore selling those books, we'd have nowhere to shop.

Jesus did confront sin when he saw it . . . he was honest with the woman at the well, he did not excuse the woman taken in adultery, he did not dismiss Zacchaeus's greedy cheating . . . but in each of those cases, he was gentle in his honesty and his confrontation. As I search my memory of the Scripture, I try to think of situations where Jesus became angry or confrontational—when he chased the moneychangers out of the temple, rebuked the Pharisees, and cursed the unfruitful fig tree.

He confronted the religious people—and an unfruitful tree—with righteous anger. He met sinners with loving firmness and truth.

For the first time in our marriage, I find myself questioning my husband's methods.

The little gremlin pounding in my head increases his volume and tempo. I click back through the secular bookstore pages and close my eyes, suddenly weary of my excursion through titles sympathetic to immorality, pedophilia, rampant consumerism, hedonism, and debauchery.

Why are we surprised when sinners sin?

Christopher's question haunts me. Why, indeed?

CHAPTER THIRTEEN

$\mathcal{T}$he sun struggles to rise Tuesday morning; by seven-thirty it is barely glowing through a cloud-dark sky. Abel and I part after exchanging the fewest possible words. He reminds me that he needs me to proof a draft of a letter about the bookstore boycott; I counter with a promise to return to the office as soon as possible. I even promise to bring him a cinnamon roll from the diner if they have rolls hot from the oven, but not even the offer of his favorite food penetrates the tent of grimness that encloses him.

As I park at the curb in front of a boarded-up dime store, I remind myself to ask Christopher why he is so fascinated by our decaying downtown. Ten years ago the streets would have been crowded by this time on a weekday morning, but I have no trouble finding a vacant spot on Sixth Street.

Chilly fingers brush my cheek as I get out of the car and slip two quarters into the parking meter. Above me, a swollen sky sags toward the gray buildings. I would rather be meeting Christopher under sunny skies and warm breezes, but I would not exchange this moment for the world.

Careful not to overlook Jackson's Photo, I take off down the street and clutch my coat collar to ward off the frigid wind. It's not cold enough to snow, thank goodness, but in this part of Kentucky the temperature can drop in a flash if the winds change.

I am reading signs when my eyes spy a dilapidated hanging board shaped like a coffee cup—Chris said the place was next to a diner. I quicken my pace and hurry forward, looking for the photo shop, then halt in mid-step.

Jackson's Photo lies behind a wall of iron burglar bars, through which I can see a window papered with what I can only describe as movie posters featuring photos of scantily clad women. A neon sign with three X's gleams from the window, while a cheery note hangs from suction cups on the door: *Open. Come in!*

I am wondering if I have managed to wander onto the wrong street when movement from behind the glass catches my eye. A balding man in a cardigan and reading glasses is standing behind the cash register and gesturing for me to come in.

I whirl away, my cheeks burning. I don't think I've ever consciously walked past an X-rated video store, and I've certainly never entered one. This has to be a mistake.

I clutch my purse, grateful that I remembered to recharge my cell phone. It's already eight-thirty-five and Christopher is not here, which means he's probably waiting for me in front of Arnold's Photo or Johnson's Photo Shack or something similar—maybe I wrote down the wrong name. In a little while he'll call and ask where I am. I'll tell him I'm a scatter-brain, and within a few minutes he'll come running down the street and profusely apologize for embarrassing me to death.

I'm standing on the sidewalk, my eyes intent on the inter-section, when the first raindrops begin to fall. Big and fat, they splat on my coat and wet my cheek, the first spits of a major deluge. I look up in time to see that the threatening cloud has darkened to the color of weathered slate, then the skies open.

Shivering, I close my eyes. I should run back to my car, but what if Christopher comes looking for me on foot? I'll never recognize him in this deluge if I'm sitting a block away; it's as thick as fog, morphing people fifty feet away into gray, faceless figures. I could retreat to the wall, where the overhang pro-vides a thin ribbon of shelter, but the thought of standing next to pictures of nearly naked women appalls me.

While I'm debating, I hear the metallic squeak of a door, then footsteps splash across the sidewalk.

"Lady, come inside." The man in the cardigan holds his umbrella over me. "You'll catch your death out here."

I shake my head. "I'm waiting for someone."

"You can wait inside and watch through the glass."

Abel would *die*.

"Thank you, but no." I strengthen my voice. "I would prefer to wait out here."

The man sighs heavily, then presses the handle of the umbrella into my palm. "Then at least use this. I can't have you catching pneumonia on my front stoop."

I would have protested, but surprise leaves me speechless. With wide eyes I turn as the bare-headed man splashes back through the rain and ducks beneath an absolute waterfall pouring from the tattered awning above his door.

I am still gaping when I feel the pressure of a hand on my elbow.

"Emma!" Drenched to the skin, Christopher draws me into a light embrace, kisses my wet cheek, then grins as he cowers beneath my unexpected shelter. "Didn't get your umbrella open in time, huh?"

"It's, uh . . ." Floundering like a fish out of water, I jerk my thumb toward the adult video store. "It's his. This man just came running out and gave it to me."

"That's George. You couldn't tell by looking, but he's got a real chivalrous streak in him." Christopher takes my arm and leads me toward the store. For a moment I think he's just moving me to the shelter of the awning, then he *opens* the door.

"We had to see George anyway," he says, pulling me forward. "He has my pictures."

Like a shell-shocked soldier, I am led into the kind of store that didn't exist when I was living on the streets. In those days lewd old men resorted to dirty magazines, dingy theaters, and strip clubs; if the posters are an accurate indication, this place offers magazines, videos, and interactive DVDs, all the latest in pornographic technology.

Caught by my son's firm grip, I follow Christopher into the room. We are standing in an aisle facing the counter with the cash register; behind me is a half-wall topped by a glass panel. For a moment the arrangement seems odd, then I remember that state law requires children to be shielded from the sight of X-rated materials in public places. A toddler walking in here would see nothing but a beige wall; a toddler in his father's arms, however, would take in rows and rows of videos and posters and magazines.

The warning sign at the entrance to the video area should have been posted on the front door—no, at the beginning of the *block*. No one under the age of eighteen should be permitted within a mile of this place.

Averting my eyes, I stare at the floor. Seemingly unaware of the moral cesspool behind him, Christopher calmly takes the dripping umbrella from my hand, closes it, and slides it across the counter. "Thanks for the use of the umbrella, George."

"No problem. The lady looked like she was drownin' out there."

"George, this is Emma. Emma, I'd like you to meet George."

Drawn by the sound of my name, I find myself mechanically offering my hand to the man in the rain-splattered cardigan. He takes it with surprising civility, then offers me a tobacco-stained grin. "You a friend of Christopher's?"

Thank the Lord, he doesn't know who I am.

After nodding helplessly, I lower my gaze to the spot where his belly is tugging at the lower button of his cardigan.

George releases my hand. "Christopher's a good lad. The world could use a few more like him."

I am struck dumb. And my son, who has not even turned to glance over his shoulder, seems completely oblivious to the sort of establishment he is patronizing.

The vendor turns, flips through a vertical stack of rectangular envelopes, then pulls one out and slides it across the counter.

"Here you go. Twenty-four color prints."

Though this transaction is perfectly legitimate, I can't bear to watch. I step back and stare at the black and white floor tiles.

"Well, George." A note of laughter underlines Christopher's voice. "I don't see any Disney posters on your wall yet. I'm still waiting for you to see the light."

George coughs slightly, then squeaks out a forced laugh. "Ah, Christopher. You never let up, do you?"

The door opens; a woman in wet tennis shoes and jeans comes in. In a quick glance I see that beneath her raincoat she's wearing a gold T-shirt emblazoned with the Wiltshire Warhawks logo, so she must have a son on the high-school soccer team.

I keep my head lowered, mortified that a woman would voluntarily enter this place, but I can't help overhearing her words.

"These are *yours*." I hear the sound of something sliding across the counter. "I found these in my bedroom, hidden under the mattress. I'd throw them all into a Dumpster, but then you'd come after me to pay for them, wouldn't you?"

Christopher seems to be counting out bills in his wallet, but George clears his throat with a phlegmy rumble.

"Uh . . . yeah, these are ours."

"I shoulda smashed 'em with a hammer." The woman's voice is so heated I'm surprised the videos don't spontaneously combust.

George clears his throat again. "Appreciate you bringin' 'em back."

"You people make me sick." She speaks in a soft voice

laced with venom. "I kicked my husband out, you know. I can't have that kind of filth in the house, not with two teenage sons. But now I'll have to deal with them and a divorce, all because you people make this kind of stuff available to men with dirty minds and too much time on their—"

"Lady, nobody put a gun to his head," George interrupts. "It's a free country. People can do what they want, and your husband wasn't hurting nobody."

"Are you kidding?" Her voice rises to a shriek. From the corner of my eye I see Christopher place a five-dollar bill on the counter, then he edges between me and the woman.

"My husband—this filth—has destroyed everything!" She clenches her fist and waves it in George's face, then she erupts into tears as something within her breaks.

Christopher picks up the packet of photos, then takes my arm and leads me toward the door. As we pass, I look at the woman's face for the first time. I know her—the woman is Eunice Hood, wife of one of our deacons. She's one of our people . . . and I saw her just the other night at the deacons' dinner.

Eunice does not see me—her hands are over her eyes, as if she would hide her tears of anger and shame. Her face is quite pale, with deep red patches at her neck and on her cheeks. Her wedding band twinkles at me from her left hand, but if what she said is true, she won't be wearing it much longer.

I don't know Eunice well, but I am suddenly overcome

by an urge to draw her into my arms. When I hesitate, Chris halts in mid-step. I stand behind Eunice for a moment, debating my options, then lower my head and move toward the door.

A hug might have helped her . . . but merciful heavens, what would she think if she found her pastor's wife in a pornographic video store?

I resolve to catch Eunice at church as soon as possible. If I don't see her in the crowd on Wednesday night, I might have Celene call her to my office. I can say, quite truthfully, that I am worried about her and would like to know how we can pray for her family . . .

Having resolved to wait, I hurry into the rain.

The coffee shop next door is, thank goodness, clean and neat as a pin. Annie the waitress is a small, quick woman with a tight white perm. She seats us at a table near the heater, and after a few minutes in its warm breath I feel myself begin to thaw.

Annie drops two plastic-covered menus on our table, then spins off to pour coffee at another station.

Chris doesn't look at the menu, he looks at me. "You okay? You seem a little upset."

I can't deny the truth. "That woman in the video store—I

recognized her as we were leaving. She's married to Tim Hood, one of our deacons. Abel's going to be so disappointed when he finds out. We'll have to ask Tim to step away from his leadership role, of course. And if that marriage breaks up, there are two children to consider. And poor Eunice . . . well, I just don't know what she'll do. She has no training, no job experience."

Chris's eyes shimmer with sadness, but I can't tell if his sympathy is for Eunice, Abel, or me. "Has your church no programs for wounded people?"

I'm startled by the question. "Well . . . the entire purpose of our ministry is to keep people from getting into these situations in the first place. We try to make sure people honor the Lord in their marriages, and we promote righteous living. Eunice's husband should never have set foot in that video store."

It seems a natural time to add a bit of advice. Surely a mother has the right to share a little wisdom.

"Chris," I begin, carefully choosing my words, "I can't believe you patronize that store when you could get pictures developed at Walgreens. You saw what kind of place it is. And maybe it's a good thing, even a God-thing, that Eunice Hood came in when she did. Now you see what kind of damage pornography can do."

His eyes soften as he smiles at me. "I don't go there to look at posters, Emma. And I don't rent those videos."

220

I can't stop a cough. "How can you help but see them? They're everywhere!"

He shrugs slightly, and transfers his gaze to the gingham tablecloth. "I'm a man, yes, and those pictures bother me, so I don't look at them. I go there to see George. And people like Eunice."

Instead of growling in frustration, I scrape my nails through my hair. I didn't raise this kid; I don't know how to read him. Just when I think we've landed on common ground, he launches a comment like that one and I'm left with no answer.

"Jesus never worked himself into a moral panic when he saw sin," Chris continues, calmly moving his cup toward Annie when she approaches with the coffeepot. "We tend to be staggered by sin, but Jesus was always calm in the face of immorality. He knew people; he knew they were sinners. The situations that ticked him off were those involving egotistical mind-sets, and he found more of those in the religious people than in the fallen ones."

I stare wordlessly across the table, my heart pounding. I'm not certain, but I think I've just been rebuked. First my husband throws Scripture at me, now my son.

Annie looks at me and waves the steaming pot. "Coffee, ma'am?"

"Yes, please."

Chris dumps two packets of sugar into his cup, then stirs. When Annie moves away, he leans toward me.

"You see, God built a sense of natural law inside man. Almost without being taught, people know that it's wrong to kill and steal and be unfaithful to their marriage partners. Nearly every religion in the world acknowledges that natural law."

Nodding, I pour sugar into my own cup.

"But Jesus introduced a completely revolutionary idea. The thing that sets Christianity apart, the thing most people don't get, is that Jesus asks us to give up our rights to ourselves. When we do that, when we allow him to have complete control, then we are actually living for him and not ourselves. If we fail to do that, we are like all the other religious people who follow a list of dos and don'ts they have attached to natural law."

Feeling as though I have stumbled into quicksand, I pull the menu closer and stare at the list of breakfast selections. Christopher and I share a genetic string and a common faith, but our differences might yet come between us.

"'I'm not asking you to take them out of the world,'" he says, his voice thicker than before, "'but to keep them safe from the evil one. They are not part of this world any more than I am. Make them pure and holy by teaching them your words of truth. As you sent me into the world, I am sending them into the world.'"

I look up, unable to make sense of his familiar but misplaced words.

"Jesus' prayer." Chris answers my unspoken question. "In the Upper Room, remember? That prayer was meant for us, Emma. We were never meant to hide in our churches or in our sheltered social circles. Jesus wants us to advance into the world, not retreat from it."

For an instant I cannot believe a twenty-eight-year-old unmarried kid is preaching to a woman who has been involved in ministry more than half her life.

My defenses kick in. "I have not retreated. Abel and I have spent our lives trying to reach the world."

"Really?" His lips are smiling, but his eyes remain serious. "I don't know you well enough to judge, Emma, and it's not my place. But in my travels I've seen too many Christians cocooning as if the outside world doesn't exist. They build huge churches, Christian schools, recreation programs, even medical centers for their members—anything and everything possible to ensure they never have to venture into the world Christ wants us to embrace."

I can quote Scripture, too, and a verse springs automatically to my lips: "'Come out from them and separate yourselves from them, says the Lord. Don't touch their filthy things, and I will welcome you.'"

"There's a difference," Chris says, his eyes gentle, "between walking in the world and wallowing in it. We are the light of the world, but we have hidden our light inside our buildings and Christian programs. When the world looks at us, too often they see petty, self-absorbed people who wag their fingers and scold everyone else for misbehaviors, then retreat into ivory towers—"

"Hold on a minute." I lift my hand. "You haven't lived long enough to see the big picture. Jesus established the church and he has blessed it through the ages. I'm not sure I understand what kind of ministry you're doing, but—"

I bite my lip, suddenly realizing that I have no idea how my son has lived or ministered. And the purpose of this meeting is for me to understand the things that have made him the man he is.

"I'm sorry." I spread my hands on the table in an attitude of surrender. "I'm cold and wet, plus I didn't get a lot of sleep last night. You're not finding me at my best."

"I love you anyway."

His smile makes my heart contract like a fist.

When the waitress approaches again I order two scrambled eggs and toast, no butter, then listen as Chris orders scrambled eggs and toast, lightly buttered.

"I learned to like it." He hands the menu to Annie, then grins at me. "My mom slathers butter on everything."

As the waitress whirls away, I attempt to guide him toward the purpose of this meeting. "I'm so glad you wanted to see me again, Chris. I felt like I talked mostly about myself the other night, and I want to know about you."

"I want to know you; I want you to know me," he says

simply, and suddenly I am hearing Abel's voice: *Don't you see? He's calling you to relationship.*

Well, why shouldn't I have a relationship with my son?

Chris swipes a hank of wet hair from his forehead, then pulls the folder of photos from his coat pocket. "I've been taking pictures so you can see the kind of work I do." He opens the folder and slides the first photo from the stack. I find myself looking at a picture of a young girl, probably fifteen or sixteen, but it's hard to tell with girls these days.

"This is Melinda." He slides the picture toward me. "She's only fourteen, but she was kicked out of her home about six weeks ago. She's using drugs, drinking, suffering the abuse of practically every man who enters the crackhouse where she's staying. But the house is warmer than the street, and I've been taking her a couple of hot meals every day."

I blink. "You're working for Meals on Wheels?"

He laughs. "No. I told you, I'm a minister."

"But you don't work for a church."

"Call me self-employed and God-directed."

I digest this answer; it's one I've never heard. "If you're self-employed . . . who pays your bills?"

His features soften; his smile becomes coy.

"God takes care of my needs."

"He feeds the birds and bees, too, but people need money to pay the bills."

"Well . . . have you ever heard of Lewis and Coombs?"

Of course I have. Lewis and Coombs is the biggest maker of household products in America. The company is older and bigger than Procter and Gamble; they manufacture everything from toothpaste to foot powder.

I gasp as the reality strikes home. "You are Christopher Lewis . . . of Lewis and Coombs?"

He nods slowly. "My father is Paul Lewis, the grandson of Geoffrey Lewis, the man who started it all with Edmund Coombs. The Coombs have all died off, but the Lewis family is still going strong. I'm an only child, but I have more cousins than I can count."

I bring my hand to my mouth, but a giggle slips from beneath my fingertips. And Abel thought Christopher came here looking for money!

"So you don't need help to pay the bills."

He grins. "My father supplies everything I need."

"But isn't he disappointed that you've chosen something other than the family business?"

Smiling, he tucks a lock of damp hair behind his ear. "In Dad's eyes, what I'm doing *is* the family business. The manufacturing part is just a day job. The real work of our family is ministering to the world where we find it, when we find it." He taps the photo of the young girl. "I find kids like Melinda all over the place. Last year I worked six months in Manhattan . . . on the Lower East Side."

I lean back against my chair as an unexpected warmth

surges through me. I can see the hand of God in this—my Lord does all things well. Imagine, Chris working to rescue people where I myself had been rescued!

I'm still smiling when the waitress approaches with our breakfast. The food smells wonderful, but I am far more interested in the young man sitting across from me than food or photos.

"Tell me about how you grew up."

Chris waits until the waitress sets his plate on the table, then he pauses to give thanks. As I bow my head, I am struck by the way he prays. He uses no formality or elaborate address, just "Thank you, Father, for this food and fellowship."

I keep my head down, waiting for the customary closing words, but they do not come. When I peek through my bangs, I see Chris unrolling his napkin.

I hurry to keep up with him.

"Growing up?" he asks. "I was as ordinary a kid as anyone."

I pick up my knife and smear jelly on my toast. "I imagine you went to a nice private school."

"No, public school, kindergarten through twelfth grade."

"That can't have been easy."

"I enjoyed it. When I reached sixth grade—right about the time peer pressure increases—I told anyone who asked that I was a follower of Christ. No one ever taunted me for my faith. In some ways, I think they respected me for taking a stand. And I did take a stand—I had to, after going public like that. I debated abortion and other life issues in speech class, talked about creationism in biology, brought up abstinence and purity in health ed. Sure, I bore a few taunts for my faith, but nothing I couldn't handle."

I stare at him. I'd been thinking that it couldn't have been easy for a fabulously wealthy kid to suffer insults from his envious peers, but Chris seems to be communicating on a different wavelength.

I take a stab at bringing the conversation back to familiar territory. "I like the way you say that—a 'follower of Christ.' It sounds . . . more active, somehow."

"My dad always said that. He said the rest of the world assumes 'Christian' means 'American,' and most Americans don't have any idea what Christians are really supposed to be."

At a complete loss for words, I glance at the photos. "Who's next?"

"Oh, right." Chris lifts the next picture and holds it before my eyes. I see a wizened middle-aged man in dark blue pants and, judging by the collars at his neck, at least three flannel shirts. A blanket is wrapped around his shoulders, a quilted plaid fabric that rings a bell in my memory.

It's the bum I saw sleeping on Fourth Street.

I force down a bite of toast. "He was outside O'Shays."

"Yeah." Chris's smile is as innocent as a two-year-old's. "His name is Judd. I met him the other night, got him some coffee and solid food."

I rub the bridge of my nose. "But all Jim the bartender had was peanuts."

"Yeah, I know. So I took him to my apartment and pulled a few things out of the fridge. After a shave and a shower, Judd began to look a lot better."

I drop my fork as horror snakes up my backbone. "Chris, honey, you can't go around doing this kind of thing, even in Wiltshire. You got lucky this time, but some of those street people are dangerous. What if he'd pulled a gun or a knife or something? Why, he might have robbed you blind!"

Chris shrugs. "All he'd take is money."

"He could take your life."

Again he shrugs. But I'm steaming like an overheated radiator, so he pulls another photo from the stack in an obvious attempt to distract me.

His gesture works. I shove all thoughts of Judd aside and gape at the picture. It's the lush at the bar—what was her name?

"Is that . . . Shirley?"

"You know her?"

I transfer my gaze to Chris, convinced that this child-man is too naive for his own good. "Well, no, I don't know her, but I talked to her the other night."

"Then you know her story."

I shake my head. "We didn't get that far."

He is about to launch into what I'm sure will be a dazzling

tale of Shirley's woe when my purse begins to play Mozart. I lift a finger, silently asking him to excuse me, then I pull the phone to my ear.

Abel's calling. Josh wants to run through details of the press conference scheduled for Sunday afternoon, and they need me back at the church ASAP.

I drop the phone into my bag. "Sorry, Chris, but I need to run."

He pushes his chair back. "Want me to walk you to your car?"

I look through the glass door. The streets still gleam with wetness, but the rain seems to have stopped for the moment.

"Don't let your breakfast get cold. Eat up, enjoy it."

I reach for my wallet, fully intending to drop a twenty on the table, but Chris catches my hand. "It's my treat, remember?"

"Oh, okay." I smother a smile. "You know, I'm probably the only new mother in Wiltshire whose kid is wealthier than she is."

His grin deepens into laughter. "I don't own much more than a few books and the clothes on my back. But Dad supplies everything I need."

On an impulse, I bend and kiss his forehead. "Listen, I'd love to see the rest of your pictures and hear more about your work. And I want you to meet Abel."

"That'd be great. I really enjoyed his Sunday sermon." Chris slides the loose photos into the folder, closes the flap, and offers them to me. "I took these for you. There are some great stories behind those pictures—great needs, too."

"I'm sure there are." Touched by his thoughtfulness, I tuck the folder into the pocket of my purse, wave good-bye, and leave the coffee shop. And as I lower my head and hurry past Jackson's Photo and X-rated video store, I can't decide whether I am relieved or irritated to be called away from my sweet, naive son.

CHAPTER FOURTEEN

I find Abel in the TV studio at the back of the worship center. We televise our regular worship services, but for heart-to-heart messages and appeals, Abel wants our viewers to feel they are visiting with him in a more personal space. So the studio features an office set, where a pair of tall false windows look down upon a fiberboard desk artfully arranged with my photograph, a few typed pages, and a blank desk calendar.

Abel, Josh, and Celene are gathered around a TV monitor when I walk in, and over their shoulders I glimpse a scene of two couples lined up against the headboard of a king-sized bed.

Celene is the first to hear my approach. "There you are." I hear relief in her voice, and at the sound of it I realize Abel has not told her about my meeting with Christopher . . . which can only mean he hasn't told her *anything* about Christopher. If Celene's in the dark, Josh must be, too.

I give her a diplomatic answer: "I had a breakfast meeting." I lean over to squeeze Abel's shoulder, then nod to Josh. "You've been busy, I see."

Josh is as excited as a kid with a new toy. "This is an old movie—remember *Bob & Carol & Ted & Alice*? This is vintage stuff, but the visuals are just what we need to roll at the beginning of the telecast introducing our bookstore boycott. They're decent enough to air—not a lot of flesh or anything—but the idea comes across loud and clear."

I glance again at the monitor. Natalie Wood, Elliott Gould, Dyan Cannon, and Robert Culp are sitting in a bed with expressions ranging from bored to confused. I vaguely remember my mother mentioning this movie when I was a kid; the footage certainly seems dated now.

But it's just what Abel needs for his campaign—sanitized sin, perfect for driving home his point about the dangers presented in *Your Wife or Mine?*

"By the way, Emma . . ." Josh pauses to reach for a clipboard on the desk. "This just came in from the direct marketing folks. It's powerful, but I need you and the Reverend to look it over and sign off before I give them the okay for printing."

The clipboard contains a short stack of glossy double-spaced pages. The bold letterhead proclaims that the letter comes *From the Office of Abel and Emma Rose Howard*, and the Courier font is reminiscent of an old typewriter. I doubt any of our Praise Partners actually believe Abel or I typed this, but the old-style font reeks of the days when business-men pecked out their letters on clunky old machines.

Dear Christian friend, the letter begins, *Emma Rose and I recently received the shock of our lives when we learned that a book called* Your Wife or Mine? *is being aggressively sold at Books & More bookstores, the largest retail bookstore chain in America. You probably have a Books & More store near [city-field]—I know we have one in Wiltshire, only miles from Sinai Church.*

Frowning, I reread the paragraph. I don't know that anyone is *aggressively* selling *Your Wife or Mine?* at Books & More—unless I'm mistaken, it was only one book on shelves containing thousands of titles. The direct marketing people tend to take poetic license when they lay out a case for action.

Make no mistake, the letter continues, *this book is designed to erode the fabric of our society by destroying the God-ordained institution of marriage. Such a book should never find a place in a family bookstore!*

When I called Barry Zilhoff, president of Books & More, Inc., I was told that his chain would not stop selling the book and

Books & More stores are, in fact, "committed to meeting the needs of its customers in every conceivable area."

Heavy red lines underscore the next sentence: *Do you understand what this means, [firstname]? Can you believe that the leadership of this company considers a handbook for swinging couples a "need" for our communities? This is outrageous! It is one more example of how far we have fallen away from the ideals established by our forefathers who intended that America should be a nation under God, a country committed to honoring divine principles in public and private life . . .*

On and on the letter continues. The direct marketing folks, writing under our names, go on to rail against liberal politicians, feminist mothers, delinquent fathers, television producers, and atheistic schoolteachers who *"have all contributed to the decline of American society. But ours is not a 'society' anymore—we're living in a cesspool! Emma Rose and I need your help to drain this sewer of the filth polluting our lives so we can clean up America!"*

The letter ends with a heartfelt plea for support—money to continue the fight against this sort of filth, and, if the reader is unable to contribute, we solicit their prayers.

Please,[firstname], reads the text above a replica of Abel's signature, *even if you cannot send a contribution, encourage me and Emma Rose by signing your name and returning the enclosed support card. When we see it, we'll know you have joined us in the fight against indecency, and we'll be able to tell the CEO of the Books & More chain that you are standing with us in this fight for righteousness.*

We are counting on you.

I lower the clipboard as an inexplicable sense of discomfort gnaws at my gut. That line about the store "aggressively selling" the book has to go. Such exaggeration is an outright lie. The rest of what they've written is true; I certainly can't find fault with their comments about the need for morality in our society.

But I can't help wondering what Christopher would say if he were reading this. He might say the entire letter is misleading because the average viewer has no idea that professional writers from an expensive direct marketing firm actually wrote these pages and spent hours quibbling over every exclamation point and underscore. Our viewers probably think their response cards come directly into our offices, when in fact we never see them.

And the way this letter asks recipients to reply . . . it's common procedure to request some kind of response, because that's how direct mail companies judge the success of a campaign. A ten percent response rate is phenomenal, five or six percent is pretty good. Most of the people who send in a card also enclose a check, and even small amounts add up.

I know that thousands of pieces of mail flood our correspondence department every week—hundreds of women pour out their hearts to Emma Rose Howard and receive a channel letter in reply. But how else can we handle the situation? Too many letters crowd our mailroom; there's no way I can read and respond to them all.

I close my eyes as guilt pricks at my soul. What if Christopher had written instead of calling? If he wrote a letter as guarded as his first phone message, he would never have reached me.

"So, Emma, what do you think?"

My eyes fly open. Josh stands in front of me, his hands in his pockets, a confident grin on his face.

"Well . . . the line about Books & More aggressively selling that book needs to be cut. That's just not true."

The corner of Josh's mouth tightens. "They were pretty aggressive in their defense of it when we called them."

"But that's not the same thing as aggressively selling it."

Always the peacemaker, Celene lifts her hand. "I'll bet they will be aggressively selling it once the publicity begins. They've refused to ban it . . . so once news of this campaign hits the papers, you can bet that book will be front and center in their stores."

"But is that what we want?" I look at Abel, who must make the final decision. "If we give this awful book publicity, aren't we indirectly encouraging sales? Nobody had ever heard of this title until we got that letter from Mr. Keit. But if we go on the air and talk about it, all the people who support banned books will put it at the top of their lists. People who could care less about wife swapping will buy a copy just to defend their right to read whatever they want."

Abel's brows knit together in a scowl. "You're way off base, Em."

"Am I? I don't think so." I tilt my head, thinking of all the questionable books I discovered in my Internet search last night. If we must protest a book, I can think of far more dangerous books than *Your Wife or Mine?*

I hand the clipboard to Josh, then lay my hand on my husband's arm. "Honey, I don't think this bookstore boycott will do the cause of Christ any good. It may actually hurt."

Three heads turn toward me as if they are controlled by a common string.

"What?" Josh glances at the clipboard. "What else is wrong with this letter?"

"It's not just the letter." I look to Celene for help, but she seems as puzzled as the men. "I'm bothered by the entire idea. I looked that wife-swapping book up on the Internet last night, and no, it's not a book I'd recommend to anyone. But it's no worse than dozens of other titles I found in several other bookstores. Are we going to boycott them all?"

A line appears between Abel's brows. "If something is depraved, we need to resist it. Are you saying we should sit around and keep our mouths shut?"

"No, it's just . . ."

Why are we surprised when sinners sin?

I draw a deep breath. "I'm beginning to think the world won't understand our frame of reference. A few years ago, maybe, but things are different now. I mean, have any of us even read the book? I saw a description on-line, and from what I can tell, it doesn't advocate infidelity as much as it examines the practice from a social and psychological perspective. I didn't see anything to make me think it's a how-to guide for immorality."

The line between Abel's brows deepens. "I talked to Mr. Keit on the phone, and he said the book definitely does not condemn infidelity. The author says people who do this are merely maladjusted; he takes the position that while spouse swapping may not be for everybody, to each his own—"

"Okay, Abel, but—"

"Sin is sin, Em, and I've been called to preach against it. I can't sit back and let the world change its standards just because some expert changed the terminology. Wife swapping is not maladjustment, it's adultery; abortion doesn't kill a fetus, it kills a baby; gays are not happy, they're people who distort what God intended—"

"All right." I throw up my hands, acknowledging defeat. "But I think we're going to take heat for this one. They'll accuse us of censorship."

Abel snorts. "As if they've never censored Christian books—"

Celene and Josh have fallen silent, waiting to see who will win this battle of wills. But Abel will always win because God called Abel to ministry, and me to Abel. My husband must do what he thinks God is calling him to do. As his wife, I can advise him, but then I must stand back.

I meet my husband's gaze. "I won't argue with you."

"Good."

I close my eyes as my memory flits back to the image of Chris bending beside the homeless man on the street. People respond to him, not because he's on a crusade, but because they see how he cares.

People responded to Jesus for the same reason.

"I just want to say one thing before I go." I speak slowly, spacing my words for maximum impact. "What will this campaign do to bring people into the kingdom of God? That letter"—I point to the clipboard in Josh's hand—"may result in new names, more money, and a lot of publicity, but those things will be the result of human efforts. Will this campaign make the world hunger for Jesus? Somehow I doubt it."

I turn and begin to walk away.

"It's not our job to make Jesus look good," Abel calls after me. "He's the fairest of ten thousand; he doesn't need our help. He's called me to preach against sin, Em, just as he did. Do you think the Pharisees were attracted to him when he called them snakes and vipers? No, but still he told them the truth. He never pulled his punches, never ran away from a fight."

I step outside the heavy black studio door and lean against

it, reveling in the quiet of the hallway. I'm not sure what happened in that encounter, but I feel as if I've spent the last seventy-two hours on a tilt-a-whirl.

The world may never look the same to me again.

I'm in the break room, a converted closet off the office hallway, when the door opens. Celene crosses her arms when she sees me, then lowers her gaze to the carpet.

"What's up?" I ask, recognizing the body language that always accompanies somber news. After I left, Abel may have said something to Celene and Josh about Chris . . . but I have no idea what he'd say.

"The Reverend says you've been under a lot of pressure." Celene raises her gaze to meet mine. "He thinks you need to take some time off—maybe stay home and just relax awhile."

"I see." I lower the coffeepot to the burner, then pick up my steaming mug. "Did he mention how I came to be under all this pressure?"

Celene takes a half-step back. "Um . . . I didn't ask. But, you know—" She looks at me with such open friendliness that for a moment I am tempted to let the story of my past spill out.

But for Abel's sake, I have to be careful.

"You know I consider you a friend," Celene says. "And

though I know you and the Reverend are as close as bark and a tree, I'm sure there are times when you'd like to confide in a girlfriend." She lowers her voice to a whisper. "You can trust me, Emma. I wouldn't betray a confidence."

I am honestly touched by her assurance. "I know you wouldn't, Celene, and I appreciate the offer. But I've been dealing with some issues I can't share without Abel's permission, personal matters that really shouldn't affect anyone else."

A small grimace of pain crosses her features, as though I have wounded her.

"Listen." I lean against the counter, hoping to soothe her feelings. "There's nothing I'd like better than to tell you about all the crazy things that have been happening to me lately. But, frankly, I'm not sure I'm thinking straight. The Lord is showing me things I never dreamed I'd see, leading me to places I've never been. I'm beginning to question things that always seemed right—"

"Doubts come from the devil." Celene nods, secure in her conviction. "Tell the enemy to leave you alone."

I shake my head. "These aren't doubts, Celene. I've never believed more in the sovereignty of God. Lately, though, I've begun to wonder what God really wants of me . . . and I know he's big enough to handle my questions."

Celene gapes at me like a woman who's just been told to prepare for an IRS audit.

"I'm going to be fine." I step toward the door and give her a smile. "Now, shall we go ask Louise how the Bible study went this morning?"

Obeying Abel's admonition to get some rest, I leave the church early and go home. The tile man's car is parked at the curb, so I call out a cheery hello as I enter the house. He doesn't answer, but he may not have heard me from the depths of the bathroom. Or maybe it's bad homeowner etiquette to speak to tile men while they're working.

I drop my purse on the kitchen counter and check the answering machine. Though we received twelve calls today, no one bothered to leave a message. Most of them had to be telephone solicitors who assembled our unlisted number on one of those random digit dialers.

Not wanting to disturb the tile installer, I go into the bedroom, kick off my shoes, and peek around the corner. The fellow is on his hands and knees in the bathroom, delicately placing floor tiles around the tub.

My first inclination is to honor the man's silence and back away, but a stray thought makes me hesitate. What would Christopher do, finding this man here? In the short time I've known him, I have never seen him walk by another human without trying to make contact in some way. Even at that awful video store, after I'd stepped back out into the rain, I saw him murmuring something to Eunice Hood.

I glance again at the tile man, whose white jeans are riding low and exposing more of his backside than is socially acceptable. Abel would ignore him. He'd be polite, of course, but once the man set to work Abel would maintain his distance, not wanting to interfere. If he found himself in a situation where he absolutely had to speak, he'd make small talk for a moment, then ask where the man went to church. If the fellow didn't immediately accept Abel's invitation to join us for worship next Sunday, at the completion of the job he'd find a gospel tract inserted in his payment envelope.

How many people actually read those pamphlets?

I search for a reason to speak, then pick up the shoes I've kicked into the corner. Stepping into the doorway, I lift my gaze from his receding beltline and focus on the fellow's ponytail. "Hello," I say, striving to make my voice pleasant, "will we be able to get to the closet tonight?"

"Sorry," he answers, "but I'll have to ask you not to step on these tiles till tomorrow morning."

What do you know, the man will talk to me.

"That's okay, we have other bathrooms, but all our clothes are in that closet." Goodness, did that sound pretentious?

Giving up on the closet, I drop my shoes to the carpet. "Um . . . can I get you anything? A soda, maybe? I think we might have some cookies in the pantry if you're in the mood for a snack."

Good grief, he must think I think he's poor and starving.

He turns, and his eyes are bright when he looks at me. "No, thank you, ma'am, I brought my lunch. But it's kind of you to offer."

Heat sears my cheeks. "Okay, then. If you need anything, just call, okay? I'll be in the den."

He shakes his head and returns to his tiles, but a warm feeling seeps through my belly as I reach under the bed for my slippers. He didn't seem offended, so what I said must have been okay. When and if he ever mentions that he did work for Reverend Abel Howard, perhaps he'll add that the Reverend's wife even offered him soda and cookies.

No, that's absurd. What I offered wasn't much, but it was more than I'd have offered last week.

And who can say what Christopher would have done? For all I know, his version of ministry might be befriending blue-collar workers down at the local bar where he is just one of the gang.

Why am I thinking these things about my son?

I go into the den, wrap a chenille throw about my shoulders, then sit cross-legged on the couch, reveling in a sudden sense of freedom. Maybe Abel was right; I did need a break. I can't remember the last time I sat down to watch daytime TV. Abel rails a lot about the garbage on television, but we rarely see any of it. When we do have the television on, Abel watches the news. When we were younger, he used to watch ESPN, but he hasn't had time to follow his favorite sports teams in years.

I pick up the remote and flick through channels. A series of images flickers across the screen, and my astonishment increases with every moment. On one channel I see a woman in red lace underwear and high heels slowly walking down a catwalk; another channel features a pair of big-breasted women wrestling in a mud pit. On another station a man wearing nothing but a strategically placed bow stands beside a billboard for a trendy clothing company.

The sitcoms are not much better. I flip through them slowly, trying to get a feel for each show, but as far as I can tell, they're all about twenty-somethings sleeping around, having babies, and happily accepting the lifestyles of their homosexual neighbors/roommates/relatives.

Abel is so right. Television is completely corrupt. The moral fabric of this country has eroded to the point that people don't know any better. Shame has all but disappeared, and public morality is now based on whatever prevalent opinion floats by on the wind. Heaven help the misguided man who kills a grasshopper on a reality show, but let's not say a word to malign the woman who candidly discusses her abortions with Barbara Walters.

Why are we surprised when sinners sin?

The thought strikes like a bolt from the blue, rattling me

to the core. I stare at the actors on a television show and hear the inane laugh track through a buzzing in my ears. Why is television corrupt? The answer is suddenly clear: because most of the people who write for it and produce it don't know any better. Because Christianity is no longer the salt preserving our nation and the remnant still following Christ has vacated the field of competition. We've withdrawn to the spectators' stands, content to complain and ineffectively boycott sponsors who can't understand why we're upset.

I was a sinner, I still *am* a sinner, and I often fall short of God's holiness. How can I hold the world accountable to a standard I don't always attian?

I'm sitting on the sofa, slack-jawed and stunned, when I hear my cell phone ring. Where did I drop my purse? I jump up and run toward the sound, praying the caller will not hang up before I can answer.

After finding my purse—and the phone—on the kitchen counter, I am delighted to discover Chris on the line. I have waited twice for him to extend an invitation; this time, I will do the asking.

"Chris! I'm so glad you called! I wanted to see you again, and I'd still love for you to meet Abel."

"I was hoping you'd say that."

I warm to the sound of pleasure in his voice. "Good. Listen, Abel and I always have Wednesday mornings off, so maybe we could meet somewhere for brunch? The Hilton serves a great breakfast buffet. If we meet before ten-thirty, I think we can catch it."

"Um . . ."

My heart sinks.

"The thing is, I promised Melinda I'd bring her some stuff tomorrow morning. We could always go somewhere after that, I suppose . . . Hey, you wouldn't want to meet her, would you? You two have a lot in common, and I think meeting you might give her hope."

Grimacing, I try to remember what he said about Melinda. She was the girl in the photo, the one who could have been twelve or twenty. I'd really rather not spend my day off talking to a runaway, but how can I say no?

"Okay." I shoehorn a smile into my voice. "I'll meet you first, then maybe we can join Abel at the Hilton. If we miss the buffet, that's okay. We'll just make it an early lunch."

"Thanks, Emma. I really do want to meet Abel, and I want to introduce you to Melinda before I go."

"You're leaving? So soon?" The words come out as an agonized croak.

"I have to go." A note of ruefulness lines his voice. "My father wants me to help him handle some family matters, and I can't let him down. But I'll stay in touch—I'll call whenever the Spirit leads."

I can't speak for a moment; disappointment weighs too heavily upon my heart. I don't know why I thought he'd be around forever; perhaps pride led me to imagine he'd be so enthralled with our relationship he'd never want it to end. I may have been secretly hoping Abel would eventually hire Chris, who would work in our church and be part of our lives forever . . .

Chris interrupts my pity party. "Let me give you the address."

I reach for a pen.

He rattles off the name of a street near the downtown district, and I scribble the numbers on a sheet of notepaper.

"Chris?"

"Yeah?"

"Thank you," I whisper, and I'm not merely thanking him for the assurance of continued contact. I'm thanking him for being the way he is, for persevering in his search, for loving me enough to overcome insurmountable obstacles. "By the way," I ask, "I've been wondering about something."

"What's that?"

"Why do you do ministry . . . well, the way you do it? You could always get a degree and work for a church."

"I have a degree in biblical studies." He names a prestigious seminary that would impress even Abel. "And don't misunderstand—though I love the body of Christ with all my heart, I don't think we can ignore those who are dying outside the body."

"People in the church are sick, too. You should listen to

the problems Abel deals with every week. Family problems, drug use . . ." My thoughts drift toward Eunice Hood and her husband's problem with pornography.

"I know church people have problems, but if they choose to trust and obey, they also have the answer. But what do people outside the church have? They're living in darkness, and most of them have no idea how lost they are."

I think of my next-door neighbor Cathleen. She's one of the people Chris is describing . . . she desperately needs Jesus, but she's completely unaware of her need. Worse yet, unless she comes to me and asks me to explain the plan of salvation, I have no idea how to reach her.

"I think I see what you mean, Chris. The church has programs to reach lost people who reach out for help, but—"

"What programs do you participate in, Emma?"

I laugh as I reach for my purse. A copy of our church bulletin is peeking from within the recesses of my bag, and it lists the more than two hundred weekly programs of Sinai Church.

With one hand I lift the bulletin and flatten it on the counter. "Well," I run my hand down the list of activities, "there's the TV program, of course. And we have Sunday school programs from the cradle to the grave. We offer a Scripture memory program for children, and our youth pastors are really on the ball with ministries for our students. There are Bible study groups for women during the day, and other groups for working men and women on most evenings. We run a summer camp for our children and teenagers, and couples weekends for married people—"

"But what do you do to reach people who aren't *in* your church?"

I make a face at the phone. "I just told you—the *Prayer and Praise* program is capable of reaching forty million homes."

"And that's good—assuming that the unbelievers in those homes are willing to watch your program. But what are you doing to reach those who aren't?"

I search the bulletin for a moment, then tap the appropriate listing. "Abel and the deacons meet every Monday night for visitation. Abel has always believed in visitation; it's how he built our church."

Christopher laughs. "So they get a lot of cards?"

"Sure, anywhere from twenty to thirty every Sunday morning. It takes fifty or sixty people to cover all the cards, plus they also try to do nonurgent hospital visits on that night."

"That's great, Emma. I would never criticize effective programs or the people who run them. But tell me this—what is your church doing to reach people who have never visited one of your services?"

My gladness shrivels like an emptying balloon. "Well . . . Abel and I used to visit all the newcomers in town."

"Do you still do that?"

Silence swells between us as I try to make sense of what he's saying. "Well, no. There isn't time. Abel has all these other visits to make. He has to constantly put out fires among the church people, he travels and speaks, and the TV program keeps us busy raising funds. Airtime is expensive, you know."

"We certainly can't expect one couple to reach an entire city. But your church is huge—how many members?"

"Ten thousand." The number is boldly printed in the bulletin, along with the offering amounts for each Sunday of the month.

"So what are those other ten thousand people doing? Surely you have programs to train your people to reach folks like Melinda and Judd and Shirley?"

Do we? We have classes that teach people how to share their testimony in two minutes . . . but how effective is a two-minute testimony delivered to a stranger? My thoughts shift to my neighbor. Cathleen could live the rest of her life next to me and die without knowing the Savior. I could, of course, go next door and deliver my two-minute testimony like a bomber delivering its cargo . . . but I'd probably be better received if I invited her to one of the special events at our church.

"We have special events." My mind fills with a series of images from our elaborate Easter pageant, the singing Christmas tree, and the Fourth of July spectacular, complete with fireworks, honor guard, and a gigantic flag that once flew above the U.S. Capitol Building. We've always said those presentations were gifts to our community, but I know the vast majority of those who attend are our own church members.

I also know there are people in Wiltshire who so resent the media attention given to Sinai Church that you couldn't pay them to cross the threshold of our worship center.

"I'm not trying to hurt you," Chris says, his voice low and soothing. "For a long time I was afraid to climb out of the nest, too. After all, it's cozy there, I was well fed, and I was happy being among friends-of-a-feather. But one day I clambered up on the edge, looked out at the world, and realized I was no longer a fledgling. I asked God to help me fly, and he's been guiding me ever since."

I remain silent as my mind reviews the list of programs Sinai Church has instituted to keep our people busy. Abel likes to brag that the lights at Sinai burn constantly, for even in the dark of night we have people working for the cause of Christ. They go to the church at all hours to stuff envelopes and attach "Clean Up America" pins to cardboard gift cards, but should they be doing more?

"Think about it," Chris says, jolting me out of my assessment. "When the average American is physically sick today, he goes to the doctor. If he's critical, he goes to the hospital. But where does he go if he's spiritually sick? The man who discovers a hole in his soul will try to fill it with anything and everything until he learns only God can fill that void. But he'll visit bars, singles clubs, the beds of other men's wives in search of meaning and fulfillment. Where are we Christians going to find those people? They're not in our churches. They're in the bars, they're in Kiwanis Clubs, they're leading PTAs and running for local office. The world's people are in the world, Emma, but too many Christians are hiding in the church."

"But the church," I pluck one of Abel's favorite sayings from the air, "is the only institution Jesus ever founded. He didn't give his life for the Kiwanis Club; he gave his life for the church."

"He gave his life for the *world*, Emma. I'm not denying that the church is our foundation, our strength. We're a body, and we need each other. But too many people are billeting at the base camp when Jesus wants us to advance onto the battlefield."

I lift my gaze to the ceiling, silently imploring heaven for help. Chris and I aren't arguing, exactly, but still I feel we're at odds again and I don't want to be at odds with my only child. "Abel understands this," I finally whisper. "That's why he's worked so hard to build Sinai Church. That's why we established a TV ministry. We are doing what God called us to do."

"God calls each of us to the same thing," Chris answers. "We are to surrender ourselves and conform to the image of Christ. By doing that, we become salt and light just as he was. I never planned to become involved in urban ministry; I just learned to see the people I encounter in my path. Along the way, I've realized that the world doesn't hunger for what most of our churches offer. The people I meet don't yearn for sermons or pageants or crusades against immorality, yet Christians do produce the one thing they desperately want and need."

I think I know what he is going to say because I've spent the last four days watching him. Still, I ask. "What?"

"Love." Ruefulness fills his voice. "Unfortunately, even in the church love is often in short supply. Christians who forget that Jesus calls us to give up our rights to ourselves are prone to wanting their own way. And where selfishness abounds, love withers."

I am suddenly grateful he can't see my expression. He couldn't possibly imagine what I've experienced in twenty-four years as a pastor's wife, but he's right. Though Scripture says the world will know we are Christians by our love for one another, I can't count the times I've had to moderate feuds between church members.

"When I meet an obedient Christian, someone like you," he says, a smile in his voice, "the human part of me figures everything's pretty cool with the world. But then I meet some-one like Judd sleeping on the street, and the human part of me is depressed. But Jesus was never prone to those kinds of feel-ings. He knows there's hope for people like Judd, and he knows you aren't perfect. He sees us as we are, Emma . . . and that's what my ministry is. I go where the Lord leads and ask God to let me see people as they are."

I open my mouth, but no words come.

"And so," Chris continues, speaking more slowly, "whenever I meet a person and feel the tug of the Spirit, I ask myself, 'What can I do to show God's love?' Sometimes it's something as simple as offering a glass of water. Sometimes it's as easy as buying somebody a plate of bacon and eggs."

"And sometimes," my voice clots with emotion, "it means taking a man home with you and giving him your bed?"

"That's right." His voice is tender, almost a whisper. "Sometimes it means meeting your biological mother and putting her mind at ease."

With a heart too full for words, I stare at the fabric of my skirt as comprehension begins to seep through my confusion. Until this moment, Chris's behavior had baffled me; now his actions make perfect sense. Like a dandelion seed blown by the breath of God, he has drifted throughout life, sharing God's love where and when he could.

But how can people who are tied to responsibilities live that way?

"The key is being obedient," Chris murmurs. "It's not so difficult. When you see a need and hear the Spirit's voice, you obey."

Is it that easy? For him, maybe. For me . . . it's never that simple. I have too many obligations, too many demands on my time.

"I have to go." The words spring from my tongue almost

of their own accord. "Abel will be home soon, and I need to find something to make for dinner."

"All right, then. See you tomorrow."

As I lower the phone, I realize it's been a long time since I consciously stopped in my busy routine to listen for the voice of God. Oh, I've heard him pounding against the walls of my heart a few times, but how often have I missed his still, small voice?

I have spent my entire adult life doing what I thought Christianity required me to do while Chris has been walking with an ear cocked to hear the voice of God.

Such a simple concept . . . and so difficult to implement.

I'm not sure I can live that way.

Chapter Fifteen

J'm in the kitchen, taking pleasure in the aroma of sizzling bacon and buttery eggs, when Abel comes through the garage door. I wipe my hands on a towel as I greet him. "Hi, honey."

He comes toward me like a man approaching a bomb he expects to go off. "You okay?"

"I'm fine." I smile as I realize it's true—I haven't felt so energized in ages. Chris's random thoughts have done more to open my eyes than all the Bible conferences I've ever attended.

Abel places his hands on my hips and nuzzles my neck. "Bacon and eggs for dinner?"

I laugh as his whiskers brush my cheek. "It was all I had in the house—and who says you can't have breakfast for dinner?"

Actually, I cooked breakfast because after Chris's call I needed to do something with my hands. My thoughts were racing so much that I couldn't sit still, and it felt good to beat the eggs in a bowl and drop the bacon into the skillet.

Abel sinks onto a barstool and spreads his fingers over the flecked granite counter. "I think everything is finally ready for the press conference Sunday afternoon. Josh sent out the press releases, Celene gave the local stations a heads-up, and Esther organized all the quotes we've assembled from Books & More managers. The production guys are working on the video with the women you contacted, so that'll be ready on time. We'll hand out the quotes in a press kit beforehand, before you and I step onto the platform—"

"I don't want to be on the platform, Abel." I turn a slice of bacon in the popping grease. "I thought I made my feelings clear."

He lifts his fingertips from the counter. "Fine." His voice is clipped. "You don't have to be on the platform, no problem. I'll go solo on this one, and if anyone asks why you're not with me, I'll say you're taking a sabbatical."

"I'm always with you, Abel." I pull the last slice of bacon from the pan, then drop it onto a paper-towel-covered plate. "I'm your wife, so I'll always support you. I see what you're trying to do, but I don't think this is the way to go about it."

"And what would you do?"

At first I think he's being snippy, but when I look up I see honest curiosity in his eyes.

I pause to turn off the gas range. "I think I'd tackle the problem from the opposite direction. Barnes & Noble doesn't stock that book, did you know that? I think I'd begin the press conference with praise for that company, maybe even urge Christians around the country to patronize their local B&N. Economic power can be wielded both ways, so why not try urging people to spend money instead of saving it?"

"I can't tell our people to spend money at a secular company—they'll write and tell us they spent their monthly pledge money down at the bookstore. Besides, not everything at a secular bookstore is good, so if we send them there, someone's going to find a book about soap operas or rock music and raise all kinds of Cain. We'll get letters, Em; you know how our supporters love to write letters."

He shows his teeth in an expression that is not quite a smile. "We can't support anything secular. I might be able to send them to Christian bookstores—"

"There's not a Christian bookstore in this country that doesn't contain some book you'd disagree with." I spoon the still-warm eggs into a bowl. "So why not let people support what they like and not support what they don't?"

Abel snorts. "Have you taken a close look at the people around you lately? Too many Christians have developed a taste for too many bad things. They go to R-rated movies, they watch horrible TV—"

"So they need us to tell them what's right and wrong? I thought that was the Holy Spirit's job."

He gives me a look that is anything but tender. "That's not fair, Em. Some of our people wouldn't recognize the Spirit's voice if he broadcast through their microwave ovens. They're spiritual babies. We have to lead them because they don't know how to decide for themselves."

"What would you know about babies, Abel?" I speak in a light tone, but Abel flinches at the snap in my words.

"What are you saying?"

I drop the spatula and fork into the sink, then spin to face him, my hands rising to my hips. "I've never been a parent, but I've heard the purpose of parenting is to teach children how to think for themselves. And you can't shepherd your flock forever—sooner or later people have to follow Jesus and learn to listen for his voice."

Abel shakes his head. "That's easier said than done."

"Really? Well, maybe we need to listen more closely ourselves. I've looked at the people around me—what I see are a lot of nice folks trying to get through life like the proverbial monkeys that see no evil, hear no evil, and speak no evil. If we live in the world, occasionally we're going to see and hear evil. We might even brush up against it."

From some dark place deep in my memory, the image of

a drunken, abusive stranger rises into my consciousness. Despite the strong aroma of bacon, I can almost smell the whiskey on his breath.

I turn back to the sink and brace myself against the edge of the counter. If God brings another whiskey-soaked stranger into my life, will I be able to see him through the fog of unpleasant memories? If I can't handle my past, I'm the last person on earth who should be talking about brushing up against evil.

Jesus, help me.

I take a deep breath as the memory fades. With the Lord's help, I could talk to almost anyone. In O'Shays the other night, I didn't waste a thought on my past because I was too focused on meeting my son. In that video store this morning, I could have talked to George . . . if I hadn't been so embarrassed to be in such a place. If I keep my heart and mind focused on Jesus . . .

Unaware of my thoughts, Abel continues to preach at me. "We shouldn't have to live in darkness. We shouldn't have to pay good money for bad books."

Sighing, I run my hand across my face, brushing the last remnants of the sordid memory from my mind. "No one is telling anyone to buy bad books, Abel. It's just . . . well, I've been wondering if we've done our people a disservice by keeping them squirreled away in the church." I turn to face him. "If our members attended every program we offered, they'd be at the church ten or twelve hours a day, seven days a week."

"And what's wrong with that?" Abel lifts a brow. "We are to center our lives around the Lord, we are commanded to fellowship together, we are to build up the body of Christ."

"Going to church does not equal living for Jesus. Church is part of the Christian life, but it's certainly not all of it. It *can't* be all of it."

I drop the skillet into the sink, where it clatters with more noise than I expected.

"We have visitation programs." Abel lowers his gaze. "We go into the community. We visit prisons and hospitals—"

"I'm glad you go into prisons and hospitals. When I had my appendectomy, our church people nearly killed me with kindness." I pull two plates from the cupboard and set them on the table. "But I know how few community contacts are made in the hospitals. Most of the time our pastors visit our church members, say a prayer, and go on their way."

"That's not true—we visit anyone who requests a pastoral contact."

"And how many lost people even know what a *pastoral contact* is?"

The question hangs in the silence. I know the answer because I've seen the hospital visitation reports on Esther's desk. Every once in a while we will get a call from a frightened hospital patient who is reaching out for spiritual guidance, but our pastors are so busy taking care of our ten thousand church members that they rarely have time to befriend sick people who might not even know they're in need of spiritual healing.

Abel thumps the counter as I spoon eggs onto a plate. "Well, your idea about sending our people into other bookstores just won't fly. It's harder to convince people to spend money than not to spend it, and besides—if some little lady gets ahold of a book with profanity, we'll never hear the end of it. After taking such a strong stand against immorality on television, the media would fry us."

"I don't like profanity," I scrape the bottom of the bowl, then spoon the dregs onto Abel's plate, "but I don't think anybody's going to fall captive to the dark side if they happen to read a bad word. Jesus didn't walk around with his fingers in his ears."

Abel presses his lips together. "Garbage in, garbage out, Emma. Scripture tells us to think on whatsoever is lovely, true, and of good report. Furthermore, it says we'd be better off at the bottom of the sea than in a position where we cause a little one to stumble."

"A child, yes." I wave the salt and pepper shakers over our plates. "Or a weaker brother who's such a new Christian that hearing profanity or the like might tempt him to fall back into his old lifestyle. But you've been a Christian most of your life, Abel, so you're not a weaker brother."

Abel looks at me as if I have suddenly begun to speak a foreign language. "What's gotten into you, Em?"

I sink onto the stool next to his, then lower my cheek to my hand. How can I explain thoughts and ideas I don't understand myself? My life has looped backward in the last few days, and in meeting a part of my past I have begun to question my present.

I close my eyes and try to force my confused emotions into order. "I honestly don't know. I only know that lately our methods seem . . . ineffective. In our quest to be holy and pure and protected, have we closed ourselves off from the people we need to be reaching?"

His hand, comforting and strong, falls upon my shoulder. "Don't we send thousands of dollars to the mission field every year? Aren't we spending our lives in an effort to broadcast the gospel throughout this country? Over forty million people could watch our program every time it airs, Em. We've done our best to be faithful and do our part, and I'm trusting God to do the rest."

He's right, of course. My husband has always been able to slice through my emotional fog and see the heart of the matter.

I sniffle, rub my nose, and lift my head from his hand while we bow our heads for grace.

"Our Lord and Father God," he prays, "we thank you for this food and the day you have brought us through. Give us strength for the day ahead, Lord, and wisdom to know what we should do. Guide us, protect us, and keep us on the path that is straight and narrow. I ask these things in the name of my Lord and Savior, Jesus Christ. Amen."

The prayer has changed the subject, and the set of Abel's jaw tells me he has no desire to talk further about his press conference, boycotts, or books of any kind. He searches the table a moment, then walks to the refrigerator and pulls out a bottle of catsup.

I look away, squinching my nose. I've never been able to eat catsup on eggs; Abel can't tolerate them any other way.

"Sorry." I pick up my fork. "I forgot to set it out."

"No problem."

I slice off a bite of egg, then edge toward another topic Abel won't be eager to discuss.

"I got a call from Christopher today. He'll be leaving town soon"—that news, at least, should please Abel—"and he'd like to meet you. Tomorrow he's taking me to this place where he's ministering to a teenage runaway on Fourteenth Street. I thought you might like to come along."

Abel picks up a slice of bacon and bites off the end. "I thought," he mumbles around the bacon, "you and I were going to have brunch at the Hilton."

"We can still do that. If we miss the brunch buffet we can always do lunch."

His brow wrinkles, and in that instant I know he is not going to meet my son. Not unless the Lord himself comes down and gives my husband a direct command.

"I don't need to meet him." Abel reaches for the catsup. "He's part of your past and he's going away. Let's leave it at that, shall we?"

"Well . . . I think he'd be honored to meet you. He's watched the program, Abel, and he came to church Sunday morning."

Abel slams the meaty part of his hand against the bottom of the catsup bottle with a trifle more force than necessary. A slurry of catsup spits across the counter, spraying his eggs, the edge of his plate, and about six inches of my formerly clean countertop.

I take another bite of egg, knowing his decision is irrevocable.

"I don't understand," he says, speaking in the clipped, curt voice he uses when he is truly angry, "why you keep trying to force this kid on me."

"He's not a kid. He's a wonderful young man."

"Fine. But he has no claim on us."

"He's my son."

"He belongs to the people who raised him. You were only the baby factory."

He has gone too far again, and he knows it. In the abrupt silence I hear all the unspoken words that bubble behind his closed lips—questions about why I wasn't able to give him a child, unvoiced suspicions about my abortion and our subsequent infertility. But he will not say these things, because our childlessness could be his fault. That fact alone prevents him from dropping the entire burden of our empty home upon my shoulders.

"I won't mention it again." I stab my egg, then frown as a chunk of white eggshell cracks beneath the tines of my fork.

"He doesn't even treat you like a lady," Abel mutters, swiping a dishtowel across the messy counter. "Taking you to a bar! How can you think I would be glad a man like that has come into our lives?"

I am suddenly very glad that I haven't told Abel about my meeting with Chris at the video store.

"My son has always shown me the utmost respect. He looks out for me."

"You should never have been anywhere near downtown."

I lift my chin as my mind fills with images of Shirley and George and Judd, who is no longer sleeping on the sidewalk. "Maybe I should go downtown more often. Maybe Chris is doing the real work of the ministry while you're spinning your wheels."

Abel flinches as my words strike deep . . . and instantly I wish I could withdraw the barb. My husband is a good man, a godly man, and he is giving his best to the Savior. I have never seen him do anything to bring dishonor on the Lord or the church he serves.

"I'm sorry, honey." My eyes brim with tears as I reach for his arm. "You didn't deserve that; I know you're doing everything you can for the kingdom. But Christopher has done nothing to deserve your scorn."

Abel looks at me, his eyes damp with pain. "What I feel for him isn't scorn. I'm . . . I'm not sure what it is."

"I know. This has been a confusing time for all of us."

Abel drops into his seat, then picks up a fork and slices a piece of egg. "I suppose I could be a little more open-minded—after all, the Pharisees called Jesus a winebibber because he consorted with drunks. They accused him of wickedness when he socialized with sinful people. His family even called him insane."

I laugh, a wild sound that echoes crazily in our kitchen. "I've been wondering if *I'm* losing my mind, but Christopher definitely is not."

We eat the rest of our meal in silence.

I am putting the dirty dishes in the sink when I hear the three-noted beep that sounds whenever a window or door in our home has opened. I look across the kitchen to the study and see Abel's foot on a leather hassock—he hasn't moved, so who opened the door?

I go to the window and watch as the tile man lowers his tools into the back of his pickup truck. Guilt avalanches over me when I realize he was in the house—our expansive, high-ceilinged house where voices float up to the ceiling and echo to every room—while we were arguing at dinner.

Arguing over Chris. My son.

For the first time in years, an outsider has seen a chink in our armor.

I sink to a stool. Here I am, thinking of myself as Lady Bountiful because I offered the man a soda and cookies . . . now he'll go home and tell everyone that Reverend Howard and his wife fight just like other couples. If he heard us clearly, he has some powerful information.

Lord, forgive me.

I walk to Abel's study and stand in the doorway, watching him as he reads a commentary. Under the pressure of my gaze, he looks up, a question on his face.

"He had to hear us." I jerk my head toward the front door. "The tile guy."

Abel turns a page. "I'm sure he's heard worse in hundreds of other houses. Besides, he doesn't know us."

"But he knows who we are. And I was trying to—" What? My offer of a snack was a far cry from witnessing Abel Howard style.

I was trying to show concern and caring . . . and I'm sorely out of practice.

But Abel's nonchalance calms me. I'm overreacting. The tile guy doesn't care about who we are or what we've done. He probably didn't listen in to our conversation. But he undoubtedly knew we were arguing.

Leaving Abel to his reading, I turn and move toward our bedroom, weary and more than ready for my pajamas. So the tile guy saw our humanness, what's so terrible about that? Everybody's entitled to be human, right? And if he didn't hear what we were specifically arguing about . . .

No . . . I feel awful because I wanted him to see a man and woman united by God's love and his purposes for their lives—the pair our TV audience sees. But that couple doesn't live in this house, if in fact they ever did.

I breathe deep and feel a stab of memory, a broken remnant of a conversation with Christopher.

Jesus . . . knows there's hope for people like Judd, and he knows you aren't perfect. He sees us as we are, Emma.

I've been the Christian superwoman for so long, I can't imagine being human . . . yet the freedom to be human at this moment would be sheer relief. God knows my frame and its weaknesses. If I could take all the energy I invest in maintaining my virtuous image and transfer it to simple trust and obedience . . . maybe then I could leave my reputation and other people's expectations in the Lord's hands while I walk through each day with an ear cocked for his voice.

After dressing for bed, I crawl beneath the covers and lie in the soft gray glow of the television. When Abel has not come to bed by the time the clock strikes eleven, I turn off the TV and close my heavy eyes.

CHAPTER SIXTEEN

I don't know when Abel came to bed. When I wake Wednesday morning, I leave him sleeping while I tiptoe into the bathroom, step carefully over the perfectly spaced tiles, and head toward the shower.

Before opening the shower door, I take a moment to admire the tile man's work. Every piece is perfectly placed, with a uniform quarter-inch gap between each tile, even in odd spaces like the diagonal corners of the bathtub.

I find myself wishing I could stick around and sound out the installer when he comes in to do the grout. Maybe he didn't hear last night's dinnertime conversation . . . but the odds are against it.

I lean into the shower and turn on the hot water full force. While the water heats, I peek into the closet and find myself wishing I owned a pair of blue jeans. Jeans and a sweater would be the perfect attire for a blustery February day, but the most casual pants I own are beige khakis. I pull them from the shelf, then select a blue Oxford shirt to go beneath a cream-colored cashmere sweater I've owned at least ten years.

After a quick shower and a cup of instant coffee, I head into the garage and start the car. I keep looking toward the door, expecting Abel to stick his head out to say something—anything—but I haven't seen him since I left the bedroom.

He'll go about his business, then, without even trying to find out when I'm meeting Christopher. And I'll catch up with Chris and offer some lame excuse about why Abel couldn't come, even though he had the morning off and had nothing more urgent to do than sleep.

Then I'll take my son to the Hilton for lunch, hoping to run into Abel . . . and if he doesn't show, I'll know the breach between us has widened. We have not had a major disagreement since our horrendous first year, but this feels like the beginning of something significant.

Am I sacrificing peace in my marriage in order to pursue this relationship with my son? I shouldn't have to—a woman should be able to love her child and her husband without either one fearing the other. But unless Abel changes his heart, I'm afraid Chris will always be a thorn between us.

After turning on the radio, I find myself listening to Amy Grant as I take the interstate and head toward the downtown area. Abel doesn't approve of Amy—he thinks she sold out a few years ago when she recorded songs for the secular market, and he completely wrote her off when she remarried after her divorce—but I'd bet my bottom dollar that Christopher likes Amy Grant. A lot.

I am cautious on the highway, for last night's below-freezing temperatures left patches of ice on the overpasses and in areas shadowed by hills. The highway leads me through the timbered outskirts of town, meandering through leafless trees that stab at the winter white sky with black, bony arms.

Fifteen minutes later I catch my first glimpse of down-town Wiltshire from the exit ramp. The dingy sky hangs over this urban area like a dustsheet over threadbare furniture. Soon I'm navigating narrow, hilly streets boarded by old clap-board houses that have seen better days. I glance at the address on the sheet of notepaper—1089 Fourteenth Street lies just ahead.

A patina of grime covers the slanted house with boarded-up windows. A leafless vine clings to the clapboards and cov-ers a window at the front, giving the place a furtive look. I park on the curb, then shiver as I look around. Not a sign of life on the block. Iron burglar bars adorn the windows and front door of the house across the street; the two-story next door nestles in the embrace of a thorny hedge, formidable even in the grip of winter.

The building at 1089 Fourteenth Street looks uninhabited. No smoke curls from the crumbling brick fireplace; no lawn beckons the visitor forward. There's no car in the driveway, no door on the mailbox, no light shining around the edges of the boarded windows.

For an instant I think I've made a terrible mistake, then experience reminds me that Christopher never does what I expect. I unbuckle my seat belt and look around, hoping to see a vehicle or any sign of civilized life. I am not getting out of the car unless I feel safe, and I definitely do not feel safe in this neighborhood.

Then I catch a glimpse of movement. I turn to see Christopher standing on the concrete slab that probably used to be a front porch. He is wearing jeans and a thin pullover sweater—where is his coat?—and he is smiling at me.

Thank the Lord, for once he has managed to arrive on time. I pull my purse out of the passenger seat, then step out and click the remote to lock the car—probably a senseless gesture in this neighborhood. After I cross a carpet of crisp dead weeds, Chris greets me with a hug.

"Thanks for coming, Emma."

I step back and give him a look of maternal rebuke. "You'll catch your death of cold out here without a jacket."

"I'm okay." Smiling, he takes my arm and leads me into the house. "Melinda's inside. I told her about you. I think she really wants to meet you."

What did he tell her? I haven't time to wonder, because he opens the door and leads me into the house. I am not sure what I expected to see, but never in my wildest dreams could I have imagined this.

Pigsty is too mild a word to describe what I see once my eyes adjust to the gloom. The scarred wooden floor is littered with newspapers, crumpled food wrappers, and brown paper bags. A man sleeps—at least I think he's sleeping—on the floor before a brick fireplace that's been decorated with profanity and obscene words. Another man sits with his back to the dark window, puffing on a hand-rolled cigarette . . . and I don't have to ask what he's smoking. A sweet, acrid aroma mingles with the sharp tang of body odor and the pungent smell of urine.

Christopher walks through the rubbish without flinching. He turns to catch my eye, then nods toward the hallway. "Melinda's back here."

A kitchen opens up off this hallway, and the room is filthier than the first. In the shadows beneath a sagging cupboard, a rat nibbles on what looks like a shriveled apple. A roach scurries into a flattened pizza box on the chipped orange Formica countertop at our approach, but the girl sitting on the floor does not move. Her hands rest on the tops of her knees while lank hair, caked with grease, straggles around her face. Her eyes are closed.

"Melinda?" Christopher reaches for a white plastic bag on the counter, the only spotless object in sight. "I've brought you some soup. You need to eat it."

Slowly, her eyelids lift, revealing glassy blue eyes. I finally recognize the girl in the photograph, the child with whom Chris thinks I can identify. She looks younger in person.

My son has lifted a foam container and plastic spoon from the bag. "It's beef and barley." He kneels on the dirty floor. "You need to eat something. Starvation is not good for you or the baby."

I take an involuntary half-step back. The baby? Good heavens, how did this child come to be with child?

Melinda looks at Chris with a slightly perplexed expression, as though she heard his voice but couldn't understand what he was saying. Finally a light gleams in her eyes. "I . . . don't . . . like . . . soup."

He flashes me a quick grin, as if getting her to respond at all is a major victory, then returns his attention to the girl. "What do you like, then?"

Even in her stoned condition, a mischievous smile quirks the corner of her mouth. "Pepperoni pizza. Thick crust."

Chris looks at me. "I think we can manage a pizza. Can't we, Emma?"

For an instant I am struck dumb and senseless, then I

understand. "Oh! Of course." I pull my cell phone from my purse, then realize I haven't the faintest idea what company to call in this part of town.

Shrugging helplessly, I hand the phone to Christopher. "I don't know who to call."

He laughs. "I do."

Standing, he punches in a number from memory, then proceeds to order a large pepperoni pizza with thick crust. As he gives the address, I walk back to the hallway and peer into the other rooms of this hellish house.

The bathroom stinks to high heaven—either the plumbing is not working or it's been months since anyone cleaned the toilet. Rust stains crowd the aqua tile, the stool has no seat or handle. Gingerly, I turn the faucet at the sink—no water. I flip the light switch—no power. A candle sits on the edge of the rusty tub, burned down to a nub.

I peek into the bedrooms. A thin, stained mattress crowds most of the floor in the first room, and the bed is occupied by a man and a woman who seem dead to the world. The woman opens her eyes as I walk by the doorway, then closes them with no more reaction than if I were only a figment of a dream. On the floor beside her, a little girl with dark hair calmly plays with a broken mouse trap. She can't be more than two or three.

Almost instantly, my mind fills with a scene from the old black-and-white version of *A Christmas Carol*. One of the ghosts who visits Scrooge shows him two pitiful children, Ignorance and Want. "Beware them both," the spirit warns in a booming voice, "and all of their degree, but most of all beware this boy, for on his brow I see that written which is Doom, unless the writing be erased . . ."

I bring my hand to my mouth as my gorge rises. It's bad enough that people make choices that degrade themselves to this point, but must their children be forced into this miserable sort of existence?

I stumble into the hall, where I nearly run headlong into Christopher.

"Hey." He catches my shoulder. "You okay?"

I can do nothing but nod.

He looks at me for a moment, then drops my phone back into my hand. "The pizza is on its way, but it'll be a while before it gets here. While I go out and watch for the delivery guy, would you mind talking to Melinda? I've been trying to get her out of here, but she won't leave." His eyes soften as he looks at me. "She doesn't trust men, but I think she'll listen to you."

Finding my voice, I gesture toward the room where the little girl is playing in filth. "What about the others? We need to do something about that situation; we can't just leave that child. We should call social services."

Chris glances toward the room, then shakes his head. "If you call social services, they'll disappear. They'll go out the back window the minute that car pulls up, and then that little girl will be living on the streets. As bad as this is, it's a roof over her head."

Frustration percolates beneath my breastbone as I stare at him.

"One person at a time, Emma." His hands, warm and steady, fall upon my shoulders. "I spoke to the Father this morning; this is Melinda's day."

My frantic restlessness calms under the power of his gaze.

"Okay." I swallow hard. "Today we help the pregnant girl. But where will she go?"

"Any place is better than this, don't you think?" His eyes are glowing with purpose and pleasure. "I'm sure the Lord will provide a place."

When he turns to leave, I am suddenly terrified by the thought of being alone in that house. "Wait, Chris." I catch his sleeve. "Do you have to wait outside? I mean, won't they bring the pizza to the door?"

He gives me a wide smile with a touch of irony behind it. "Delivery people don't like to stop in this neighborhood, Emma. You kinda have to catch them as they go by."

As he strides away and opens the front door, I take a deep breath and feel a dozen different emotions collide—fear, loneliness, irritation, hope, despair, hopelessness. For an instant I am sixteen again and standing alone in Grand Central Station, then I remind myself that the past is past. I have become an adult, I have been redeemed, I have . . . overcome. Through the love of Jesus, I have been saved from far worse than this. And I owe an unspeakable debt.

Nola Register swept me off the street and into loving arms. It's time for me to reach out and rescue someone else.

I walk down the hall and go back into the kitchen where Melinda still sits on the floor, her arms limp at her sides, her hands palms-up on the cracked linoleum. She is staring straight ahead, her eyes as remote as the ocean depths. The cup of soup sits on the floor, untouched.

I pick up the soup, slip the plastic lid back onto the container, and place it on the counter. When I've completed that small chore, I realize I have two choices: I can either begin to clean up this kitchen or sit down and try to clean up a life. The kitchen would be far easier to tackle, but Chris asked me to come here for reasons that have nothing to do with my domestic skills.

Reminding myself to buy a pair of jeans as soon as possible, I sink to the floor in front of Melinda. "You know," I link my arms around my knees, "I was about your age when my mom kicked me out of the house. My dad had died a few months before, and my mother was an alcoholic. Anyway . . . she caught me making out with my boyfriend and she couldn't handle it. Actually, I don't think she could handle anything by then. She was looking for a way to simplify her life."

Slowly, Melinda's eyes focus on my face.

"I didn't know where to go." I lean back against a sticky cupboard, realizing that this sweater will never be the same. "I was living in New York State at the time, so I caught a bus to Manhattan. Seemed like a glamorous place to go. Broadway, Madison Avenue, Greenwich Village . . . all of it sounded better than hanging around my hometown."

Melinda tilts her head slightly as her eyes drift away. I draw a breath, assuming I've lost her, then she closes her eyes. "I'm from Cason's Holler, back in the hills. My daddy"—she pronounces it *diddy*—"he took a new wife, and she didn't like me at all. So she turned me out. And my daddy didn't say nothin'."

Grief wells in me, black and cold. I am tempted to draw Melinda into my arms and weep for her, but I don't want to frighten her away. Instead I drop one hand to cover hers . . . in much the same way Nola Register reached out and comforted me.

"I hitched a ride here." Melinda finally meets my eyes. "And the guy who gave me a ride was a college boy, all sweet and nice, until we got to the school. Then he turned me out, too. But before that . . ."

Her eyes fill with tears as her voice trails away. I slide across that dirty floor to place an arm around her slender shoulders. "I know."

"He . . . he put a baby—"

"You're going to be okay, Melinda. Believe me, honey, I've been where you are, and I know you're going to be okay."

Suddenly she is holding me like a drowning girl clings to a life preserver. Her tears are coming in sobs so strong they shake her body, and I realize I am crying only when I taste the salt of my tears running into the corner of my mouth. Holding her, I rub her back and whisper soft shushing sounds while the walls of her resistance come tumbling down.

It is a small victory, but I cherish it nonetheless. I haven't led her to Christ or found her a home or helped her toward the future, but I have drawn her into my arms and shown love.

Yet if not for Chris, I wouldn't be here.

When Melinda's weeping slows to a trickle of tears, I pull away, push the hair from her eyes, and lift her chin. "You're going to get out of here, honey. We're going to find you a place to stay, and then we're going to take care of you and your baby."

She blinks, and for a moment I wonder if she has again retreated behind the wall of indifference. "Christopher says you're on TV."

I'm a little perplexed by the change of subject, but I nod. "That's right."

"What do you do on TV?"

"Well, I sing. On a program from our church. My husband preaches."

"What does he preach about?"

What do I say? He preaches about sin and morality and

indecent books and the importance of having your kid play on a Christian Little League team?

None of those things matter one whit to Melinda . . . or anyone like her.

I meet the girl's wet eyes. "He preaches about Jesus' love."

A slow, shy smile blossoms on her face like a rare and radiant flower. "I know about how Jesus died for our sins and all like that. Mama brought me up in the church before she died."

I nod again. "That's good."

Melinda wipes her nose with her sleeve. "So what else does he talk about?"

I am staring at the stained plaster ceiling, trying to come up with a truthful, useful answer, when I hear a man's groggy voice. "Hey—food's coming!"

I stand and peer around the corner into the front room. One of the men—the formerly comatose guy by the fireplace, I think—has opened the door.

I turn to grin at Melinda and hold up a finger. "You wanted pizza, right?"

She nods.

"Then wait right here. We aim to please."

Four steps take me down the hall to the front door. Our bearded and malodorous sleeping beauty steps aside as I approach.

"You hungry?" I ask.

He scratches his beard for a moment, then nods.

"Good. I'll be right back."

I step through the doorway in time to see Chris approaching a nervous-looking delivery man in a red SUV.

Chris wasn't kidding—the pizza guy has pulled over to the right and makes no move to get out of his truck. He takes Chris's money, then struggles in the confined space to wrestle a large pizza box from an insulated pouch.

Grateful for a blast of fresh, cold air, I step onto the porch. The sun is now almost directly overhead, spreading white light over the wet black roads. The surrounding houses stand like silent sentinels; if not for the smoke rising from a chimney down the street, I would wonder if other people still lived in this crumbling neighborhood. But across the street, the face of an elderly woman appears through a gap in the lace curtain, then vanishes. The SUV in front of her house must be making her nervous.

Scanning the street, I feel a sudden coldness that has nothing to do with the weather. I have read about urban blight in magazines and newspapers, but before this week I had never thought that it might be gnawing away at Wiltshire. Yet here are all the signs of inner-city decay—empty homes, frightened residents, the homeless and helpless living in a drug-induced haze to ease the pain of disconnection.

I shudder when I realize that I, who have always considered Abel a little out of touch, have passed the last two decades of my life in another sort of seclusion. If Chris had not come to town, I might never have seen these streets or met these people. We have been so intent upon reaching the world for Christ that we have forgotten about parts of our own city . . .

I am shivering, my hands in my pockets, when a rumbling truck crests the hill to my left. It's a Schwan's delivery truck, and as Chris accepts the pizza from the driver, I'm wondering which shut-in in this neighborhood orders packaged foods. As Chris begins to cross the street, the pizza delivery driver guns his engine and cuts hard on his steering wheel, attempting to make a quick U-turn in front of the oncoming truck.

My feeling of uneasiness suddenly turns into a deeper and much more immediate fear. Time slows as I shift my gaze to the driver of the delivery truck. The young man, close enough now for me to see the expression of surprise on his face, utters a one-word exclamation and braces himself against the steering wheel. I hear the squeal of brakes; I see the back of the truck swing wide. I am moving down the concrete steps and breathing in the acrid scent of burning rubber by the time the vehicle spins on the wet road.

My feet stutter to a stop on the broken sidewalk. I see the side of the truck hit Chris and jettison him across the asphalt; I watch as the pizza box flies from his hands. The Schwan's man glides by me in the safety of his cab; the front of the truck turns its pale yellow face away.

Somewhere, a drum begins to pound to the rhythm of my pulse. The young man stumbles from the vehicle, the pizza guy has left the scene, and Chris, my beloved son, lies on the pavement a few feet away.

I take a step forward, then retreat, torn between running for help, rushing to his side, and melting into helpless panic.

The delivery truck driver shocks me out of my stupor. "I'm calling an ambulance! Get him warm, lady!"

His voice is all the impetus I need. I run to Chris's side.

His eyes are closed when I first approach, but they open when I kneel and touch his cheek. He is so perfect, so unbroken, that for an instant I am certain God sent an angel to deflect the force of impact. Soon he'll stand up and laugh; he only needs to catch his breath . . .

But then he smiles, and blood trickles from the corner of his mouth. I yank at my sweater, pulling it off, then shape the cashmere into a pillow for his head. A smear of blood wets my palm as I withdraw my hand. He is bleeding from the ear, too, and something in me knows this is not good.

I sink to the road and pull his hand to my cheek. "Hang on, Chris."

His blue eyes are glowing brighter than I have ever seen them. "Mom?"

"I'm here, baby."

"I have to go home."

And he leaves me, just like that. The light in his eyes dims and after a moment I find myself staring into blank, empty windows that no longer house a living soul. Though his palm is still warm and his lips curve in a smile, I know he is no longer with me.

He is with the Lord.

"Chris—?" Pressing his hand to my heart, I rub the pale skin of his arm as if I could massage life back into his frame. "I love you, son. I love you so much."

I am still sitting there when the ambulance arrives. One of the paramedics gently lifts me up so they can take care of Chris. Though he is gone, they hook him up to machines; perhaps, I am told, his organs can be used to help someone else.

One of the paramedics, a young woman, asks if I want to ride along. I am about to say yes, but then I glance behind me.

The accident has drawn a small crowd—mostly elderly people, but also a few small children who seem to have materialized out of thin air. Melinda stands in the midst of the gaping strangers, her arms crossed over her chest, her hair whipped by the wind. I cannot see her eyes, but I can imagine what she is thinking: Someone came, someone cared, and someone left. Something bad happened again, and she is once more alone.

I can get into the ambulance and ride with a lifeless body to the hospital . . .

I spoke to the Father . . .

. . . or I can remain here with the girl Chris came to rescue.

. . . this is Melinda's day.

Somehow I find the strength to tell the paramedic I will go to the hospital later.

I walk to Melinda and slip my arm around her shoulder as tears stream down my face. And as the ambulance pulls away, I hear my heart break with a sharp, snapping sound.

Chapter Seventeen

$\mathcal{F}$atigue oozes from every pore as I wait for Mr. and Mrs. Lewis to arrive. I'm sitting in a pale green visitor's lounge with some ugly vinyl chairs, a sofa, and an industrial-sized waste can. The glass-and-chrome table at my knees is littered with copies of *Sports Illustrated*, *Guideposts*, and *Good Housekeeping*, but I have not felt like reading since my arrival.

Next to me, Abel sits silently, his ankle resting on his knee, his foot jiggling. I am grateful he has come, but I know he is not comfortable. He has waited in this room a hundred times before, always in complete control, but never has he waited to comfort the parents of his wife's son.

The scene is beyond bizarre.

My husband and I have scarcely spoken. I called him from the scene of the accident to tell him what happened and that I would not be going to the office today. I planned to wait at the hospital until Mr. and Mrs. Lewis arrived, no matter how long it took.

To his credit, Abel walked through the doorway half an hour later. He pulled me into his arms, offering comfort in the best way he knew, then took the chair at my side.

We've been sitting for three hours, not talking, not even looking at each other. When a candy striper comes by to ask if we want coffee; Abel accepts her offer and follows her in search of the coffeepot. He returns a few moments later and hands me a cup; I place it on the horrid chrome table.

The big black-and-white clock overhead is striking five when the door swings open again. A man and a woman enter, both of them pale and glassy-eyed. The man looks at Abel, the woman looks at me.

I see her see me, and I know she knows.

I push the boulder from my throat as I stand. "Mrs. Lewis—"

"I'm Georgiana; my husband is Paul. And you are Emma Rose."

"Emma," I tell her. "Call me Emma."

And then she falls into my arms and we hold each other, two weeping mothers bound by tears and love for one remarkable son. I don't have to describe the accident; through the sounds of our sobs I hear Paul Lewis explain that they heard the story from the police and came as quickly as they could.

I'm not sure how long we stand there, but eventually Paul tugs Georgiana away. They sit in the awful chairs across from me and Abel; their eyes scan our faces. It occurs to me that Abel is the only one whose eyes are not swollen from weeping.

It is time to talk, but I'm not sure how this conversation should begin.

Georgiana begins. "Thank you." She pulls a tissue from her purse and wipes her streaming eyes. "Thank you so much for being so generous with your time this past week. He kept calling with reports of how well you were getting on —meeting you has been an answered prayer. He has wanted to know you for so long."

Her gaze shifts from me to Abel, and through the thickened, awkward air I sense my husband stiffen. To spare him the embarrassment of confessing he did not know Chris at all, I lean forward to capture Georgiana's attention.

"You did a wonderful job of raising him." I give them a wobbly smile and hope they can see my sincere gratitude. "He was . . . remarkable. Truly the most unique young man I have ever met. I was so happy to know—to be able to *see*—how God answered my prayers."

Paul's chin wavers. "For so long we prayed for a son. You

answered our prayers when you chose to give him life. We will never be able to properly express our gratitude."

"You don't owe me anything." Heat enters my face as I meet their eyes. "Chris owed his life to an old woman on the Lower East Side and a widow in Hudson Falls. I owe my life to them, too."

"It's like"—Georgiana's voice breaks, but she turns the sob into a cough and continues—"God gave him to you, you gave him to us, we gave him back to you, and you gave him back to God." Her green eyes are swimming. "Though I can't believe the Lord has taken him so soon, somehow it seems right that he was with you when he went home. Like a complete circle."

I close my eyes, unsure how anything about this can seem right. I have sat beside scores of grieving parents who have lost children, and accidents like this never seem to make sense. We always assure parents that God does not make mistakes, yet this time I wonder if I'll be able to believe the standard assurances.

Is it right that God took a strong young man in the prime of his life? Chris gave so much, but he had so much more to give. Who knows what sort of ministry he could have had if he'd been allowed to live fifty more years? He might have worked at one of the nation's largest churches; he might have even joined us to work with *Prayer and Praise.*

I turn my head, unwilling to let the Lewises read whatever bitter emotions might be reflected on my face. And as I wrestle with my rebellious feelings, the rational part of my brain reminds me that Chris did not measure his effectiveness in the same way Abel and I always have. He didn't count honors or numbers or donors. I don't think he counted anything. He just . . . cared.

Georgiana opens her purse and pulls out a small photograph album, the simple plastic kind favored by middle-school girls and doting grandmothers. "I threw this together in a hurry, but thought you might like to have these . . . since you missed his growing-up years."

Gratefully, I accept the photograph album and set it on my knee, holding it to the side so Abel can see, too. He says nothing, but slips his arm around me as I flip through the pages.

Here, encased in plastic sleeves, are frozen moments of Christopher Lewis's life. On one page I see him waddling in a sagging diaper; on another he is riding a pony. Flipping through the pages, I see my son kissing the cheek of a little girl, wearing a baseball uniform and ball cap, belly-down on the carpet with a video game controller in his hands. He is handsome in a tuxedo with a pretty girl on his arm; he is the all-American boy in graduation cap and gown. He is adorable in a college sweatshirt; silly in reindeer antlers beside a glittering Christmas tree. In the final shot he's standing between Mr. and Mrs. Lewis—his mom and dad—with a diploma in his hand.

"Thank you." The words come out as a strangled croak; my throat is too tight for natural speech. I find myself wishing I had some similar token to give these people, then I remember.

"I have pictures, too." Delighted by the sudden memory, I look at Abel. "Chris took them just the other day. He said he had taken shots of all the people to whom he was ministering."

I pull my purse to my chest and sort through the pockets until I find the white envelope from Jackson's Photo.

"Here." I lift the flap and pull out the glossy pages. "I haven't had a chance to look at more than a couple of these, but maybe you can get an idea of what he was doing here in Wiltshire."

The first photo is a shot of Melinda, and my throat aches with regret as I slide it over the coffee table. "That's a fourteen-year-old pregnant girl Chris befriended at a house in the downtown district. Chris and I were visiting her when . . ." I bite my lip. "She saw the accident, and she was pretty shaken up about it. So I drove her to my assistant's house, where she'll sleep in a warm bed tonight."

Georgiana lifts the photo, then tenderly traces the outline of Melinda's face. "He always had a soft spot for outcasts."

Her gentle words stab at my heart. "Did he?" I look at Georgiana, whose eyes are soft with pain. "Did he think I rejected him? I never meant for that to happen. You've got to believe I never meant to hurt him."

"Oh, my dear." Georgiana drops the photo, then reaches forward to take my hands. "Emma, we know you had the best of intentions for him. Children don't always understand the ways God works in our lives, but in time, they learn."

Featherlike lines crinkle around Paul Lewis's eyes as he smiles. "I can't tell you he never went through hard times. Like any other kid, he had his insecurities and his questions. But he matured past all that. And after a while he wanted to find you . . . if only to tell you how grateful he was for what you did."

Georgiana picks up Melinda's picture again. "What will happen to this girl?"

I glance at Abel. A plan has been percolating in my brain these last few hours, but I haven't yet found the courage to speak to my husband about it.

"I know a place." I meet Georgiana's eye. "Mercy House, in central New York. I'm hoping to take a few days off to drive Melinda up there. She'll have the best of care, an opportunity to continue her education, and a wonderful Christian influence."

Somehow, Georgiana finds a smile. "I think I know the place. There's an adoption agency right around the corner."

Our eyes meet, silently acknowledging the bond between us. "That's the one."

Our paths crossed at Mercy House and the place changed both our lives.

Georgiana opens her mouth, then holds up a finger and

dabs at her eyes as fresh tears begin to stream down her cheeks. Her husband drapes his arm around her, drawing her close, but she looks at me and forces words through the crack in her voice.

"Despite this"—her hands sweep outward to indicate our surroundings—"I'm so glad he came to you." She swipes at her nose, then balls her tissue in her fist. "I wouldn't ever want you to think it was wrong for him to come here. All his life, he yearned to know you. I knew he loved me, so I was never really jealous. Chris just had this great big heart."

I manage a choked laugh. "Did he have you visiting street people, too?"

A look of surprise crosses her face, then she glances at the photo of Melinda and shakes her head. "We've always believed that to follow Christ means just that—we follow him wherever he leads. The Lord led Chris into the inner cities. He led my husband into the corporate world. Me, I've followed Jesus into the Junior League and the Garden Club. I was a little reluctant to join those groups because I'm not really into meetings and social events, but Chris reminded me that society women need Jesus, too."

Where have I followed the Lord? Over the last twenty-odd years, have I been following Jesus . . . or Abel?

A memory opens as if a curtain has been pulled aside. I am sitting on a bunk bed in the dorm, and I am telling my college roommate that I think the Lord might be calling me to work with teenage girls because he has brought me through some really rough waters . . .

In believing that God called Abel to ministry and me to Abel, have I missed the ministry God intended for me?

Sobs rise in my throat again, threatening my speech, and Abel, bless him, tactfully changes the subject. He nods at the other photos in my lap. "What else do you have there?"

Grateful to be distracted by the question, I look at the photos in my lap. "I'm not really sure. Chris was going to tell me about all of these people, but . . . we never finished."

I lay the stack on the table, then run my fingertips over them, spreading them like a deck of cards. We all lean forward as if we could discern the meaning of a lost life in a few glossy rectangles.

Recognizing a flip of blonde hair, I slide a photo from the row. "This is Shirley, from O'Shays. The man next to her is Jim, the bartender. And this one"—I pull out another photo—"is Judd, who was sleeping on the sidewalk before Chris took him home and gave him a bed." My voice softens. "I scolded him for that, but he said he knew he was doing the right thing."

"Chris was fearless like that." Georgiana's voice trembles. "He said as long as he was being obedient, nothing could happen to him except what the Lord willed."

Abel abruptly reaches for a photograph. "What are you doing with a picture of Eunice Hood?"

My breath catches in my lungs. The photo in Abel's hand is Eunice the way I saw her last Tuesday, her face flushed, her eyes red from weeping. She's even wearing a wet raincoat and the Wiltshire Warhawks T-shirt.

Impossible. Chris couldn't have snapped this photo before we met Eunice . . . could he?

A shiver rises from the core of my belly as I examine the scattered photos on the table. There are pictures of strangers as well as people I recognize—a photo of the little girl in the crack house, the man hungry for pizza, the frightened old woman peering at me from behind a lace curtain and iron bars. There's a shot of the cardigan-clad clerk in the video shop, a picture of some other down-and-outer on a downtown street.

And in my mind, as sharp as reality, other images form in glorious living color: my neighbor Cathleen, with her new puppy, the tile man standing beside his truck, Eunice weeping before a sink in a public ladies' room.

My mouth goes dry. I know the others are looking at me, waiting for details, but I can't begin to explain the images in front of me. Yet I can hear Chris's voice ringing in my memory: *There are some great stories behind those photos—great needs, too.*

I may never understand how or when he took his pictures, but in a flash of insight I understand why: These people and their needs are now my responsibility.

Too shaken to talk further, I push myself up from my chair. "I'm so sorry for your loss," I say, allowing habit to take over. "But I have to go. I have to get out of here . . . I need to be alone for a while."

Leaving Abel to say a proper good-bye, I push on the swinging door and hurry away on legs that feel as weak as a newborn colt's.

Somehow I find my car, unlock the door, climb into the seat and turn the key. I have to go somewhere, stay busy, do something, then maybe these hot spurts of loss will stop burning my cheeks.

I pull the car out of the hospital parking lot and head toward the interstate. The Lewises will be at the hospital for some time yet, and I need time to say a final farewell to the son I have known only a few days.

My foot feels heavy on the gas pedal, but cars are regularly whizzing by me. I watch them pass, a little amazed that so many people can go about their business as if nothing unusual has happened. A good and godly man has just left the world—how can they not sense the sorrow that shadows our city?

From the interstate I take the now-familiar downtown exit. I check my watch—five o'clock. Too early for O'Shays to be in full party mode, but Jim should be working behind the bar. And maybe Shirley will be there. Surely one of them will know where Chris was staying.

My brain sorts through the available facts as I negotiate the one-way streets. The Lewises undoubtedly have the address of Chris's apartment, but I don't want to ask them for it. He had to be staying someplace near the downtown area, because he seemed to walk almost everywhere.

I pull into an empty space across from O'Shays, then slide out of the car and stride toward the door, ignoring the parking meter at the curb. A handful of men are gathered around the bar—the after-work crowd, obviously—but Shirley is not among them.

Jim cocks a dark brow as I approach the bar. "So . . . it'll be something stronger than hot tea today, right?"

Why would he think that? Startled, I glance at my reflection in the mirror behind the bottles. The Emma Rose Howard staring back at me has mussed hair, lashless eyes, and a swollen nose.

I look like I've been licking the inside of a gin bottle for the better part of a week.

Ignoring his comment, I lean against the brass railing. "You know Chris Lewis, right?"

Jim looks at me as if he's weighing my motives, then nods slowly. "So what if I do?"

I am about to explain what has happened, but a sudden

tightening of my throat assures me I won't be able to speak of the accident without igniting a fresh explosion of tears.

I close my eyes. "He was staying around here, right? I need to know where he was—is—staying."

"Can't help you, lady."

My eyes fly open. "You can't help—or you won't?"

"None of my business. If he didn't tell you, none of yours, either."

With that he turns to answer a summons from the far end of the bar. I draw in a ragged breath, then hear a chuckle near my ear.

"Chris is a little young for you, ain't he?"

The man next to me is barely five-foot-two, with thinning silver hair arranged in a faint halo on his head. But there's nothing else angelic about him—I can smell whiskey on his breath and see its effect in the blossoms of burst blood vessels in his nose and cheeks.

I recognize him almost immediately—he's one of the men in Chris's photo collection.

"I seen you here with him," the pint-sized wino assures me. "The other night you was here with Chris."

A flurry of hope rises in my breast. "You know Chris well?"

The wino nods again. "Ought to. We're roommates. The day he came to town he saw me standing down by the bus stop and said, 'Hey, buddy. Where can a guy get a room around here?' So I took him to my place, and the landlord said we could share the room, long as we didn't light candles or anything that might burn the place down."

"Leave the woman alone, Buddy." Jim has returned, and he's frowning at the little man by my side.

"It's okay." I drop my hand to Buddy's shoulder, then lower my head to look into his eyes. "I need to see Chris's room. There's been an accident, you see, and I need to pull his things together."

Buddy squints at me for a moment, his eyes alight with speculation, but when I pull a twenty from my purse his face melts in a buttery smile.

I can't believe I'm greasing palms like a Hollywood hot shot.

"C'mon." He slides the twenty from my hand as he waddles past me. "It ain't far."

Buddy is right, the apartment isn't far away. We leave the bar and walk a few feet, then Buddy opens one of those unadorned, dark doors that downtown shoppers pass without thinking.

I follow him through a dingy hallway with a floor of chipped tiles, then we come to an elevator shaft. Buddy jerks his thumb toward the old-fashioned expanding gate. "Don't work. Never worked since I've been here."

I follow him through a swinging door clad in only a few shreds of paint. Someone has carved obscene words into the wood, but those don't alarm me nearly as much as the sight of a fat rat scuttling into the shadows behind the stairwell.

"Second floor." Buddy is wheezing now, and clings to the banister as we begin to climb. "First door on the second floor, that's our room."

I keep pace with his lagging step, though everything in me wants to turn and race out of the building. We turn the corner at a dark landing, and I'm faintly amazed that my swollen nose can still register the strong odors of sweat and urine.

Another flight of steps, another landing, another door, this one even more bare and scrawled than the first. A naked light bulb hangs by the door, adorned only by a spider and its filmy web.

"Room two-oh-seven," Buddy says, leading me down the hall. Newspapers litter the floor, and a soiled mattress sits outside one door. I'm surprised no one is passed out on the mattress, but the hour is still early.

Finally we halt outside a door. Two rusty letters hang on bent nails, a two and a seven with a space between them. Buddy fishes a key from his pocket, unlocks the door, and pushes it open.

I am suddenly aware that I am putting myself at the mercy of a stranger—exactly what I warned Chris not to do. Despite the withered condition of the man with me, the gloom in this place feels heavy and threatening.

I tilt my head toward the open room. "You first."

Shrugging, Buddy walks into the room and flips a switch. With a loud plastic crack, an overhead bulb floods the place with yellow light, revealing a square room with a sink against one wall, two beds on rusty iron frames, a small table, and an extra lamp. One of the beds has been neatly arranged with the pillow at one end, a folded blanket at the other. The other is covered by a rumpled sheet and blanket.

Buddy sinks to the rumpled bed and gestures toward the table. "That's Chris's stuff. He doesn't have much."

I move to the desk. A small suitcase sits beneath it; an open Bible, two copies of *People* magazine, and a leather journal are stacked on its surface.

"You say Chris was in an accident?"

I pull out the rickety chair and sit in the place Chris must have occupied, perhaps just this morning. "Yes."

"Somebody drop a brick on him? Bad stuff always happens to the good 'uns."

I run my hands over the leather binding of his Bible, then open it to a random page. The words have been underlined and highlighted; the margins are crowded with handwritten notes.

"He was hit by a truck. And he died."

Buddy swears softly, and when I hear the holy name he utters I am compelled to meet his gaze. "Chris was a follower of Jesus, you know."

Buddy lowers his eyes. "I know. Talked about Jesus all the time."

"Then I'm sorry I missed the respect you must have intended when you said his name."

Buddy sits in silence a moment, his hands fidgeting with the edges of his coat, then he mumbles something about having to visit the john and leaves me alone.

Running my hands over the pages of Chris's Bible, I realize I am no longer frightened. A sense of rightness washes over me, and I understand what my son meant about having no fear as long as he was in the perfect will of God.

It is right that I be here. This room is no worse than those I slept in during my dark days. My alcoholic companion is no worse than I was; in fact, he has shown kindness by bringing me here.

The Lord has shown me a kindness by bringing me to this moment.

I pick up the journal. Will I be trespassing if I read it? For a moment I hesitate, my head bowed, but the feeling of peace persists.

I open the front page, in which Chris has scrawled his name and New York address. I study his bold handwriting for an instant, then flip to a page and read what he has written:

I believe Christ calls us to be quiet followers, not heroes. When I am following him, the simple act of offering a cup of water to a thirsty man on the street is more precious to God than the preaching of an eloquent sermon that falls on mostly uncaring ears. The Lord has not called me to a platform . . . he has called me to walk among people as he did, touching them one by one.

Sometimes I look at my bio mother and wonder if the show business mentality that has invaded our view of Christian work has blinded us to the real meaning of discipleship. Believers look at people like Emma and think they have to do exceptional things for God, when that's not what the Father wants at all. I'm learning to be extraordinary in ordinary things, to be holy in unpleasant circumstances, surrounded by confirmed sinners.

This is where faith sustains me.

Pressing the journal to my heart, I ball my fingers into hard fists, fighting back the tears that swell hot and heavy in my chest. I'm tired of weeping, weary of the holy hands that keep twisting the stubbornness from my heart, but still they persist. And it hurts, dear God, it hurts.

My son has pulled the blinders from my eyes and allowed me to see myself for what I am—a sinner, cast from the same mold as the people I've met this past week. Yet until today, I was so focused on my own joys and worries that I refused to see the souls behind those strangers' faces.

Chris wanted me to see them—that's why he took their pictures. He wanted me to understand his view of the experience I glibly refer to as the "Christian walk." Now I see how blind I have been.

Jesus never meant for me to retreat from the world. I'm beginning to think he wanted me—a woman with a past as colorful as Mary Magdalene's—to grow strong in faith and love so I could reach out to people like Buddy and Jim and Shirley and Melinda and Eunice and George and all the strangers I don't yet know. They need the Savior as much as I do. None of us deserve redemption, yet still Christ calls us from darkness into light.

Still holding the journal to my chest, I lift my face to the streaked window. A week ago I thought I had honed the Christian walk to an art form. I was living a blameless life, working in the ministry, serving a church and a godly husband, doing my part to spread the gospel over the airwaves. I loved every minute of my perfectly designed calling.

But who called me, Jesus or Abel? When Abel proposed, did I automatically transfer my allegiance to him? He is a godly man, a wonderful pastor and teacher, and by following him I have managed to lead a dutiful Christian life.

But Abel is not my Lord, nor does he understand who I am. I am the woman who came to Jesus with an alabaster jar, the grievous sinner who washed his feet with her tears and dried them with her hair. I gave him all I had—a wretched, broken life—and he lifted me up to a life worth living.

I love my husband, I will honor and submit to him as the

head of our home, but I can no longer seek Abel's will when I should be seeking my Savior's and listening for his holy voice.

Over the years I have discovered that human nature and pride can handle almost anything. How long has it been since I found myself begging heaven for a touch of divine mercy because I had utterly reached the limits of my capability? Abel and I regularly invoke God's blessing on our food, our work, our home, but when was the last time we came broken to the throne, offering up a problem we could not handle?

I'm in desperate need of divine grace at this moment. My carefully arranged life has been blown to bits by the breath of God, and I have no idea how—or if—I should put it back together.

CHAPTER EIGHTEEN

*F*or the first time in twenty years, I miss a Wednesday evening service at Sinai Church. After gathering Chris's belongings, I carry them to the hospital and present them to Paul and Georgiana Lewis. I embrace Christopher's parents, thank them again through my tears, and then drive around town and stare at the winking houselights.

I don't know how Abel will explain my absence behind the piano—he'll probably mention something about a family emergency or simply say I'm not feeling well. He'll be telling the truth in either case. I don't feel well—my eyes are burning, my nose is raw from too many tissues, and a migraine has begun to claw at the back of my left eye. Despite the lessons I've learned in the last few hours, something in me wants to die rather than face the loss I've suffered.

By nine-thirty I am heading home, and by nine-forty-five the garage door opener hums to let me in.

A lamp is burning in the bedroom when I enter the house. I drop my purse onto the kitchen table, slip off my shoes by the mat, then slip silently through the kitchen and hallway.

Abel is sitting on the bed, his gaze downcast. As I draw closer, I see that he is studying Chris's photographs. They are spread over the comforter, arranged edge to edge like perfectly spaced tiles.

Without speaking, I lower myself to the opposite side of the bed. He acknowledges me with an uplifted brow, then picks up one picture and turns it toward me. It's the photo of Eunice Hood.

"How did one of our deacons' wives end up with this crew?"

I press my fingertips to my throbbing temple. "I don't know when Chris took the picture. And they're not a crew, Abel . . . they're people."

"Not the sort . . . well." His voice trails away.

I gather my courage and attempt to explain. "Chris and I were in this downtown photo store when Eunice came in to return some X-rated videos she found in her home. Apparently they were Tim's."

Abel shakes his head, pauses for a moment. "I had no idea."

Limp with weariness, I wave the issue away. "He's a man, Abel. Even Christian men can struggle with lust."

"I should have known." Worry lines mark Abel's face, creases that didn't exist a week ago. "A pastor should know about the troubles of his flock."

"Your flock has ten thousand members. You can't know everything."

"But Timothy Hood is one of my deacons. We ate dinner together just the other night. He was praying and testifying right along with the others."

"You can't see into a man's heart, Abel. So don't beat yourself up about it."

I curl up beside my husband and place one hand on his arm. "I love you, Abel. I know you are a righteous man who loves God. I know you try to do your best to lead the flock. But you know what? You're a sheep, too. Though the lambs can learn a lot from you, there comes a time when they have to grow up and learn to follow Jesus. He's the true Shepherd."

Abel hauls his gaze from the photographs to my face. "You were in the sort of place that rents X-rated videos?"

I close my eyes. "I wasn't there to rent anything."

"But you were there."

"Chris had befriended the owner. And you may not believe this, but I think I was supposed to be there that morning. I felt a tug at my heart when Eunice came in and started crying, but I was too preoccupied with my own embarrassment to see her need. Now I know I should have stood right in the middle of that store and wrapped my arms around her."

Surprise has siphoned the blood from my husband's face.

"I disobeyed the Spirit, Abel." I look up and meet his gaze. "I heard him, and I ignored him. And now I'm wondering how many other times I've ignored him to further my own interests."

"You've always followed Christ." Abel speaks in the raspy voice of frustration. "We've spent twenty-four years praying together, being a team—"

"We've spent twenty-four years following your vision, Abel. My prayers have been echoes of yours; my goals have always been whatever you put on my to-do list. I think it's time I asked the Lord what he wants me to do."

"He wants you to keep on being the way you are."

"No—he doesn't. He wants me to look back to where I've come from. I know that world, and I know how to help the people who are mired in it."

I send up a silent prayer for wisdom, then take a deep breath. "You reflect what you know, honey, and you've always known God as holy and pure. He is those things, but he is also passionate love—love strong enough to reach into the pits of despair and depravity. That love rescued me, Abel, and delivered me from my miserable life. In the early days, you were a great example for me to follow. But now I've matured, and it's time I learned what God wants me to do."

My husband's handsome face and bright eyes, which can intimidate most men even from a distance, are full of beaten sadness. When he speaks, his voice is rough. "I don't understand what you're getting at, Em. We've always tried to win souls to Christ. We've always worked together."

"And we'll still work together. I'm not leaving you, Abel. I just think it's time I opened my eyes to the work God might have for me *outside* the church."

He shakes his head. "What else could you do? We've never tried to limit God."

"Maybe we've been limiting ourselves." I turn the thought over in my mind, examining it from all perspectives. "I mean, think about it—we have built our ministry to be a lighthouse and we expect it to draw people like moths. But there are some valleys where the light doesn't reach. Even in Wiltshire, some people can't see it. So we need to take the light to them."

Abel considers a moment. "So you think we should go out and live in the gutters?"

"I think we should live circumspectly as we move through the world . . . being as wary as serpents and as harmless as doves. Isn't that what Jesus told us to do?"

Abel looks at the ceiling as if appealing to a higher authority, then grips his arms. "I understand what you're saying, Em, but I just don't see how it applies to us. I'm already doing all I know to do. I don't have many free hours as it is."

"I'm not saying you have to do it all, but you can train our people to think differently. Instead of inventing so many programs to keep people within our walls, let's think about sending our people out. Instead of creating Christian baseball teams, let's send our Christian coaches into the city leagues. Instead of boycotting books about swingers, let's write something to promote the ideal of a Christ-centered marriage. Let's light a candle instead of cursing the darkness."

"You've thought a lot about this."

"I've had a lot of time to think . . . and I'm not done yet."

As he slides the photos into a neat pile, I hug my pillow. "I drove around town tonight, Abel, and I asked the Lord why he brought Chris into my life. I mean, look at it from an eternal perspective—I knew Chris only four days. If God meant to take him home today—and I believe he did—then he could have just as easily kept Chris in New York with his parents. But God sent Chris to Wiltshire, and to me. The Lord used Chris to pull me out of my usual places and patterns, and he had to have a reason. I want to understand it."

He lifts one eyebrow at me, suggesting in marital shorthand that I'm overtired and in need of sleep. "Sometimes things just happen, Em."

"I don't believe that." I run my hand up his arm. "I've already figured out one thing I'm supposed to do. Tomorrow

I'm going to do whatever I must to get Melinda safely situated at Mercy House, but I can't do that for every runaway girl in Kentucky. So I want to think about beginning our own home for throwaway kids . . . girls *and* boys. And I think we need a place where alcoholics can learn about Jesus while they dry out. And we need to establish a ministry for families who have been torn apart by pornography and drug abuse. Downtown real estate is cheap, Abel, and that's where some of the neediest people are. We could buy a building there and get started by summer."

Abel scratches the stubble at his chin. "You're talking about a lot of work and money, Em."

"It couldn't be any harder than cleaning up television."

When he lifts a brow again, I know I've scored a point.

CHAPTER NINETEEN

*T*hursday morning I rise with the sun and dress in slacks and a casual cotton sweater. While Abel stumbles sleepily to the shower, I pull a suitcase from a closet shelf and toss in lingerie, socks, a change of clothes, and a pair of pajamas.

By the time Abel comes out of the shower, I'm packed, with my purse and car keys in hand. He comes forward, scrubbing a towel through his hair, then looks at me and blinks hard.

"I'm going to Celene's house to pick up Melinda." I lift my chin. "Then I'm driving Melinda to Mercy House. I'll stay there overnight, spend a little time with Lortis June, then I'll drive back Saturday morning."

"You're driving her? Why, that's more than five hundred miles!"

I pull my purse to my shoulder. "Ten or eleven hours in the car will give us a chance to know each other. And I could use the time alone on the way back. I need to think and pray about some things."

"But—"

I rise on tiptoe to plant a kiss on his cheek. "I've already spoken to Celene. She's going to cancel all my appointments, and she's already spoken to the folks at Mercy House. So it's all settled."

I linger a moment, waiting for his reaction, but Abel seems too stunned to object. I move toward the door, then turn to blow him a kiss.

I don't know much about teenagers, but Melinda and I settle into guarded conversation as we set out. I learn she is from a small town back in the mountains, with seven siblings, a father, her evil stepmother, and "a passel of hound dogs" her father uses for hunting. Her favorite possession is an old transistor radio that looks like it was manufactured during my high-school years. Her greatest fear is that God will punish her for getting pregnant by doing something bad to her baby.

I tell her that God doesn't operate like that, but my assurances have no credibility with her now. So we stop for lunch at a Cracker Barrel and I tell her bits and pieces of my story. Her gaze keeps drifting over my shoulder, so I'm not sure how intently she's listening.

She interrupts as I'm explaining how I met Nola Register.

"You know that guy who got killed?"

I nod. To speak Christopher's name would spur more tears.

"You have his eyes. The way you talk sometimes, you look just like him."

I pick up my fork and stab one last green bean. "That's probably because he was my baby."

Melinda's bushy brows shoot up to her hairline. "That ain't right. He told me his people lived in New York."

"The wonderful couple who adopted him *do* live in New York. I'm the woman who gave birth to him. I'm the girl who was pregnant and scared half to death because I was living on the streets in a big city."

Melinda doesn't answer, but her eyes stop wandering as I continue. I tell her about Nola, about how that brave woman took me in and fed me when I was hungry, and about Lortis June, who gave me a bed and a home and love when I had nowhere else to go.

Melinda eats, she listens, and when we're back on the interstate heading north, I catch her studying me with an intently curious expression.

Night has fallen by the time we pass the Hudson Falls city limit. The town has sprawled farther into the wooded hills since I left it, but Hillside Drive is still the first right after Central Avenue and Mercy House is still the first house on the left.

Melinda and I get out of the car. I reach for our small suitcases; she tugs nervously at the hem of her new shirt as we walk up the narrow sidewalk.

The porch light blazes out of the darkness, then the storm door opens with a metallic screech. "That you, Emma?"

At the sound of that voice I am seventeen again, happy to exchange my heartbreak for the security of home. I drop my suitcase on the sidewalk and run into the soft, sachet-scented arms of Lortis June Moses.

"Why are you troubled, child?"

I give Lortis June a look of skepticism. I have just finished telling her about the four days I spent with Christopher; I have wept my way through another box of tissues as I described his death. I knew I didn't have to share every detail, but something drove me to describe the smile on his face, his last words, his last look. Talking about it brought him back, if only for a moment . . .

So how can she ask me why I am troubled?

"It's just—" Unable to find the words, I wave my hand. "It's everything, Lortis June. My heart feels so heavy. Something in me wonders if I'll ever be happy again."

"That's grief, honey. You'll feel that way awhile, then the grief will ease. Part of your heart will always feel a little lonely for heaven, though."

Sighing, I rest my cheek against my palm. We are sitting in Lortis June's little room, and I can't help but wonder how many other brokenhearted females have curled up in this wicker chair and let their hurts flow into this cozy space. She sits on the other side of a chintz-draped table cluttered with silver-framed baby photographs.

Looking at the babies, for a moment I look for Christopher's face, then I decide not to try. I'd rather remember him as a man who came into my world and somehow sharpened the focus.

"I know grief," Lortis June's faint smile holds a touch of sadness, "and I know trouble. And the look you're wearing has as much trouble behind it as sorrow."

I swallow hard and blow my nose. She's right, of course—even though her eyes are weaker than they were twenty-eight years ago, she doesn't miss a trick. "It's just—" I halt when my throat clogs, then clear it and press on. "Well, Christopher worshiped and loved the same Lord I do. But he lived so differently! He talked about Jesus as though he and the Lord had breakfast together every morning. And he was so dedicated to his work, though it was the most disorganized ministry I've ever seen."

"Is that what's troubling you? His ministry?"

"Not really . . . maybe I'm jealous. Maybe I'm wondering if I've somehow missed the boat. I've always thought I was fulfilling God's plan for my life by being Abel's right hand, but now I don't know what I'm supposed to be." I hiccup a sob. "I'm a forty-five-year-old woman who has no idea what she's supposed to do with her life. I have all these ideas. . . . My mind is racing."

Silence falls between us, broken only by the clank of the radiator in the corner of the room and the pinched sound of Lortis June's labored breathing. Giggles of passing girls seep through the door, and for a moment my thoughts wing after them. I had hoped to work with girls once . . . before I met Abel.

"Not everybody is gifted to work with people on the streets," Lortis June says, "and not everybody is gifted to be a pastor's wife. But we are all called to follow Jesus, and to be lights where we are planted. If you're using your gifts, and shining your light, I don't think you have any reason to be troubled."

I know she intends to comfort me, but one phrase sticks in my mind: *If you're using your gifts . . .*

I'm using my talents—I'm playing a piano and exercising my voice. I'm using the knowledge I acquired in college to edit a magazine and teach Bible classes. I know my spiritual gifts are teaching and administration, and I am using those in our ministry.

But aren't Christ's love and mercy also gifts? And I, who have been so completely bathed in his forgiving love and grace, should be splashing that same love and mercy onto everyone I meet . . . yet I can't recall the last time I met anyone who didn't profess faith in Christ.

An image focuses in my memory. Wait—I met the tile man. And Shirley. And Jim. And George. And Judd. And Buddy. But at the time I met most of them, I was far more concerned with my own feelings than their lives. I have met my neighbor Cathleen . . . and I have repaid her kindness and her invitations with marked indifference.

God, forgive me.

I bow my head and cover my eyes with my hands. Lortis June says nothing, but begins to hum tunelessly as she picks up her crochet.

She will wait until the Lord is finished speaking to me.

I will wait, too.

Chapter Twenty

*T*he nine A.M. service at Sinai Church opens in predictable, comforting splendor. As the organ swells to the strains of "Holy, Holy, Holy," Abel stands beside the pulpit, Kenyon Glazier aerobically directs the congregation, and my fingers move smoothly over the piano keys.

I'm a little weary from my marathon drive, but I doubt anyone will notice. I pulled in before dark last night and caught up with Abel when he came in from speaking at a Fellowship of Christian Athletes rally.

We exchanged little more than the usual pleasantries—I asked about his meeting ("Went well, thanks"), and he asked about Melinda ("Settling in nicely, I think. Lortis June will take care of her").

I asked about his big press conference ("Everything's on schedule for tomorrow"), and he asked if I had changed my mind about joining the bookstore boycott ("No, I haven't. Thanks for understanding").

A stranger might have thought we were enjoying one of those comfortable silences long-married couples routinely share, but I knew something had changed.

Half-afraid to begin working our way through the fog between us, we went to bed early in preparation for a busy Sunday at Sinai.

Now, as my fingers automatically slip into the chords my ears have selected, I realize that though my environment has not changed, my perspective is radically different. My emotions have been rubbed raw by the harsh events of the past few days. Lortis June was a comfort as always, and so were my prayers on the long drive home. But I could not pray for consolation without asking God to open my eyes as well. The Spirit filled my heart and mind with new thoughts, and by the time I reached home, I knew things in my world were about to change.

Tomorrow morning, I'm going to talk to Abel again about beginning a different kind of ministry—something designed to get our people out of the church and into the community. That's what struck me most about Chris—everything he did was motivated by his desire to show love to a lost world. I don't want to scold or chide or challenge the world. I don't want to boycott anything. I want to dish up love to people who hunger for it because I have been a starving soul.

Even as I stand on the brink of a new adventure with Christ, the dependability of this worship service comforts me as much as the hundreds of tip-tilted faces involved in worship. I have always been moved by the power of community, but through the music and sights of this service, I feel as though this body has slipped its arms around me. I see love in the faces that occasionally glance my way and smile; I feel the strength undergirding the aged saints who are lifting wizened hands to the Lord.

The body of Christ is a mighty force, and Abel is not wrong to serve it. He is a guardian of the sheep obeying the Lord's command. He is feeding them with what he has been given, he is teaching the young ones and helping them grow strong in wisdom and faith.

But I pray I will never again cocoon in this comfort. There are too many absent from this building, too many people waking to a Sunday morning filled with despair and loss.

I relax, letting my hands slide over the keys, relishing the tension in my fingers as I manage the octave reach to emphasize the notes in the chorus. My eyes fill with tears of gratitude in the swell of the song. I am so grateful God is holy, and that the sacrifice of his blameless Son is enough to cover my past, present, and future sins . . .

When I look up, my heart does a double beat. Through my blurred eyes I see Christopher standing in the congregation, his head tipped back, his hands slightly raised as if the song has lifted him somehow. He's wearing the black leather jacket he wore the night we met in O'Shays.

My vision clears when I blink the tears away. The dark-haired man isn't Christopher at all, yet he is still familiar. I look away, puzzling over his identity, then the answer comes—the stranger in Chris's jacket is no stranger at all. Judd—the man who'd been sleeping on the sidewalk—has come to church.

After church, Crystal Donaldson stops me as I'm getting into my car. "Emma Rose?"

I hesitate, my hand on the door. "Yes?"

A blush burns her cheek. "I hate to bother you, but I still need to get your impressions of the National Prayer Breakfast. The deadline for the April issue is nearly on top of us."

I tilt my head. The girl has everything—a tenacious personality, pleasant looks, a talent for words.

"Crystal, you're a good writer. Have you ever thought about getting a job with the *Wiltshire Record*?"

The smile on her face vanishes. "Are you firing me, Emma Rose?"

I laugh. "No, honey, I'm just asking a question. When you were studying journalism, did you ever think about working for a city paper?"

She grimaces, but I can see thought working in her eyes. "Well . . . no. I always thought I should work for a Christian publication."

"Think again, sweetheart." I open my car door, then pause to squeeze her shoulder. "You're as good a writer as anyone, honey, and the world could use a few more Christian journalists. Pray about it. Stay if that's what the Lord tells you to do, but who knows where he'll send you if you're willing to go?"

When I pull out and wave good-bye she is still standing in the parking lot, her eyes alight with speculation.

After leaving the church, I stop by our local T. J. Maxx and pick out a pair of jeans. The teenage girl at the cash register stops chewing her gum when I hand her the price tag and tell her I plan to wear them out of the store. After giving me a slanted look, she runs my credit card through the register and I'm on my way.

Abel is having a special lunch for the pastoral staff before his big press conference. I was invited, of course, but I told him I needed to go back to the house where Chris died. Melinda is safely in Lortis June's care, but she wasn't the only person in need of help.

I spoke to the Father yesterday. Today belongs to the mother and the little girl.

The pieces fell into place on my long drive from Hudson Falls. Chris was right when he said the church shouldn't send young Christians into difficult situations, but I've been tested, tried, and prepared in over twenty years of hands-on ministry. Furthermore, before Chris appeared I had been praying that God would reveal more of himself to me . . . and God took me at my word.

Another paragraph from Chris's journal replays in my mind: "The things that tempt me from following God daily aren't sinful things," he wrote. "They're good things—duty to my family, to my father's company, to the people at my church. But if I am going to devote myself to following God, I must be willing to leave the good things behind as I seek the best thing—total submission and obedience."

I have been so wrapped up in good things—Christian forms, Christian functions—for so many years that the idea of breaking free is a little frightening. And yet I must do it. I'm not sure how the Lord will use me to reach the world, but I know where I can begin.

Before leaving for church this morning, I found Cathleen's invitation to the progressive dinner. Before tossing the note, I asked the Father about it . . . and received a surprising answer. So I dialed Cathleen's home and told her that if it wasn't too late, I would be delighted to participate because I looked forward to getting to know my neighbors.

Every year Abel and I attend an average of two hundred

services at Sinai Church. On Sunday night, February 22, I will obey the Lord by meeting the lost lambs on Martingale Place . . . and I hope Abel will come with me. Church attendance is a good thing, but obedience is better.

Now obedience is leading me back to the place where I lost my son. A look of decay still clings to the neighborhood when I park at the curb outside the dilapidated house. I get out of the car and hesitate at the place where Chris died. Nothing marks the spot; no gravestone or cross will ever call attention to this particular patch of asphalt.

But for me it will always be one step shy of holy ground. Christopher, the son born of my sin, brought me back into the world from which I had been miraculously, gloriously saved.

Thank God for that.

I cross the walk in a few steps, then pause on the porch. The stale odors of the house waft through a gap between the door and the framing, and I instinctively take a deep breath of clear air to fortify myself for the stench inside.

When I open the door, I find that little has changed. The pizza Chris paid for with his life has vanished, but the empty box litters a corner of the living room floor. Someone has drunk the soup Melinda wouldn't touch. The empty container lies on the counter, but at least Melinda is no longer crouching beside a cabinet.

"One person at a time," I whisper. "That's how Jesus met people."

I find the woman I'm seeking when I reach the back bedroom. On my last visit I thought she had to be at least forty-something; today, seeing her in the afternoon light, I realize she's probably in her mid-twenties. The little girl, obviously her daughter, squats beside her on the floor.

Despite the chill, the toddler's feet are bare.

Ignoring the snap and crackle of my knees, I crouch to look them both in the eye. The mother won't meet my gaze.

"I'm Emma." I reach out and touch the child's soft cheek. "I saw you here the other day."

The woman's mouth curls in a one-sided smile. "You're the one who took the girl away?"

"Yes." I sink all the way to the floor. "And I can help you get out of here, too, if you want."

"Why would I want to leave? One house is as good as another."

"Not really. I was thinking maybe you and your little girl would like a hotel room, some place with clean water and a nice bed. And then I was thinking maybe you could use some help getting a job and finding someone to watch your little girl during the day."

She gives me a guarded look. "Why would you do that for us?"

"Because someone did it for me."

I am about to offer my hand to help her up when the front door creaks. I glance over my shoulder and look down the hall—a tall man in dark slacks and a sweatshirt has come into the house, and his stiff posture sends a shiver of unease up my spine. I can't see his features in the windowless gloom, but I see him survey the room, then look down the hall toward me.

A gasp catches in my throat when I recognize his silhouette. The newcomer is my husband, a man who hasn't ventured out of the house in anything this casual in more than twenty years.

He looks around for a moment, his hands in his pockets, then lifts his chin when he recognizes me. He strides forward, glancing to the left and right, and hesitates in the bedroom doorway.

"Hi," he says softly, his gaze falling upon the little girl. "I have some food and blankets in the truck. Want me to bring them in?"

For a moment I'm too surprised to speak.

"I saw your car." He shrugs toward the street. "You weren't hard to find."

I glance at my watch. "But you're supposed to be at the press conference."

"I canceled it."

Visions of invoices and conference calls and fund-raising letters flash through my mind. "You *canceled* it?"

"I called off the entire campaign." He lowers his head a moment, then slips his hands into his pockets. "Boycotting one rotten book didn't seem very important after . . . well, after everything that's happened."

335

I can't stop a grin from sneaking across my lips. "I'll bet Josh didn't appreciate you upsetting all his carefully laid plans. And the direct mail people—"

"Well . . . you know what they say about the best-laid plans of mice and ministers. The direct mail people will survive; we'll just change the focus of our next campaign. And Josh quit."

I stare at him, my mouth open.

Abel shrugs. "Apparently he didn't care for the new direction of our ministry."

With an effort, I close my mouth and take my husband's arm. After escorting him out of the bedroom, I tilt my head back to study his eyes. "Are we moving in a new direction, Abel?"

Beneath the smooth surface of his face there is a suggestion of movement and flowing, as though a submerged spring is trying to break through. "I've been thinking all weekend, and while you were gone I kept looking at those pictures."

He seems hesitant to continue, but then he looks at the little girl who clings to the leg of my jeans. "This morning during my sermon, I kept thinking that it wasn't a preacher who reached you, Em. It was a cook."

I nod, remembering his morning text. In order to prepare our people for the big boycott campaign, he had preached on bearing one another's burdens and building up the church.

"Actually, Nola was a restaurateur. But mostly she was a follower of Christ."

"Right." His gaze drops to the floor. "Anyway, I realized

that in my own home I haven't been practicing what I preach. I've not been fair to you, and I have to apologize for that. I should have rejoiced when you rejoiced and wept when you wept . . . and I should have listened when you were trying to explain what God was teaching you. I forgot to sit still and listen to what God wanted to teach me. I've been all caught up in thinking that nothing we do *outside* the church is as important as what we do *in* it."

"I don't think you can separate the two." I stand and take two steps forward, moving close enough to lower my voice so my words reach Abel alone. "We don't stop following Christ the moment we leave the church property. We have to be lights wherever we find ourselves . . . even when we are led to places like this. And God doesn't call just preachers—he calls restaurateurs and dentists and real estate agents and teachers to light up the world. You're not responsible for saving the world all by yourself."

"Well . . . I know one thing. I want to help you obey the Lord."

In that moment, I realize again why I married him.

"And I want to help you." I rise on tiptoe to kiss his cheek, then melt into the circle of his arms. "I love you, Abel, and I always will. But I can't obey God through you . . . I can only follow him beside you."

He kisses my forehead, then we both look down. The little girl is clinging to Abel's leg and looking up at us with mirror-black eyes.

I hear my husband's breath catch in his throat.

"There are others like her," I whisper. "Enough to keep us busy for a long time to come."

I release my husband, then turn him toward the kitchen. "Let me get the counter cleaned off and we'll serve lunch for anybody who's hungry."

As Abel heads to the car to fetch the food, the young mother comes out of the bedroom, then lifts the toddler to her hip. She props one shoulder against the wall, then twirls a strand of hair around one finger. "I don't know you people," she says. "Why are you here?"

I have scooped up a few pieces of trash, but at her question I drop everything onto the counter so I can reach out and squeeze her shoulders. "We're here because we care about you, honey, and we want to know your name."

Distrust flickers in her eyes, hot and bright as a Kentucky sun in August, then her lower lip trembles. For the first time since my arrival, she meets my gaze. "I'm Julia, and this is Liane."

"What beautiful names." I brush a lock of the baby's hair from her eyes, then outline the curve of her cheek with my fingertip. "You can call me Emma."

Questions for Book Discussion Groups

1. Did this book shock or surprise you in any way? Why?

2. Some parts of this story are allegorical—they are meant to represent other characters or events. Which characters might be allegorical representations? Who do you think Chris represents?

3. Emma says that Christopher was born of her sin. Who was born as a result of mankind's sin?

4. *The Debt* is also intended to illustrate the parable Jesus told in Luke 7:41. How does Abel's love for the Lord differ from Emma's?

5. Why do you think Christopher had Emma meet him in such odd places?

6. Compare Emma's encounters with people at O'Shays, Jackson's Photo, and the abandoned house to Jesus' encounter with the corrupt tax collector, the woman caught in adultery, and the woman at the well. Did Jesus worry about his reputation when he dealt with people? Did he worry about his reputation at all?

7. What did you think of Abel? Is he a good Christian? A good husband? A good neighbor?

8. Has this book challenged your thinking in any way? How?

9. The Bible says that some are gifted to be pastors, teachers, and prophets—abilities that minister to the body of Christ. When Scripture speaks of our "callings," however, it speaks in general terms—we are called to be disciples, to be obedient, to follow Christ. Are those who are gifted to serve the body also called to minister to the world at large?

10. Not everyone is led to the sort of "street ministry" Christopher practiced . . . nor is everyone led to work with the body of Christ. So what are some ways you can walk in the world and shine the light of Christ to those who don't know him? When was the last time you went out of your way to befriend an unbeliever?

11. At the end of the story, Emma realizes that she has been depending upon Abel for far too much—he is not only the spiritual head of their home, but he has stepped into the role she ought to reserve for Christ. What other figures in our lives might fill the place that rightfully belongs to Christ alone?

12. Chris urges Emma to venture out of the church so she can act as "salt" in the world. As we go into the world, what must we do in order to avoid becoming "salt licks"? In other words, what things can we do to prevent our testimony from being eroded? What sort of personal standards should we establish to be sure we remain as "wary as snakes and harmless as doves" (Matthew 10:16)?

Author's Note

Like Emma, I am a long way from perfect obedience, but in the past few years the Lord has brought me out of a cloistered place to a more exposed place. The cloister is safer, to be sure . . . downright cozy, in fact. When in the world, I find that I must be more vigilant, more watchful, more cautious of my words and attitudes.

In my high-school youth group we used to glibly chant, "You're the only Jesus some people may ever see."

Truths often come from the mouths of babes.

This is my third attempt at writing an author's note. I filled the first two versions with reasons and explanations, but if a story does what it's supposed to, why should explanations be necessary?

My job is simply to tell the parable. I've had help along the way, and I need to acknowledge it:

Thank you, Jesus, for tenderly teaching me what it means to listen for your voice.

Thank you, members of my prayer team, who supported this project in the heavenly realm.

Thank you, Bill Myers, for giving me advice and a great line for George's video store.

Thank you, Susan Richardson, Marilyn Meberg, and Marty Briner, for giving me excellent feedback on a rough draft.

Thank you, Bob Briner, for writing *Roaring Lambs,* a book that reinforced things I had been thinking and feeling for years. I can't wait to personally thank you in heaven.

Finally, thank you, B. J. Hoff, for telling me that love is what the lost world most hungers for . . . because that's the seed from which this story grew.

An Excerpt from the Bestselling Book

THE NOTE

BY ANGELA HUNT

CHAPTER ONE

WEDNESDAY, JUNE 13

The sultry breeze carried not a single hint that the summer afternoon would give birth to the worst aviation disaster in American history. At New York's bustling LaGuardia Airport, thousands of passengers clutched belongings, flashed driver's licenses, and gripped boarding passes before departing for far-flung destinations across the globe.

Every one of them had made plans for the evening.

At gate B-13, 237 passengers waited for a jet that would carry them to Tampa International Airport. Their reasons for traveling were as varied as their faces: some hoped for a few days of fun, others looked forward to work, others yearned to see family. A pleasant mood reigned in the lounge area despite the jet's late arrival. Chuck O'Neil, one of the PanWorld gate attendants, told jokes to pass the time. Four standby passengers smiled in relief when they were told seats were available.

PanWorld Flight 848, which had originated at TIA, touched down at LaGuardia at 2:38 P.M., almost an hour late. Two hundred fifty passengers and crew disembarked from the Boeing 767, which had developed problems with a pressure switch in the No. 1 engine. The trouble was nothing unusual, considering the age of the twenty-two-year-old plane, and Tampa mechanics had corrected the problem while others performed routine maintenance.

In the gate area, families kissed their loved ones good-bye while other travelers placed last-minute calls on their cell phones. Five passengers were PanWorld employees utilizing one of their employment perks: free travel on any flight with available seating. Debbie Walsh, a ticket agent with PanWorld, was taking her nine-year-old son to visit his father in Florida.

Forty-nine-year-old Captain Joey Sergeant of Tampa stepped out for a cup of fresh coffee before returning to the cockpit. With him were flight engineer Ira Nipps, sixty-two, of Bradenton, Florida, and first officer Roy Murphy of Clearwater. Together the three men had logged more than forty-six thousand hours of flight experience.

On the tarmac, PanWorld employees loaded the belly of the plane with golf bags, suitcases, backpacks, and two kennels— one occupied by a basset hound belonging to the Cotter family from Brooklyn, another by a ten-week-old Siberian Husky, a present for passenger Noland Thompson's grandchildren in Clearwater. While baggage handlers sweated in the afternoon sun, mechanics poured twenty-four thousand gallons of fuel into the jet.

The flight attendants boarded the waiting travelers with little fuss. Among the 237 passengers were Mr. and Mrs. Thomas Wilt, who planned to cruise the Caribbean from the port of Tampa; Dr. and Mrs. Merrill Storey, who hoped to buy a condo in St. Petersburg; and the Darrell Nance family—two parents and four children, all bound for Disney World after a day at Busch Gardens. First-class passenger Tom Harold, defensive coach for the Tampa Bay Buccaneers, boarded with his wife, Adrienne. To celebrate their fortieth wedding anniversary, the couple had taken a quick trip to New York to catch her favorite play, *Les Misérables*, on Broadway.

Forty-eight of the PanWorld passengers were students from Largo Christian School—recent graduates whose senior class trip had been postponed until mid-June to avoid conflicting with final exams. The students and their nine chaperones had missed an earlier flight, and many were openly thanking God that the airline could accommodate the entire group on Flight 848.

Shortly before 4:00 P.M., flight attendants sealed the doors, then airline workers pushed the 767 back from the gate. On the flight deck, Captain Sergeant started the four Pratt & Whitney engines. After checking with air traffic controllers in the tower, the plane taxied to its assigned runway.

At 4:05, controllers cleared the jet for takeoff. By 4:15,

Flight 848 was airborne, her wheels tucked back into the well, her nose lifted toward the stratosphere. After a short circling climb over New York Harbor, Captain Sergeant began a graceful turn to the south, toward Florida and sunny skies.

The pilots couldn't have asked for better weather. Temperatures in Tampa were in the high eighties, the humidity a sultry 70 percent. No clouds marred the horizon for as far as the pilots could see. The captain took the jet to 35,000 feet, typical cruising altitude for the 767, and held it at 530 miles per hour. Once the plane was safely settled into her flight path, he checked the passenger list and noticed that he flew with two empty seats. Florida flights often sold out at this time of year.

The passengers set about the business of making time pass as quickly as possible. They closed their eyes to nap, clamped on headphones, browsed through magazines, or peered at dusty paperbacks they'd picked up from the airport bookstore. The high school graduates in the back of the plane laughed and shouted across the aisles as they shared stories of their Manhattan adventure.

The flight attendants unfastened their seat belts and whisked out the drink carts, murmuring "Watch your elbows" with every step they took down the aisle.

One of those flight attendants was Natalie Moore. She had joined the flight in New York at the last moment, filling in for a steward who had taken ill. Before leaving New York she told a roommate she was looking forward to her first visit to Tampa. A rookie with the airline, she had graduated from flight school in Atlanta and moved into Kew Gardens, a New York neighborhood primarily populated by young flight attendants who worked out of LaGuardia and Kennedy Airports.

As the hands of her watch moved toward five o'clock, Natalie and her coworkers began to serve dinner. Passengers had a choice of entrées: baked chicken breast or sirloin steak, both accompanied by green beans and salad. As soon as the flight attendants served the last of the dinner trays, they cleared their cart and pushed it aft to begin cleanup. The flight from New York to Tampa did not allow much time for lingering over dinner, and only because Flight 848 flew during the dinner hour was a meal offered at all.

At 6:06, after nearly two hours of uneventful flight, Captain Sergeant began his descent. At 6:18, air traffic controllers at Tampa International cleared the incoming flight to drop from 15,000 to 13,000 feet. As usual, the pilot responded by repeating his instructions: "PW 848, out of one-five for one-three."

On board, passengers on the right side of the plane caught a dazzling view of Florida's Sun Coast—white beaches, pool-studded backyards, and green treetops, all bordered by the wide, blue expanse of the Gulf of Mexico.

In the galleys, flight attendants locked the drink carts into their stowed positions, getting ready to make a final pass down the aisle. Natalie Moore moved through the cabin reminding passengers to be sure their seatbacks and tray tables were in their upright and locked positions. As she waited for a rambunctious teenager to comply, she bent to glance at the horizon. The sun, slipping toward the ocean, had painted the sky in a riot of pinks and yellows.

At 13,389 feet, while Natalie and the other crew members went about their work, the torrent of air rushing past a loose screw on the fuselage outside the fuel tank created a spark. The electrical fuses tripped, and at 6:29 the plane's radio and transponders fell silent. Captain Sergeant sent a distress call, but no one heard it.

The loose screw continued to spark.

A few moments later, a man sitting in row 24, seat C, noticed three of the attendants huddled in the galley, their arms around each other. One wiped away a tear, while another bowed her head as if to pray.

"Isn't that nice." He nudged the woman sitting next to him. "Look—they've had a tiff, and now they're making up."

Their disagreement must not have been serious, for the flight attendants immediately separated. "Ladies and gentlemen," a male voice called over the intercom, "this is the captain. Please give attention to the flight attendant in your section of the plane. We have experienced a loss of power due to an electrical disruption, but we can still land safely. In order to prepare for this event, however, we ask that you remove all eyeglasses, then give your attention to the flight attendants as they demonstrate the crash position."

Leaning forward, the man in 24-C looked out the window and saw that they were descending in a curving path, moving over water toward land. Though the atmosphere in the cabin hummed with tension, he remained hopeful. The jet was coming down in a relatively smooth spiral above the choppy waters between the Howard Frankland and Causeway Campbell Bridges. The airport lay just beyond.

As the people around him fumbled to obey the flight attendants, he pulled a sheet of paper from his coat pocket and scribbled a message. Glancing out the window again, he saw the blue of the water and felt a flash of inspiration. Digging in another pocket, he produced a plastic bag, then tucked the note inside and secured the seal.

Smiling, he looked up at the pale stewardess standing in the aisle, her mouth a small, tight hyphen. "Sorry," he said, noticing that everyone around him had already bent forward to prepare for an emergency landing. "I wanted to take care of something. I'm sure we'll be all right, so tonight I'll laugh and give this to my—"

He never finished his sentence. A spark from the fuselage ignited the fuel vapors, and Flight 848 exploded. At 6:33 P.M., pieces of the plane began to rain down into the waters of Tampa Bay.

Among the shards and debris was a note.

Available from Angela Hunt

THE CANOPY
by Angela Hunt

Neurologist Alexandra Pace races to find a cure for a deadly disease that is already ravaging her own mind and body. Can she trust British physician Michael Kenway and his unbelievable story of mythical healing tribe living deep in the Amazon jungle? Are Alex and her team willing to confront the unknown dangers lurking in the dense forest? Is her faith in Michael enough to lead them through the black waters to an antidote that can save her life?

THE PEARL
by Angela Hunt

Talk-radio show host Dr. Diana Sheldon has made a career out of giving advice to irate daughters-in-law and spurned lovers. But when her whole life changes in one moment of bad judgment, the carefully built life she's built begins to spiral out of control. She'd give anything—and everything—to get her family back.

From the best-selling author of *The Note,* a heart-wrenching story about the sovereignty of God and the peace he offers he children if only they'll receive it

Also Available from Angela Hunt

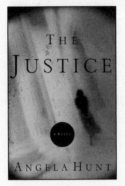

THE JUSTICE

Destiny propels Vice President Daryn Austin to the pinnacle of power when President Parker dies unexpectedly. She now controls the White House. To help her through political and legal quagmires, she hires Paul Santana, the brilliant lawyer she loved in law school. When she nominates Paul to fill a vacancy on the Supreme Court, however, her grand plans begin to crumble. After being influenced by another justice, the man she loves begins to love God, a rival with whom Daryn cannot compete. Daryn's obsession with the changed Paul leads to an emotionally charged battle of wills from which neither can escape unscathed.

THE NOTE

When PanWorld flight 848 crashes into Tampa Bay killing all 261 people on board, journalist Peyton MacGruder is assigned to the story. Her discovery of a remnant of the tragedy—a simple note: "T - I love you. All is forgiven. Dad."—changes her world forever. A powerful story of love and forgiveness.

THE IMMORTAL

A man claiming to be 2000 years old says he is on a holy mission to prevent a global cataclysm. To uncover the truth, Claudia must re-examine her beliefs as she delves into ancient legends of the Wandering Jew, biblical warnings about the Antichrist, and eyewitness accounts of the Crucifixion, the Inquisition, and the Holocaust.

The Heavenly Daze Series

THE ISLAND OF HEAVENLY DAZE
By Lori Copeland & Angela Hunt

To a casual visitor, the island of Heavenly Daze is just like a dozen others off the coast of Maine. It is decorated with graceful Victorian mansions, carpeted with gray cobblestones and bright wild flowers, and populated by sturdy, hard-working folks—most of whom are unaware that the island of Heavenly Daze is also populated with a group of unforgettable angels.

GRACE IN AUTUMN
By Lori Copeland & Angela Hunt

Authors Lori Copeland and Angela Hunt revisit the *Island of Heavenly Daze* in the second book of the highly acclaimed series about a small town where angelic intervention is common-place and the Thanksgiving feast a community affair.

A WARMTH IN WINTER
By Lori Copeland & Angela Hunt

In *A Warmth in Winter*, the unforgettable characters and humorous circumstances offer poignant lessons of God's love and faithfulness. The story centers around Vernie Bidderman, owner of Mooseleuk Mercantile and Salt Gribbon, the light-house operator, who despite the vast differences in their struggles are being taught about the ultimate failure and frustration of self-reliance.

A PERFECT LOVE
By Lori Copeland & Angela Hunt

Despite the blustery winter chill, love is in the air in Heavenly Daze. Buddy Franklin is searching for someone to change his lonely life, Dana and Mike Klackenbush are trying to reestablish the friendship that led them to marriage three years before, Barbara and Russell Higgs are contemplating babies, and Cleta Lansdown is determined to keep Barbara, her married daughter, close to home.

HEARTS AT HOME
By Lori Copeland & Angela Hunt

Edith is trying to lose weight in every way imaginable to get into a certain dress by the time Salt and Birdie's April wedding rolls around. Annie has to learn how to find God's will . . . and open herself up to a new love that's been under her nose the entire time.

WestBow
PRESS

WOMEN OF FAITH℠

Women of Faith partners with Word Publishing,
Integrity Music, *Today's Christian Woman*
magazine, International Bible Society, World
Vision, and Campus Crusade for Christ to offer
conferences, publications, worship music, and
inspirational gifts that support and encourage
today's Christian women.

For more information about Women of Faith,
call 1-888-49-FAITH.
www.women-of-faith.com